FREE TO BREATHE

K. L. SHANDWICK

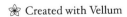 Created with Vellum

ACKNOWLEDGMENTS

Author: KL Shandwick
   Publicist: KL Shandwick
   Cover Design: AM Creations
   Editor: Andie M Long Editing and Proofreading
   Formatter: Kris Vellum
   Beta readers: Elmarie Pieterse, Lisa Ashley Perkins, Sarah Lintott
   Proof reading, Kim Gray, Sue Noyes and Lisa Ashley Perkins

CHAPTER ONE

Maggie

"*A*re you feeling okay?"

I forced a nod even though I wasn't. The January climate was warm and dry in Sydney, much different to the biting cold weather I had left when I flew out of New York the day before.

"Are you ready? If you'd care to follow me, you can see your sister in a few minutes." I stared blankly but I could see he was moved by my horrible situation.

I'll never be ready for this.

Holding my breath, I fought the sick sense of panic I was barely suppressing. Only someone walking in my shoes would know the debilitating emotions controlling my thoughts in that moment. My aching head began to swim as I rose from my chair and stood to follow him. I lost my balance and landed heavily back down on the chair again.

"Do you want a glass of water, Margaret?" Jeffery enquired. His concerned gaze registered with me when he saw my difficulty in following his instruction.

"No, thank you. I just need a minute, do you mind?" I asked as I wrung my hands together. It was overwhelming.

"No, of course not. Take your time. I'm right here with you. Just tell me when you want to do this."

1

Staring up at him, I saw his eyes soften in sympathy because he realized his mistake. No one would ever want to be in this position, to do what I had to do. Strangely, his recognition of that fact calmed me. Then I figured I'd been hard in my initial judgment of him. What had happened wasn't his fault, yet he looked sorry. I felt my throat roll as I swallowed back my tears and drew in a deep breath, right before I heard a voice that I realized afterward was mine.

"Okay, Mr. Barker. Please would you take me to Shona now? I'm ready." My voice carried a level of quiet confidence I didn't feel inside. It sounded brave to my ears.

The heels of my shoes clicked loudly against the polished concrete flooring as we walked in silence along a long corridor. The clinical odor of bleach and disinfectant made my stomach roll. My mind flitted, distracted between long term memories of Shona and the events I had learned about in recent days.

As a young woman I'd already had more than my fair share of distressing events to deal with and asked myself if the death of my father and mother was preparation for the biggest, saddest challenge of my life? If those tragedies were, they hadn't worked because nothing could have prepared me for this.

The previous forty-eight hours were in part blurred and part vivid and painful. Each thought vying for the most prominent position in my mind. Then again, I was exhausted from all the harrowing information and subsequent legalities I'd had to cope with. By the time I had met Mr. Barker face-to-face I had become so worn by the burden of my responsibilities I was prepared for anyone else to tell me what to do. By then the only thing I could focus on was seeing my sister.

During the previous ninety minutes I'd completed a full day of travel, with changes, and arrived in Sydney International Airport from New York. The flight was long and indirect which added to my misery. I had felt like I was on a never-ending journey. A consulate official was already waiting to meet me on my arrival and after a polite, somewhat impersonal introduction, I was ushered to a waiting black sedan parked in the drop-off zone.

Once inside the car his manner appeared different. His sounded calm and the way he appeared at ease when he spoke about my sister told me he was probably well versed in receiving people in my situation.

I had barely caught my breath by the time he began reeling off the agenda he'd planned like some script he had learned with the optimum amount of sympathy in his tone as he delivered all the words someone in my position needed to hear. His sincerity may have fooled some, but he didn't convince me in the slightest. I knew he was only doing his job.

The journey from the airport didn't take long before we arrived at our destination at Westmead Hospital. A renewed sense of horror washed over me from the moment I saw the name of the place where my sister was being kept.

Silent tears streamed down my face as I stared at the tall building full of rectangular glass windows. I left them unchecked and trained my eyes on the entrance doorway thinking there was nothing else I could do except cry to relieve some of the sadness in my heart.

Seconds later, Jeffery Barker, the US embassy representative, slid across the seat and exited onto the sidewalk. He waited for me to alight and guided me silently into the building, resting a hand on the small of my back. It occurred to me how intimate his gesture was for someone so formal, and that I was a stranger to him. When he stopped in front of one of the white, shiny doors, it drew my attention back to the present and I knew part of my journey was almost at an end.

Being led into the quiet, seemingly airless room, my eyes were drawn to the short mustard-colored velvet drapes on the opposite wall, as soon as he opened the door. They were the sole focus for my attention. A stab of pain tore at my gut as blood rushed to my ears and swished rhythmically as my anxiety levels instantly escalated. My heartbeat fluttered irregularly in response to my acknowledgment of the imminent gruesome task ahead of me.

I'd been so distracted that I hadn't noticed when the solemn faced male doctor entered the room because I had been concentrating on not passing out from the trauma of the whole ordeal.

"Hello, Margaret. May I offer my sincerest condolences? My name is Dr. Colin Spence and I'm the lead pathologist here. I'm very sorry to have met you under these circumstances. As you are obviously aware, your sister Shona requires formal identification before we can continue with the next stage of our preparations for her body's repatriation to the USA. We're going to try to make this as easy for you as possible."

His voice was soft, but devoid of emotion and I wondered if it was because of the work he did. *Was he desensitized to breaking bad news?*

Colin was the second person I'd spoken to since I'd arrived in Sydney, if I didn't count the immigration staff at the airport. Neither man appeared willing to say what I needed to hear, their blunt words obliterating any remote hopes I had of them being mistaken. The sedation medication I had been given had made it easier to bear and at times I felt it was all a bad dream.

Except I knew in my heart none of it was a dream. I was wide awake and at that moment, I knew what I was about to see was heart-breakingly real.

Jeffery reached out and put his hand on my upper arm, squeezing it gently. His touch instantly comforted me. By then any human touch was welcome.

"Would you like me to stay with you, Margaret?"

I dragged my tired eyes away from the drapes, scanned them across his chest and looked up toward his face. Eventually they met his. *What a horrible job he has if this is how he earns his living. Do I want him to stay?* My numb robotic-type behavior suddenly left me, like a cliff face shearing off into the sea, and I was filled with the impact of the moment. I felt crushed under the weight of the burden I had to find the strength for. *No one should do this alone.*

"Margaret?"

The young Australian doctor's accent pulled me out of my reverie and my frightened eyes darted from Jeffery's eyes to his.

The question in his tone made me think for a second he'd asked me something else, but I looked back at Jeffery and then I remembered what he wanted to know.

"Yes." My voice was small and distant. I cleared my throat and said it again. Louder.

"Yes, please stay with me." Fear led me to seek comfort, and I reached out, grabbing his huge warm hand. His fingers instantly clasped around mine and he gave me a gentle I-got-you type squeeze.

For the next few minutes, Dr. Spence explained the process before he opened the door. He informed us he would come back afterwards to explain the next steps. *What happens next? What did that even mean? Next for Shona? Next for me and my family?*

As he left the room the lights dimmed, and I looked toward the ceiling. The lower lighting was strangely comforting and suddenly the whole scenario seemed weird as I stood in the semi-darkness with Jeffery from the American Consulate holding my hand tightly like we were a couple.

"Are you ready, Margaret?"

No one called me Margaret, everyone that knew me best called me Maggie.

My throat rolled once more as I swallowed hard and then I took the deepest breath I could manage. "Please... no... I... I'll never be ready for this." I stared at the velvet drape again and felt my stinging eyes brimming with tears until they were so full they blurred, and I could hardly see anything.

As if he anticipated my tears Jeffery produced a crisp white cotton handkerchief and instead of handing it to me, he gently held my chin and turned my face toward him. Like one would do with an infant he wiped my tears away. As soon as we made eye contact again he spoke.

"This is a horrible, terrible thing you have to face here, Margaret. No one should ever have to do this, but the longer you prolong it the more distressed you'll become. You know you *have* to do it, right?"

Reluctantly, I nodded. I felt helpless as I took a deep shuddery breath. Inclining my head toward the small braided cord that dangled down to his right, I heard myself say, "Okay. Do it." My voice sounded flat, emotionless, despite the turmoil I felt inside.

My heart pounded so hard I felt it pulse in my mouth, until Jeffery reached over and began to draw the curtain back to reveal a tinted window, then Shona, my baby sister, was slowly unveiled with every inch the drape retracted.

The first thing I saw was her familiar soft platinum blonde hair. It was swept back from her face—all the way back. Not like she wore it at all. My eyes painstakingly scanned from her face in profile down to her body. Lying completely flat, I noted the contours of her breasts, the dip of her flat belly and the rise again of her thighs covered by the white linen sheet that shrouded her, laid from her neck to the end of her feet.

Instantly, an imprint of her appearance etched forever in my mind as I noted the pale white skin on Shona's unsmiling, yet peaceful face. Taken before her time, even in death, I saw how incredibly beautiful she looked, and my fears of looking at someone who'd died left me. She looked as if she were asleep, but not. And then suddenly it hit me again; my chest walls contracted, and it felt as if all the air was being sucked out of the room. Any denial I had been holding onto left me, and I saw Shona for what she was—lifeless.

I scanned her appearance much closer, memorizing every line. There was a small dark stain at the corner of her mouth and I became fixated by it. My right hand slipped from Jeffery's and I reached out, placing my fingertips on the window close to her hair.

A million jumbled thoughts collided and squeezed through my mind all at once, mainly about Molly's future, and how I would manage to care for her and work full-time. For a few seconds, I felt incapacitated by all the new legal responsibilities I had to face.

Another huge wave of emotion swept through me and fresh tears fell. The agonizing ache in my heart was even greater than those I had felt when my parents had passed.

Jeffery leaned in, "Do you want me to give you a minute alone, Margaret?"

My head jerked up, and I looked at him in dismay. I didn't. It was the last thing I wanted. In that moment I'd never felt more lonely or afraid. *What good would that do?* I glanced back to my sister and the sadness I felt was instantly replaced by anger and resentment... resentment she could do this to me... to Molly.

"No. I want to leave now."

Jeffery gave me a thoughtful, deliberate nod, "You have to say it, Margaret. Then we can leave."

I stared at him, ignoring Shona's still body on the other side of the glass. "It's her. That's my sister, Shona." My voice sounded distant, detached, like someone else said it, but my heart almost broke because I had done my duty.

Identifying Shona had felt like a pointless exercise because it wasn't as if there had been any doubt as to who she was. She had sent all her identification to the management of Fr8Load and after all—the authorities had contacted me.

My sister had been found unconscious in her room with her identification in her back pocket. The initial autopsy findings were death by asphyxiation. Basically, Shona had been doing what she was known for —living life to excess, regardless of her responsibility to her daughter. For Molly, whom she had abandoned to seek excitement in the first place, it was left to me to take care of my niece.

Even as I stared at Shona in death, my impatience with her festered within, and my mind wandered. For years, I had put up with everyone who knew her making excuses for her personality and personal conduct. 'A free spirit', they said by way of excusing her disregard for rules and social restraints.

No matter what else was going on in the world, Shona always lived her life her way, often ignoring the impact of her actions on others— mostly me. Personally, I loved my sister, but I hated the selfishness of her ways.

Any goodwill I had toward her diminished rapidly the day I arrived home from work to find Molly had been left with our elderly neighbor, Mrs. Richie. All Shona had left me was a hastily written note asking me to take care of her daughter. I had no idea she'd stoop to the new low of abandoning Molly to follow her infatuation with Noah Haxby by joining Fr8Load band's crew as a styling assistant.

My sister's head had always been in the clouds and she'd spent her life chasing and stalking the celebrity lifestyle. She was obsessed with one rock star in particular—Noah. God alone knows how she managed to con her way onto his road crew, but I shouldn't have been surprised because she'd have walked to the ends of the earth to be near that man.

Shona was a fantasist and always spoke about the stars she loved like they were personal friends, and it was my bet she left thinking Noah would meet and fall in love with her on sight. From the couple of short emails she sent after she joined the crew, I knew she was bitterly disappointed.

It was apparent from those communications she had never gotten

7

anywhere near her rock star crush and found her less than glamorous job of Fr8Load's image stylists' assistant dull as dishwater. She was more of a runner, dealing with anything from laundry to sewing and everything else they deemed themselves too qualified to deal with.

A noise in the distance pulled me out of my daydream and back to the sad reality of the situation. Shona's chase for the high life had ended in a very degrading death when she was found blind drunk and choking on her own vomit by another crew member who had accidentally knocked on the wrong door.

Apparently, she was still alive when they found her, but her lungs were so swamped, the medical intervention she had came too late. The roadie in her room with her had been one of the crew she had gotten friendly with. His addiction of choice was Heroin, and because his paraphernalia was strewn around the room, they had initially treated Shona as if she were addicted as well.

As soon as I'd confirmed her identity, Jeffery closed the drape and led me out of the room.

"How soon can we go home?" I asked, as my eyes searched Jeffery's face.

"They're waiting for another round of toxicology results to come back later this morning—just to ensure there was no foul play—then they'll be able to release Shona's body to you. We can book you on the first flight back once we've finalized all the requirements to the Australian authorities' satisfaction.

Numbly, I allowed Jeffery to usher me back to his chauffeur-driven car and was driven back to the Four Seasons Hotel. Fr8Load's band management had made the travel arrangements, arranged the consulate official, and were paying for the repatriation of Shona's body back to Florida.

Was I supposed to feel indebted about that? I wasn't grateful; that was the last thought on my mind, because if it wasn't for Noah Haxby and his band, Fr8Load, my sister would be alive and at home caring for her child—not lying on a mortuary slab in some foreign country.

Thinking of the arrogant son-of-a-bitch made me seethe with temper. Life was ridiculously unfair when a guy whose name was synonymous with excess and a flagrant disregard for the morals of others could have the privileged life he led when the rest of us who stuck by the rules were dealt a shitty fate in ours.

When Jeffery reached over and took the key card from the male receptionist he passed it to me, asking if I wanted him to see me to my room. I declined. I didn't miss the look of relief on his face before he explained he'd be back first thing the next day but would call if there was any update on "the case."

It wasn't until he made my ordeal impersonal that I remembered he was just doing his job. He was a stranger, yet he had shared one of the most devastating and intimate experiences of my life.

Jeffery waited by one of the tables in the lobby until the elevator doors closed softly and the car whisked me upwards at speed to the high floor where my room was located.

Noah Haxby's personal assistant, Annalise, had made all the arrangements, and called when the front desk informed her I had checked in. I missed the call as I was in the elevator at the time and so listened to the voicemail she left. It was a courtesy call where she advised me she would pay me a visit later. I was thankful not to see her because I couldn't have faced anyone right then. I felt beat; emotionally wrung out from traveling and what I had faced when I got there.

CHAPTER TWO

Maggie

When I left the US for Sydney my mind had been full of *'What if...',* and *'How am I going to get through this?'* kinds of thoughts, but as I began to face the reality of Shona's death I felt dazed. By the time I reached the hotel, my head just wouldn't let my mind entertain the possibility of thinking what the future held.

The bank of elevators couldn't have been situated further from my room, but I had never stayed anywhere so grand before. Checking the doors as I rechecked the number scribbled on my key card folder I soon realized my room was the very last one at end of the corridor. *Where else would I be? This is my luck.*

I swear I must have used the last of any energy I had in reserve for those final steps and when I entered the room, I barely noticed the plush surroundings. One thing I couldn't ignore was the view. From the huge corner window, I could see The Harbour Bridge to my left and The Sydney Opera House on the right... well, in fact, it was kind of in front of me.

Under normal circumstances, I'd have been excited and thrilled to have had the opportunity to experience Australian culture, but my visit to Australia was far from normal. Plus, I was worn smooth and emotionally drained.

I collapsed backwards onto the bed and instantly felt surrounded by the comfort of the deep pile mattress that sucked me in as I lay staring up at the ceiling. I still held the handle of my carry-on bag. When I realized this, I let it go, and it slid down my leg onto the floor with a dull thud.

Suddenly the previous few hours and what I'd endured crashed down on me and a strangled sob tore from my throat. I'd fought back my grief since I'd stared at my baby sister in death and a tidal wave of grief washed over me. Turning onto my side I curled up into the fetal position and sobbed uncontrollably until eventually, due to extreme exhaustion, I passed out.

Feeling the vibration of my cell in my jacket pocket pulled me from my sleep. I struggled up onto my elbows, disorientated. It was day time again, and the sun cast bright yellow rays of light around my hotel room. Squinting against the brightness, I pulled my phone out and saw the same number as the one who last called me before—Annalise.

"Hello, Ms. Dashwood? It's Annalise here, how was your journey? I tried to call you yesterday, but your phone went to voicemail."

What could I say? *The journey was a living hell? I had to sit on a plane for seventeen hours before I saw my dead sister through a thick paned window whilst holding hands with a stranger to confirm she was dead because her driving license and passport with her pictures on them weren't formal enough?*

"Okay," I replied in a soft, defeated voice.

"I'm down in the lobby. May I come up to your room?"

Although, the last thing I wanted was to face someone from Fr8Load's crew, I knew it would have been rude to decline. She'd been kind to me. Despite everything, her concern throughout had sounded genuine, and she was the reason I could afford to fly to Sydney.

"Sure... I'm a mess, but... okay." I sighed heavily because I didn't have the energy or the will to resist anything, all fight had momentarily left me. The only true feeling I had was the weight of burden in the pit of my stomach that my horrible nightmare was far from over.

Rising to my feet, I wandered over to the window and pressed my hot forehead against the cool hard glass. Staring down at the people far below on the street, I connected with how far away from me they were. My thoughts flitted, and I wished I could have been any one of them rather than who I was at that moment and what I had to face.

My phone rang again, pulling me out of my drifting thoughts, and I answered, half expecting Annalise to say she was outside the door. Instead, it was Jeffery from the Consulate.

"Hello, Margaret. This is a quick update. I just put in a call to Dr. Spence on your behalf. He said he would chase the lab for the toxicology reports and he'd call you back. When he does can you update me so I can make arrangements for repatriation of Shona on my end?"

I don't know why, but I became very disappointed in Jeffery. Gone was the compassionate man from the day before, instead there was someone focused on tying up loose ends. He went on to inform me he'd arranged for the delivery of my luggage which had been left in the trunk of his driver's car. From the two sides of Jeffery I'd encountered, I could see why he was suited to the position he held.

Thanking him for his assistance, I ended the call because neither of us had anything else to say. His brisk manner during the call caught me off guard. I don't know what I expected of him or even if I expected anything at all, but the officious tone disappointed me.

I walked over to the nightstand, placing my phone down and shrugged out of my jacket for the first time since I had left the plane. The linen material was crushed and shabby, like I'd slept in it, which of course, I had.

Reaching down, I pulled my carry-on bag onto the bed and opened it. I took out the spare electric-blue silk blouse I had placed in there, along with a set of underwear and some black high waisted pants. Everything else was in my stowed bag. At least I had the presence of mind to pack a spare outfit in the event my bag got lost.

Dr. Spence's call coincided with Annalise's arrival. Opening the hotel suite door, I gestured at my phone, and waved her inside.

"Hello, Margaret. It's Colin Spence here, we met yesterday. I just want to let you know that the toxicology profile for your sister has come back clean of any other substances. The official record will state that Shona died of asphyxia due to the inhalation of stomach contents." The confirmation was heartbreaking, but I felt oddly relieved there had been no other drugs involved.

There was a pause in his delivery then he continued, "So that concludes my findings in Ms. Dashwood's case. I can now tell you I will be releasing your sister's body for repatriation. I'm just going to contact your guy at the American Consulate who I'm sure will conclude matters quickly on his end, and you can make arrangements to leave for home." He paused for a few seconds and I wondered if I should say something, but I had nothing to say, so he continued.

"Once again, I'm very sorry for your loss, Margaret, and if you have any questions you need to ask, you can contact me on this number."

I mumbled something I don't recall and concluded the conversation, then stood staring down at the plain white comforter on the bed. Nausea swept through me and my stomach began to heave. Ignoring Annalise, I sprinted for the bathroom and threw myself forward, barely making the bowl. Pale green bile spewed from my mouth and the smell was putrid. My throat burned, and my eyes stung with fresh tears.

For a few minutes I hovered, unsure if there was more to come, then I stared up at the mirror through mascara streaked eyes. A fresh new wave of grief rushed at me until once again, I couldn't hold back my sobs.

Closing the seat, I flushed the toilet, and I slumped down onto it. I lay my head on the cold marble countertop near the sink as the smell of pungent vomit in the air made my stomach roll over. Strangled noises tore from my throat. I sounded like a wounded animal, my once silent grief escaping into the air around me.

Annalise knocked softly on the bathroom door but didn't wait for me to answer. When she entered, her heels clacked rapidly on the ceramic tiles as she made her way toward me. She took a white toweling face cloth from the display by the sink and without speaking, scooped my hair away from my neck and placed the cool, damp cloth over the back of it. Her caring gesture made me cry all the harder because apart from Jeffery holding my hand the day before, no one had shown me much in the way of comfort.

"It's okay, honey, just let it out. Let it all out," she said, encouraging me to cry. Placing a hand on my back she rubbed small circles across my shoulder blades which I found instantly soothing. After what seemed like an age, I stopped crying, but my body was still wracked with sobs as it tried to recover from the prolonged bout of irregular breathing.

My cell phone rang in the bedroom. I ignored it, but Annalise left me and answered it. The low murmur of her voice from her side of the conversation continued for a couple of minutes before she ventured back into the bathroom.

"Margaret, that was Jeffery Barker, the American official dealing with... your sister," she said after hesitating. "He's asked if you want to be on the outgoing Florida flight later tonight or if you want to recover from the journey first?"

I scoffed at the suggestion I could recover from something like my sister's death by having an extra night's sleep. The flight wasn't the issue, it was the trauma of the whole situation and there was no way I could see I would ever recover from what had happened. Besides, I was desperate to get back to poor little Molly.

When I told Annalise I wanted to leave right away, her face paled. My initial thought to her reaction was she was worried about my health given I'd been vomiting in her presence. However, when I explained I had to get back to Shona's daughter she couldn't hide her shock. She had no idea Shona even had a child. Once she understood the position I was in, she made no further comment about me staying there.

I was surprised when she stayed while I rang Jeffery back; however she left promptly after she'd heard the arrangements for my return to the USA, and I figured like Jeffery, I was part of her job. With the Consulate taking care of the return flight, her work—at least until we got home—was done.

An awkward moment passed between us and it felt like she didn't know what to say, so I made it easy for her and asked her to leave because I had to bathe and take care of my appearance before Jeffery arrived.

It was Malcolm, Jeffery's driver, who picked me up and drove me to the mortuary alone. Shona's casket was being sealed for the journey, but once again, I had to go to view before they did that to ensure the correct body was being transferred. It was yet another heart-wrenching task, which along with the unexpected ones, added another layer to my traumatic experience. My ordeal appeared never-ending, and the continued suppression of my distress when dealing with officials wore me down.

Somehow, I got through it with the help of yet more strangers, and with five hours before I had to be at the airport, I found myself back at the hotel—wrung out from yet another round of grief-stricken tears.

After the second viewing, I was wracked with guilt over some of the arguments we'd had in the past. The last conversation I'd had with her the day she left, replayed those harsh judgmental words I'd thrown at her.

It had been a difficult, explosive exchange of words about her selfish attitude because she'd left Molly with our neighbor to go shopping by herself the day before. During the spat, names and labels were traded in both directions because neither of us could compromise. The vivid image of her angry contorted face that morning as she shouted into mine remained; her index finger jabbing at my chest as Shona read me the riot act, then spun on her heel and stomped toward my front door.

She had been furious when she left, banging the door with such force the glass shattered into sharp, angry shards which fell to the ground at my feet as I followed behind. Leaving me in a furious mood, I cleaned up the mess she'd made before I went to work. I had no idea of her intentions to leave the same day and it was the last time I saw her.

Since she had joined the crew there had only been two emails. No calls, not even a five-minute Facetime to the precious little girl she gave birth to. My heart clenched painfully again when I thought about poor little Molly.

An image of her beautiful innocent little face staring at me before I left came to mind, her huge brown eyes full of hope when she asked if her mommy was coming home. I didn't tell her about Shona because I would not have been able to leave her in grief to do my duty toward her mother otherwise.

When I thought of how I would break the news to her daughter, it changed my feelings of guilt to enraged anger. I was so fucking furious at her leaving Molly that way, for putting me in the position as guardian for her daughter when she should have had her mom.

Exhaustion had become a familiar feeling as I lay on the bed and slipped into a dreamless, fitful sleep for a while. Apart from emotional grief wiping me out, my body clock was all over the place. After a forty-five-minute nap I filled the tub in the hotel bathroom and got into the water. I sat motionless, fighting back the sadness that appeared to be only one deep breath away since I'd found out about my little sister.

By the time the driver picked me up, I was dressed in my outfit from earlier. He took me to the airport and led me to the desk I had to check-in at. It was obvious everyone I came into contact with had been briefed because they all behaved with the same compassion.

At the airline check-in I was upgraded from business class to first. I was surprised to be in business on the way back in the first place because I had flown out in coach... and the government was paying for my ticket home.

When the undertaker asked if I wanted to accompany my sister's body to the cargo hold of the plane, I didn't. I thought the journey home would be hard enough without the image of them stowing her there stuck in my brain.

Besides I had no more left to give because I knew I'd have to save the little I had in reserve to support Molly to the best of my ability.

I used the extra time to visit the chapel to pray for the strength to see that through instead.

Glancing at my wristwatch, I noted I had less than half an hour before take-off and panicked that I may have missed the flight. Luckily the departure gate was only a short walk from the place of worship, but I heard my name being announced in a frustrated sharp tone over the loud speaker system as I reached the check-in desk at the gate.

"Sorry, I'm here. I was praying."

The flight attendant rolled her eyes as she pursed her lips, visibly annoyed when she snatched my boarding pass out of my hand and scanned it. When she glanced at the details on her screen, I watched as shock registered on her face and her eyes instantly softened to the point where when she met my gaze they were full of pity.

"Ah, Margaret Dashwood? All right, honey, Greg here is going to show you to your seat," she said, gesturing at a tall, dark haired cabin attendant. "If you need anything, just let him know. He'll be on hand for your flight home, okay?" She handed me back my boarding pass as she nodded her head in my direction, but looked at Greg as if to say, "This is her."

Instantly, the uniformed cabin attendant stepped up beside me, gave me a tight smile that vanished as quickly as it had appeared on his face, and guided me through the departure gate by my elbow all the way to the plane. I wondered if he thought I was going to be an issue during the flight and his attitude made me feel defiant. That feeling helped me stay strong to face the journey home.

CHAPTER THREE

Noah

"*N*oah! Noah! Noah!" the rhythmic chanting of the crowd fueled adrenaline through my blood and made my heart pump rapidly. Peering out at the fans who had gathered on the sidewalk, I took a moment to collect myself before I stepped out of the limousine and came face-to-face with my Aussie followers.

"Over here! Noah, look here," several groups called out at once as they vied for my attention. Many held up their cell phones and took pictures and selfies to keep for posterity while others waved banners, proclaiming *'WE <3 YOU, NOAH'*. One looked like it had been made from a black satin king-sized bed sheet.

Another banner said, *'B MY BABY DADDY'*, on a makeshift cardboard notice which was so big it was being held by two sweet looking girls of about sixteen. *Definitely not.* Been there done that and carried the scars every day on how that worked out.

Not the underage girls you understand, the Baby Daddy part. Depression crept in with the thought and my heart ached for a second before I shook the feeling off and scanned the sea of faces. Girls stood on the sidewalk—five, maybe six bodies deep in the crush—and my chest tightened when I noticed how young some of them were.

Many were too young to be at one of my gigs alone. A lot looked fourteen or fifteen years old at most I figured, with skirts halfway up their asses. Most were displaying their small perky tits, maximized with push-up bras that I really didn't want to notice, but they had them out there on display anyway.

The one thing I despised was underage girls trying to be women by dressing provocatively to be noticed. It was an occupational hazard, and I often wondered where their parents were and if they even knew their daughters were out on the sidewalk like this instead of in school. The girls themselves probably didn't know the risks they took dressing that way, especially while hanging around a music venue with the shifty people concerts could sometimes attract.

Instead of lifting me with their adoration, I felt my mood sink, and I silently thanked God I didn't have a daughter. Don't get me wrong, I loved women, and during my career I'd had more than my fair share of groupies, but to my knowledge I'd always been careful to ensure they were legal.

I glanced to my manager, Steve, who wound his hand as his way of telling me to wrap things up and make a move inside. I drew him the stink eye and glanced at the crowd who had probably waited for hours in the rain just to catch a glimpse of me.

"Music is food for the soul," someone said, and that fact seemed to get lost in my world at times. There had always been so much bad shit and soulless people accompanying the work that I did. Not to mention that as well as the beautiful people who gathered for performances, I was surrounded by freaks of all shapes and sizes; a motley crew of people who didn't quite fit in anywhere else, but appeared to be accepted as perfectly normal in the world of live music.

Suddenly, in the sea of faces—some who were crying hysterically, some with ecstatic hopeful expressions—an attractive, curvy girl caught my eye and all concerns about my underage fans faded rapidly.

Standing in an assertive pose with her hands on her hips, she stood out. My eyes were drawn to her sexy-as-hell appearance in a white dress that clung to her in such a way it appeared as if it were sprayed on. I couldn't see an inch of material that didn't connect with her and my dick instantly responded to the visually appealing sight she made.

Her long, rustic red hair framed her pretty face perfectly and when her bright blue come-to-bed eyes met mine, we locked them in a silent stare as I continued to move along the line of fans, my head turning further as I gazed behind me in my effort to keep the connection between us. Red was definitely legal, aged around twenty-two or three, I figured.

I looked pointedly at Eamon then glanced toward her again all the while trying to appear interested in the group of fans who were waving CD cases and other shit for me to sign. Momentarily, I focused on the crowd, and when I glanced back I saw Eamon, my Irish bodyguard move in, stopping behind the girl who had caught my attention.

I gave him a sharp nod and with a practiced beaming smile and a quick wave to my fans, I turned sharply to head toward my manager.

Stepping inside to the concert hall lobby, I saw two men directly in front of me. One I knew; Larry, the promoter. The other I'd never seen before, but I instinctively knew he was the boss of the venue.

It was the same shit routine everywhere we went, so I plastered on my best 'official greeting smile' and shook hands with the guy while I sized him up as a self-important arrogant little shit. Within two minutes of talking to him I knew my assessment of him was correct. I must have counted twenty-three 'I's' in his conversation in less than two minutes.

Eventually I cut his droning conversation dead by calling out for Annalise, my PA, to direct me to my dressing room. Excusing myself, I made my way over to her on the far side of the lobby, but Eamon caught my attention as he held the heavy glass door open to allow the curvy chick from the sidewalk to enter. I couldn't help the wry smile that formed on my lips.

Glancing up at her I almost burst out laughing at the way her eyes raked longingly over my body, and after a few seconds her eyes fixed on mine. She looked in awe when she saw me standing there in front of her.

An instant look of adoration softened her eyes as I moved closer while her face flushed with excitement. I recognized that look, had seen it many times before—she wanted me.

I watched her breathless, aroused reaction, as she gathered her thoughts. Whatever was going through her mind appeared to affect her from the way her eyes began to roam over my body again.

When she licked her dry lips like she'd wandered in from the desert, I could almost see a hum of anticipation radiating from her. Once again, her eyes darted nervously from my face to my lips before dropping to my groin then back again, where her eyes met mine.

I kept my stance impassive, my narrowed eyes trained on her and as if she thought I could read her mind, her face reddened when she realized how closely I'd been watching her. I'd read her body language perfectly; she had been saying come and get me out there—luckily for her I'd been paying attention.

"Hey Eamon, what are you doing with such a beautiful woman?" I asked as I turned to address her. Smiling warmly, I leaned in, holding her by the elbow. I felt a shudder of pleasure run through her under my touch. "Honey, what the hell are you doing with this ugly little guy? A stunningly beautiful lady like you shouldn't be hanging with someone as dubious as him."

Up close, Red was even prettier, and when she smiled in response to my flirtatious comment my eyes fell to her luscious lip-glossed mouth. I wanted to kiss her the instant I did that, she had great lips.

"Jesus, Eamon, go find someone in your own league and leave this delicious female with someone who can handle her?" Eamon raised his eyebrow as if to say, "Seriously?" I knew it sounded corny, but I smirked knowingly because chicks lapped that shit up and I ignored him as I slipped what I hoped felt like a protective arm around her waist.

"Wouldn't you rather spend an hour in my company than his?" The way her large doe eyes lit up told me it was exactly what she had in mind. Nodding in the direction of the door leading to the auditorium, Annalise looked a little flustered, but took my cue and led the way to my dressing room.

"I'm taking this one with me... just to protect her from guys like him. You understand?" I said, jokingly. "What's your name, honey?" I asked as I stared intently into her eyes. Her chest heaved for air after she let out a small gasp from my attention and I knew she was all in.

"Samantha." she replied, then flashed me a coy smile. For a couple of seconds, I was confused because the way she stared me down outside was way different from the girl in front of me. Then I realized she hadn't expected to snare me so easily and was having a star-struck moment before she not only regained her confidence, but actually took the lead in the seduction phase.

In less than three minutes from when I rescued her from the foyer of the concert hall, she was on her knees in my dressing room deep-throating my dick like she hadn't had a meal in weeks.

Some girls surprised the hell out of me and Samantha had definitely been one of them. I'd expected a little more work to warm her up, yet behind the scenes she wasted no time at all before the sound of my belt buckle, metal on metal rattling, echoed in the sparsely furnished dressing room. She tugged at the leather strap and scraped roughly at my jeans in her frenzied effort to get her hands on my junk.

Samantha was a talker—no strike that comment, she was an informer. From the moment she wrapped her fingers around my thick hard dick every move she made she was preceded by a run-through of what was about to occur. "Let me take that fabulous cock in my mouth," and when she pulled me out again, "Damn, you're so thick my mouth aches."

Rising back to her feet, she rested a hand behind her on a small wooden shelf in front of the dressing room mirror, and carelessly wiped her mouth with the back of her other hand as she stared at me with a naughty look in her eyes. It was like she'd perfected her sexy-as-fuck slut move and was used to performing oral sex on guys like me. I'd have put money on her being used to having sex with random guys.

There wasn't a hint of embarrassment or shame in her actions and my initial thoughts about the innocent looking girl in the lobby bore no relation to the one that had sucked my dick with the level of exper-tise she demonstrated.

"Do you want to fuck me, Noah?"

"It's what you want, right?" I replied, clarifying why she was with me.

I wasn't in the mood for games. She had my dick as hard as nails and it was more than ready to penetrate someone—anyone. Gripping her by the arm I turned her around and bent her over the dressing table, her head to the side with her cheek pressed hard against the mirror and I threw her dress up over her hips, noting her black lace thong.

I shoved my hand between her legs and heard her breath hitch in shock followed by a soft moan when I touched her warm wet pussy covered in a small strip of sodden lace. Pulling the warm slick material to the side I slid my middle finger down the length of her entrance and pushed two fingers deep inside her. Another loud relieved moan escaped her lips, "Oh," followed by a soft chuckle when her eyes met mine in our reflection in the mirror.

"What do you want? Tell me what you want." I commanded. I always sought clear instruction so that there could be no false accusations following any action.

"Fuck me, rock star."

Her demand was a first for me. No matter how many women I'd boned, I had never had one that had actually said those words, and with so much conviction. I reacted with a belly laugh because even if someone thought it they'd never openly say something so corny. No one except the crazy-assed chick in front of me.

"Damn, you really are nasty, eh?"

"No, just honest. Why don't you try being honest for a change?" I stopped still and stared at her reflection, confused.

"What? You think that veiled attempt at winning me over from your pathetic bodyguard washed with me? Or is this the first time someone has actually called you on that stupid selection process that just went down outside?"

A woman calling me out was fresh, and I was glad for the opportunity to be straight with her. Holding her loosely by the neck I pressed my dick hard against her ass.

"Alright, you saw through that, but you're here now and you've had my dick down your throat. Still want to fuck a rock star?"

Staring up into the mirror she raised an eyebrow, "And if I said no, you'd just shove yourself back in those jeans and let me walk away?" The tone of her challenge pissed me off.

"What d'you think? I'd force myself on you? Honey, you should go take another look outside. There are a few hundred women who would love to be in your shoes right now."

Raising an eyebrow, Samantha's lip curled in a sneer, "You're one arrogant son-of-a-bitch, aren't you?"

"If saying that most of those women on the sidewalk want to fuck me is me being arrogant then yeah, I am... but I thought we were being honest? I was giving it to you. Your opinion is of no consequence to me. Anyway, the same could be said for you. You saw me and wanted me to do you, right? I mean the way you're dressed and how you willed me to pay attention to you. That was the call you made. All I did was use my judgment, and I figured you'd be up for having some fun before I went out on stage and seduced all those girls who I couldn't bring back here before the show."

Samantha lifted her head and turned back to me with an indignant expression on her face, "Get over yourself, Noah."

My dick went limp because the last thing I needed before going out to play in front of twenty thousand people was someone fucking with my mojo. And that's the only kind of fucking she appeared to be interested in.

Stepping back, I shoved my dick back inside my jeans and began buttoning the flies. She stood up straight and turned to look at me. When she saw what I was doing she hurriedly shoved her dress back down, pulling the hem straight.

Her angry face contorted. "So that's it? We're done?"

"Get out." I told her dismissively. Wandering over to a tan leather sofa I threw myself heavily onto it. "We never really got started, sweetheart. You're unreal. I'd rather be hard up than give you anything. Thanks for the blow job. There's the door," I replied and inclined my head toward it for her to leave. I pulled out my phone and texted Eamon to get rid of her before I stood again and headed over to the water jar in the corner of the room.

Eamon opened the door and without saying a word took her arm and began leading her out of the dressing room.

"You're a dick, you know that?" She spat. Eamon shoved her gently out of the door and it closed behind him. I snickered and threw the water back. "Yeah, so they tell me," I muttered.

CHAPTER FOUR

Noah

The truth of the matter was nothing really did it for me since I'd discovered depression. My moods were more low than high, and I couldn't really remember the last time I'd felt truly happy. All I know was it was before all the shit went down with my exgirlfriend.

Whenever I thought of Andrea, my chest instantly tightened. Just the memory of what I went through always made me feel like I couldn't breathe. Andrea was quite a bit older than me and when I first began dating her, I felt like the camel's nuts when I'd hooked a hot sophisticated woman. All that changed the minute she began to force our relationship and expected more.

Even after more than a decade in the charts, people still judged me for being young and impetuous at the beginning, but they had no real idea about how much the publicists and my management were behind all of that. I'd been on the road for most of the previous four years by the time I met Andrea, and I'd crammed in a lifestyle to rival the most seasoned of rockers.

Being in a band had given me a shitload of opportunities to have sex with beautiful girls and I'd be a liar if I said I hadn't taken advantage of that. If I'm honest I'd say in the early days our band were hellraisers and lived a true rock and roll lifestyle, but eventually it began to grow old—at least for me. My brothers said they thought I was overexposed to sex, if there was such a thing as that. The more I had, the more routine it felt, and the more women I did, the less connected I became with any of them.

Being more mature, Andrea kept my interest longer than most. Even with the age difference, my manager approved and thought she was good publicity for the band. In the beginning I had thought so too... then I learned she was only good to herself.

While on tour ten weeks into what I felt was a growing relationship, Andrea's heartbroken ex-boyfriend showed up one night and challenged her for just never coming back. Turned out she hadn't even told the dude he had passed his sell-by date, and she'd certainly never mentioned him to me.

The callous way she treated the guy she'd abandoned, left me questioning whether I really knew her at all. Even when she tried to appease me by trying to argue her case, she couldn't hide the self-centered attitude she'd demonstrated toward someone she had at one time been in love with.

Seeing how manipulative she was during that incident, turned me off in a heartbeat. Until then I'd been oblivious to her manipulative ways, but when I saw how callously she'd dismissed a man who obviously loved her dearly, I was done.

No matter what I'd begun to feel for her, after witnessing the scene between them, there was no way I wanted her around. Watching that poor dude standing out in the rain with his hands stuffed deep in his pockets looking utterly destroyed ended anything I had felt for her.

Unfortunately, two months later she bounced back into my life, three months pregnant with my child. Since then the contact between us was cordial at best, fractious at worst, but we were forever tied together because of our five-year old son. I guess I wasn't very mature when Rudi was born, but thanks to the shit she and the press put me through, I was now a much wiser person to the one she once knew.

No matter how my personal life had affected me, I still had a job to do. One that, with the eyes of the world watching, I couldn't afford to mess up. Our fans stood by us no matter what happened off-stage, but

I was smart enough to know they gave us that grace because each and every time we walked out to perform they could always count on a gig that would never be less than the best we could give them.

That night when I walked out on stage our fans were oblivious as to what had taken place in my dressing room between Samantha and me, and I still played my part in the band, by giving the fans the time of their lives.

Once the gig was done, I smiled and grinned through the 'meet and greet', but the incident earlier in the day still weighed heavily on my mind. Eamon had obviously filled in Steve about it because I noted they both stayed close to me during the after party.

It was the last night of the tour and the booze flowed like water. Somehow, I got through the constant offers of drink and women, and Eamon dragged me back to the hotel at the first opportunity we had, citing the long haul flight I had the following day as my excuse.

That part was true, and I dreaded the thought of it because I had a genuine fear of flying ever since I'd witnessed a light aircraft crashing into one of our fields near my family home as a child.

Steve knew the flight back to New York was playing on my mind and although I hated their intervention I had gotten used to their support in keeping an eye on me during my times of stress.

Without the emotional crutch of alcohol some nights were rougher than others, and there were times I suffered from insomnia. It was one of those restless nights I endured the night before we flew back to the USA. I tried to look at it philosophically and thought because I was tired and mentally drained I was sure to sleep during the flight home.

Transferring to the airport was uneventful once I was in the car and away from the marauding fans and as it was an evening flight the VIP lounge was fairly deserted. After being escorted to my seat on the plane I became aware of a cold blast of air from the small round air conditioning vent directly above. I reached up and closed it just as the cabin attendant dressed in her smart red uniform and white blouse, held out a small silver tray with glasses of champagne on it.

Smiling sweetly, she asked, "Would you like an aperitif, Mr. Haxby?"

"No thanks, I'm a recovering alcoholic," I stated flatly and distracted myself by attempting to plump up the inadequate excuse for a pillow behind my head. When I glanced back at her my eyes met her sympathetic ones and I felt more than a little annoyed at myself for biting the way I had.

It wasn't easy trying to take responsibility for my addiction and even though I'd been on the wagon for a long time it never felt any easier. Still, it wasn't the flight attendant's problem I lost control of myself to bourbon whiskey, she was only doing her job.

Most would call me weak-willed and I guess they'd be right. I ignored the signs and drank excessively for a couple of years, but by the time I accepted my dependency on it to get me through the day, I was a train wreck of a guy who needed it to function.

I'd been dry of alcohol for almost three years, yet it was still one painful day at a time. My sponsor from the support group, Jason, travelled with us after losing his job through alcohol dependency, instead he found support with my awesome band, as one of the road crew. He was also a reformed man, a strong man, and sometimes he was my saving grace during the times when I felt I'd hit a wall.

Blushing with embarrassment, the poor stewardess appeared both shocked and in a state of flux about what to do after my declaration, so I decided to ignore her altogether and pull the inflight entertainment magazine from the small magazine slot situated under the window. I willed her to keep moving because the tempting drinks tray she held up to my face wasn't doing me any favors.

I used to get drunk to carry me through most things: travelling, being away from home, hours of hanging around, to be sociable, feeling homesick when I missed my awesome family, but the biggest reason I drank was because I was forbidden from seeing my son. As time went on, the injustice became my main excuse for my ever-increasing drinking habit.

The ordeal of flying long haul was only one more example of when I'd normally hit the bottle to get me through. Apart from when I was both bored and nervous onboard a jumbo jet plane for hours on end.

In all the years of travel I'd never managed to conquer my nerves when flying.

As the cabin staff moved away, my eyes were drawn to an elegant, beautiful woman being seated two rows in front of me on the opposite side. Dressed demurely in black flowing, high-waisted pants and a pale-blue silk blouse she was striking. The color of her blouse contrasted beautifully with her pale skin and her delicate bone structure.

She was exquisite and something about her was vaguely familiar. I racked my brain and came up wanting, but with curiosity piqued I continued to watch her even after she sat down with her back to me.

Even from behind she still appealed to me and I sat staring at the purity of her long, platinum-blonde colored hair. Don't ask me why I felt happy that she was the polar opposite in appearance to how Andrea looked. My ex had short, dark-brown hair and was almost as tall as me at six feet. She had a slender, boyish frame; unlike this woman who looked a bit older than me; was of medium height, no more than five eight I'd guess; and her curvaceous figure was knockout gorgeous.

Pushing any thoughts of Andrea to one side I began to speculate what the blonde woman did for a living. I couldn't guess but from the way she carried herself with confidence, I would have said she was in a position of power.

I began to speculate that she may have been behind a powerful man, or even was a successful business woman in her own right. I don't know why, but I felt as if when she spoke she'd silence a room. Traveling first class wasn't cheap and that gave me another reason to suspect she was successful or well connected.

For the first time in a long time, I stared down at my usual attire of shabby jeans and felt less than well turned out. A cabin attendant spoke to her and I watched her turn toward them. Her profile came into view as she listened intently to what he said. Nodding slowly, she stared attentively as her nimble fingers tucked some silky loose strands of hair behind her ear.

For some reason I sensed an air of desperation in the seriousness of the cabin attendant's information. I couldn't put my finger on it and I couldn't hear what was said because the general atmosphere in the cabin as people continued to settle was too distracting.

I found myself straining in my effort to hear the conversation when she replied but her voice was barely above a low murmur in the drone of the sterile air-conditioned environment. I glanced to her fingers looking for rings and felt oddly pleased that she didn't appear to have been taken.

God knows why I did that because I figured we probably had nothing in common... and she'd probably have balked at being hit on by someone like me anyway. Then I became distracted when other members of the cabin crew began to prepare us for take-off.

With nothing else to see apart from the back of her head, my attention flitted to the window before I tried to settle down and read the inflight magazine. Looking through the list of inflight movies was one of the distractions I used to take my mind off impending air disasters.

A couple of short bell chimes rang throughout the cabin followed by the voice of the cabin manager who reminded us of the cabin safety leaflet before the cabin crew launched into their exaggerated safety demonstration. I looked out of the small oval window to distract myself from learning how to throw myself out of the cabin at thirty thousand feet in the case of an emergency.

Out of the corner of my eye I noticed a strange looking man dressed in a solemn black suit standing almost under the wing of the plane and I wondered what he was doing there until I became distracted by the wire caged luggage truck leaving.

Settling back into my seat I closed my tired eyes and felt the plane engine as it gently hummed; the cabin vibrated before the aircraft slowly maneuvered backwards to taxi toward the runway.

The drugs the physician gave me to make me sleep must have kicked in at that point because I dozed off until a pleasant alluring smell dragged me from my sleeping state and I inhaled the sweet smell of perfume deeply as the air shifted around me. Opening my eyes in search of the person who wore it I noticed the blonde I'd been watching earlier retake her seat. Once again, I fixed my gaze on her for a few minutes until I figured I was way too into her and I didn't even know her.

Suddenly my peace was shattered when I was interrupted by someone who made a high-pitched squealing noise, attracting the attention of most of the small section of the cabin.

"Oh, my, God. It's you. It really *is* you, isn't it? Oh my God, Noah Haxby! I've been a super fan of yours since... forever," she rolled her eyes then grinned widely. "I tweet you every day, stalk your pages, and follow you everywhere on social media. I've done it for years wishing one day you'd see one of my questions and answer me."

Suddenly she began breathing rapidly and reached over plucking a sick bag from the seat across from mine. Covering her mouth, she began sucking and blowing, the bag inflating and collapsing with every breath. She stopped after a few seconds and inhaled deeply.

"Sorry. Look, I'm shaking," she advised me, holding her hand out to show me. "I can't believe you're in my cabin. Jesus, pinch me." As she looked like she was beginning to hyperventilate again I plastered on my best sexy smile and spoke in a calm, seductive tone. "What's your name, sweetheart?"

"Sandie," she said, giggling through her name like she was suddenly a shy eleven-year-old talking to a boy she was sweet on for the first time.

"Well, Sandie. I'm pleased to meet your acquaintance, honey. Thank you for saying, *'hello'*. Glad to have you as a follower." I was determined not to open a conversation too much and went with a statement instead. For one thing, I was trying to respect the other passengers who were huffing and puffing at the disturbance.

Sandie took my statement as an opening for her to take charge of the conversation and I could have kicked myself for not being more abrupt. When she realized I wasn't going to take it any further, she fished into her pocket and brought out her cell.

"I'm sure I can switch this on now we're well into the flight. Can I have a picture with you?"

Before I could answer, she'd dropped her ass on my lap with her arm around my neck like we were old friends and took a picture of us both. She was grinning from ear to ear, and as soon as I saw the picture she'd taken I pushed her off into the aisle again and thanked her again for connecting, then told her I was exhausted and if she didn't mind I needed to rest. Even though I knew it was a shitty thing to do, I had to think of the others around me.

Sandie gushed how grateful she was toward me for allowing her to take our picture then turned and made her way back to her seat. I glanced behind me to make sure she wasn't coming back, and when I turned and looked ahead again, the blonde woman I'd been so engrossed in before scowled angrily at me. From her look I thought she found it distasteful to share the same air with someone like me.

For the remainder of the journey, even though I felt desperately tired, I was too pissed off and restless to catch any quality sleep. I must have dozed off six or seven times only to wake up and found it was only ten minutes after I'd gone to sleep before. I was also disturbed by two further passengers and a flight attendant offering me their phone numbers, which I declined.

By the time we finally landed in Dubai, I was relieved to get off the plane, but cranky and desperate for a proper bed on firm ground. Steve and the team knew me very well because I'd have probably gone insane if it had been a non-stop flight home.

CHAPTER FIVE

Maggie

*W*hen I boarded the aircraft, I sunk back into the seat and closed my eyes. I'd have given anything not to have had to endure the long journey back home. No matter how I tried to reason, I felt deeply distressed that Shona was to be placed in the hold of the plane alone. It disturbed me so much I had to use my self-restraint to stay buckled into my seat and not attempt to get off the aircraft.

As soon as we were in the air and the seatbelt light sign had gone off I unfastened my buckle and glanced behind me to find the restroom signs. When I stepped out into the aisle, I began to make my way to the back of the cabin. My gaze fell on the face of a man sleeping soundly. As far as I was concerned he was the man who had stolen my life from me and the last person I'd ever have wanted to be in a confined space with—Noah Haxby.

My heart instantly reacted with an electrical surge which coursed through me like I'd grabbed a live wire. The rhythm floundered and almost stopped when I recognized him. A strangled sob stuck in my throat as I rushed past and trained my eyes on the door of the restroom until I got inside.

The familiar tight feeling of distress gripped my chest as I sat down in the tiny space. *If God had a hand in this twist of fate he was being particularly cruel. Why did he have to send yet another test for me? Wasn't taking my sister enough?*

Fighting back my tears, I relieved myself and stood in front of the small rectangular mirror. I looked a mess. Black circles and puffy eyelids were visible signs of the ordeal I had endured. Cupping my hands, I turned on the cold faucet and splashed my face with the water. It felt cool, but somehow not cold enough.

For a couple of minutes, fury scrambled my brain, but I knew that causing a scene would change nothing. It wasn't like either of us could leave or anything. He was right there and so was I, and I had no option but to tolerate the situation I had found myself in until the plane landed.

I figured it was either a sick coincidence that we were on the same flight or Annalise knew, but had been powerless to do anything about it. I hated him, and nothing would have soothed my aching heart more than to have hurt him on my niece's behalf. His tour was responsible for Shona's daughter being an orphan and for me being left to take care of her child.

The world knew more about Noah Haxby's reputation than of any other rock star, and from what I'd seen in the papers my opinion was the same as many: he was a low-life rock star with no conscience. It wasn't all rumor and speculation either, because according to the press he'd even been banned from seeing his own son. That spoke volumes as to the kind of person he was.

Several minutes later, I was still standing inside the restroom but as anger had taken over from grief it had given me the courage to make my way back to my seat. When I opened the restroom door I saw there was less than thirty feet between me and my place, with Noah situated less than ten feet from what I perceived then to be my safe haven until we landed.

I closed my eyes briefly and a flash back in my mind produced the face of my sister lying still and lifeless. It gave me the motivation to brave my way to my seat. My eyes honed in on the back of his head as soon as I opened the door and I felt relieved he was still asleep. My stomach, which had been constantly acidic since I'd heard the news, was knotted again and I felt sick with anger that the man I held responsible for what happened to Shona was sharing her last journey with her. Even after her death it felt like he was still capable of causing more chaos for us.

Once I was back in my seat exhaustion washed over me. The least amount of effort wiped me out. I wasn't sure if it was the cabin pressure and feeling dehydrated, but whatever had contributed to it, I welcomed. Sleep gave my aching heart a break for a few hours.

Glancing out at the seamless, black night sky calmed me down. There was a sense of serenity and I hoped Shona was at peace wherever she was. It was the last thing I remembered as my eyelids drooped and I fell into an uneasy slumber.

Someone shrieked loudly, and I woke startled. My pulse raced from the sudden noise and in my disoriented state I sat bolt upright, turning my head to look at the commotion behind me. When I saw what was happening my temper rose and stopped just short of my tipping point.

A fan was flirting outrageously with Noah, and I felt both infuriated and sick. She was perched on top of his lap as they grinned shamelessly as she took selfies of them. His behavior confirmed everything I'd ever read about him. Their raucous conduct was ridiculous and disrespectful considering what had happened to my sister.

Neither showed any consideration toward any of the people around them and I felt furious. My eyes narrowed at the arrogance which appeared to ooze from every pore. I was about to turn away when he shoved the excited girl back to her feet and into the aisle where she headed back toward her seat. I watched him, watching her until he turned his face back in my direction. He obviously caught me observing his behavior and his lips curved into a slow smile. The smile felt salacious. *Did he just hit on me?* I threw him a look of disgust and turned back to face the front.

It was then I had the weirdest sensation like he was still watching me. The most fucked up part of it all was the fleeting thought that passed through my mind of how good looking he was. The notion that I'd even registered his appearance perturbed me.

I never moved from my seat for the rest of the night and sat in a paralyzed grief wondering how Shona would have reacted to him being confined in an airplane near to her. I slept again until the cabin lights went on at 6:40 am. Breakfast was served, and we were informed our descent had already begun. We landed in Dubai less than thirty minutes later. Greg, the cabin crew manager, came over to me, crouched and murmured in a low tone for my ears only.

"You will be the first passenger to leave the aircraft, Margaret. Linda here will take you to the transport which will transfer you to your hotel. Don't worry, the other passengers will remain behind until you see your sister transferred and you have departed to the gate." Greg gave me a tight smile but a nerve on his jaw ticked and the strain in his voice gave way to a hint of anxiety because he felt awkward.

There was an overnight stop before we continued on to New York. It was less than welcome, and I didn't relish the thought of another night away from home, but I was surprised at how quickly the legal issues were tied up for me to have enabled me to travel back with Shona in the first place. If I'd stayed until the following day I could have taken a direct flight, but I didn't want to stay in Australia a minute longer than I had to.

The aircraft door opened with a dull thud and Greg reached up, pulled my overnight bag out of the compartment above my head, then gestured for me to leave by nodding his head toward the door. I rose slowly to my feet and followed him to where a middle-aged, smartly dressed woman in a navy-blue suit waited to meet me.

I figured her attire was a uniform, but it wasn't the same as all the other airline staff on the plane. Greg gave me a gentle half smile, his eyes softening as I stepped out onto the mobile gangway, and I thought it was a smile of relief that his duties toward me were over.

Standing on the runway, I watched the somber men load Shona's casket again, before being taken to my hotel for the night. As stared out of the window I felt numb and thought how Shona would have loved the adventure of seeing another country.

By the age of eighteen she'd become an unruly teenager with her head in the clouds and a major fantasy crush on Noah and his band called Fr8Load. With his brooding good looks and an eye for the ladies, I could see the attraction, but Shona was obsessed... besotted with the guy.

Occasionally she had even disappeared from home and traipsed around the neighboring states, following his band with hope of meeting him. Her thoughts were delusional where he was concerned, and she had really convinced herself if he ever met her he'd fall in love with her.

Shona was intellectually smart, but dumb as fuck when it came to accepting responsibility for anything. Whenever it suited her she became an airhead, and any time I had tried to have a serious conversation with her she behaved like a petulant teenager and left me with no option but to become parental in my approach.

At eight years my junior, she was the late baby my parents never expected to have after a difficult birth with me, and as young as I'd been back then I had shared some of the responsibility for taking care of her. Our dad was already drowning his sorrows by the time she was walking and died an alcoholic after his company went bust when Shona was almost sixteen. As for our mom, she barely lasted a year after Dad died, due to a sudden deterioration of her chronic ill health. I guess she gave up.

Neither of my parents showed much interest in my younger sister, mainly because she had always displayed an awkward defiance toward them, but I reckoned Shona deserved better and continually tried to keep her on the right side of the tracks. I figured one day her maturity would catch up with her imagination and she'd settle down.

Despite her rebellion, I'd done an okay job with Shona and I thought I was finally getting through to her. Her high school grades were good and she finally settled on going to college to Major in Marketing and Advertising when she dropped the bombshell that she was pregnant. She adamantly refused to say who the father was, but was very determined to keep the baby.

Personally, I was devastated because I knew from the moment she told me, my life plan was instantly arrested. I could never have been selfish and washed my hands of her. It wasn't in my genes, so when she had the baby three weeks after her nineteenth birthday I knew my life had a new focus because Shona would never have coped alone.

Instead of using the savings I'd been squirreling away for a deposit on a better place, they were used to buy baby equipment and maternity clothing. Shona's wild behavior had caught up with her but I never expected to bear the brunt of it.

Woody, my then on-off boyfriend of four years, wasn't at all sympathetic to the situation that developed, and I guess he lost patience and grew tired of my constant excuses for not being able to commit to him. Then as soon as he found out Shona and the baby would be staying at home he called time on us for good.

Shortly afterward, he moved away from our town and never looked back. For a very long time, I was heartbroken, and it took me years to recover even after I'd decided if the focus was on himself instead of a destitute girl with a small baby then I was better off without him.

During the short journey to the hotel I began to recall all the dark experiences that had come my way in quick succession and wondered if they had been preparation for something like what I had found myself facing. If it was... it hadn't worked. Nothing could have prepared me for when Shona died. I was still brooding over that thought when the car pulled up at the sidewalk beside the hotel entrance.

My emotionally spent body was exhausted by the time I arrived at the hotel room door. It was all I could do to step into the shower quickly before I crawled onto the bed, still wet and with only a towel wrapped around me. I remember nothing after that until I woke in the darkness, feeling nauseous. I hadn't eaten much in the previous few days. With little to no appetite I had to force myself to eat and that day was no different.

Digging deep, I found the energy and made my way down to the lobby, opting to order a warm chicken sandwich and have a few cups of coffee there instead of dinner. After eating I felt slightly better.

Realizing it was almost 8:00 am on the eastern seaboard, I took my laptop out of my oversized purse and Skype called briefly with Molly and Mrs. Richie. It was good to see them, and Molly was delighted to hear from me.

Once I reassured her I'd be home the next day, I closed the call out and I looked up in time to see an elevator door open and Noah step out directly in front of me. The mere sight of the man made me upset, so I stuffed my belongings into my purse and headed for the elevators. It had been difficult enough when I saw him on the plane. I couldn't do anything about that, but I knew I'd be damned if I shared the same air on a voluntary basis.

CHAPTER SIX
Noah

*D*uring the short transfer to the hotel my mind went back to the woman who'd caught my attention for most of the flight and I wondered why she had been the first passenger to be allowed off the plane. I was a little surprised when the pilot asked us to remain seated for a few minutes and she was invited to leave by the cabin crew.

When she rose from her seat and gathered up her belongings, she looked directly at me and saw that I was watching her. I gave her a warm smile when we made eye contact and hoped for the same in return; however, she appeared to look right through me and wore a look of disdain on her face.

I recognized that look. I'd seen it plenty of times before and her snotty attitude pissed me off. I wondered whether she treated most people like that, or, if she knew who I was, she'd judged me on the reputation the media had formed of me. It was a pity because I found her highly attractive, but her arrogance stank.

It irked me because I felt she had somehow prejudged me and deduced I wasn't worth knowing simply because I sang in a band for a living, and frankly, her austere manner left me with a sour taste in my mouth.

Luckily, I didn't have time to dwell on it because I was second in line to disembark. I hated layovers, but I hated non-stop long haul more and was thankful for the quick transfer to the hotel in Dubai.

Less than an hour from leaving the aircraft I stood in the shower, thankful to have made it there in one piece. After I washed and felt a little better, I noticed the wet bar menu and scanned the room looking for the small cabinet that held it inside.

A slight tremor shook my hand as I swung open the door and found an assortment of sodas and ice teas. I sighed with both relief and a tinge of disappointment because true to form, Annalise had ensured all forbidden temptation had been removed from it. It wasn't her responsibility to keep alcohol out of my clutches; she was following orders from my manager to help keep me dry.

I pulled out a root beer and slammed the door shut, pulled the tab on the ring pull and slugged it down like it was all I really needed. Taking my drink with me I climbed onto the bed and lay naked under the colonial fan with my legs spread wide and my arms above my head. It wasn't long before the journey took its toll and I fell asleep.

Night had fallen by the time I woke and although I felt groggy, the pangs of hunger dragged me to my feet. I grabbed a fresh pair of jeans and pulled on a plain white t-shirt before texting Eamon to let him know I was on the move. I then sent another to George, one of my band mates, and Annalise, to meet me for dinner.

When I exited the elevator on the ground floor, I was stunned to see the same woman from the aircraft sitting directly in front of me when the doors opened. She glanced up and as she did I swear she winced in disapproval at my appearance before she went back to whatever she was doing on her laptop.

By then I was convinced she was stuck up and well connected. She'd been the first to leave the plane which was an obvious tell of her status. Usually, it was me who did that; the cabin crew normally gave me a head start on the passengers to ensure I arrived safely through immigration with the least amount of commotion to the other passengers. Again, I stared at her and considered what it was about her that I didn't know but all the airline staff did.

For a few seconds I considered ignoring her and heading straight to dinner, but I knew it would have bugged me if I never took the chance to change her mind about me. So, I decided to burst her bubble and show her what a gentleman I could be instead.

With time to kill and a challenge to keep me occupied, I figured no matter how I did it; I was determined to show her the kind of guy I really was and to change her bias view of me.

"Excuse me, I couldn't help noticing you were alone on the flight. As we have some time to kill I wondered if you'd mind some company... if you're not expecting anyone of course?"

When she glanced up at me her face was contorted with an angry expression. She looked horrified and dismayed to see me standing in front of her.

"I do mind. I have nothing to say to you," she snapped and pulled all her shit together without looking up.

It had been years since I'd faced rejection by any woman in conversation and I figured I at least deserved an explanation for the hostility she appeared to harbor toward me.

"Have we met before? I'm sure if we had I would have remembered such a beautiful looking woman," I asked trying again to be civil.

"Are you fucking serious? Leave me alone," she demanded, and became more visibly distressed as she sprang to her feet and hurriedly shoved her E-reader and cardigan into an oversized purse.

"Wait—"

"Stay away from me," she shrieked loudly as she hurriedly moved past me.

Without thinking I reached out and grabbed her forearm, "Hold on a minute, there's no need—"

Swiftly, she tugged her arm free, gave me a terrified look, and rushed toward the elevator. I stood stunned and watched as she rapidly pressed at the call button like she was desperate to get away from me. Glancing around, I saw Eamon walking toward me, his head turned and watching her, then I glanced around the hotel lobby. I cringed when I saw her reaction had attracted attention.

I ran my hands through my hair and turned back to look at the elevators and I was surprised when I saw her exchange words with Annalise who was in the elevator. I was even more stunned when Annalise appeared to know her. My confusion was increased when the woman appeared to reach out and slumped distressed into my assistant's arms as the doors closed.

What in Hell's name is going on? I sank down into the seat vacated by the woman and waved the waiter for a drinks service. "Soda and lime," Eamon piped up as the waiter attempted to take my order. "You didn't wait for me before you left your room," he offered, stating the obvious when he'd gone there to find me. I ignored him and sat still watching the bank of elevators and waited for Annalise to come back.

"What the fuck was that about?" he asked.

Shaking my head, I shrugged and continued to watch the doors of the elevators until Annalise came back down to the lobby. My drink arrived seconds before the elevator carrying her did and she walked toward me with a deep frown creasing her brow.

"Care to tell me what the fuck that was about?" I snapped in an aggressive tone. Annalise wrung her hands and her expression told me I wouldn't like what she said.

"Please don't be mad with me. I had every intention of telling you, but Steve said it had to wait until we got home."

"Tell me what? What the fuck am I missing? I've never seen that woman before in my life. Whatever she's accusing me of, she's a liar."

"Calm down. She isn't accusing you of anything, Noah, and I'm sure she'll view you differently in a couple of months."

"View me differently? She doesn't even know me. What the fuck is she judging me for? I'm telling you I've never even met her before."

Annalise wrung her hands again like she always did when she was about to tell me something she knew would upset me.

"Her name is Maggie. Her sister worked as a styling assistant until recently."

"So, she got fired?"

"She died. Choked on her own vomit."

The air I had in my lungs, instantly wasn't enough. I inhaled sharply as the shock of the news stopped me short of breath.

"She did what? She was one of my crew and she... *died?* Died as in dead? What the fuck? And nobody thought I should know about this?" I rose from the chair and tried to keep my voice down. "When did this happen?"

"It happened a few days ago—and of course I thought you should know. I argued that you had to be told, but Steve insisted it was a bad idea with the flight home n'all, and ordered me to wait until you were back in the USA. He knows how you feel about flying and—"

"And because Steve knows better, you did what he told you instead of what was right? Damn, Annalise, I thought you could handle my needs. Maybe you should go work for Steve instead of me. I needed to know about this... not find out about it this way." I glanced at Eamon, "You knew as well? Maybe I need a new team that will have my back," I bit in an angry outburst.

My temper rose at everyone knowing but me, and I banged my fist hard on the coffee table. It rattled my glass on the table and attracted more attention from those close by. "Very clever of you both. What was her sister's name?" I asked feeling totally inadequate because I knew nothing about her.

"Shona Dashwood."

"I didn't meet her, did I?" I asked and felt disgusted I hadn't.

"She only joined the crew a couple of weeks ago."

"What's the sister's name again?"

"Maggie Dashwood... there's something else, Noah. She arrived here yesterday to formally identify and accompany Shona's body home."

A jolt of electricity shocked my heart. "And we're all on the same fucking flight? No wonder she can't stand the sight of me. I can't believe you thought our paths wouldn't cross. What the fuck were you thinking?"

"I didn't have time to think. I didn't know Shona's body would be released so quickly and Steve had warned me not to tell you—" Annalise tried to argue in her defense, but I was too furious to let her finish.

"Now, I bet this Maggie woman thinks I couldn't give a shit about anyone on my crew."

"I'll explain."

"Explain? I think you've done enough harm. I don't care how you do it, but I want a meeting with her. Make it happen or leave. I want to speak to her. And I want as much detail about Shona as we've got. I take it there's a file?"

"There's not much to tell. She joined the crew around two weeks ago. She was in her mid-twenties, good looking, well liked, and a fun member of the crew. I had very little contact with her myself. She was vetted by some agency."

"What were the circumstances around her death?"

"She had been drinking with another crew member, got drunk, fell unconscious, and choked as far as we know. The guy she was with is no longer with us because we found he'd been using class A drugs."

I stood up and shook my head in disbelief, distressed by the news. I ran my hands through my hair. Eamon stood at the same time, like he thought I was going somewhere.

"Right. This is what you're going to do. You're going to go to her and come clean. You need to tell her I knew nothing about any of this. I can never make this right for her, but I can do my best to cover whatever she needs."

"We've already been doing this."

"Fuck. I can't believe this. I'm having a hard time that everyone kept this from me. Don't you get this? This is a huge fucking catastrophe, and I had no idea." I reflected on the incident with the fan on the plane and in a heartbeat I felt like shit. No wonder she stared at me like I was the shit on her shoe. She must have thought I was an insensitive asshole. "We were in the same cabin on the flight, for Christ's sake."

I was at a loss for how to make amends. I never thought I could. I continued to digest the tragic news and ran my hands through my hair again. "Go. I'm not doing anything else until I've spoken to her."

Annalise looked worried, like the task I'd set her was impossible. "Maybe we should wait—"

"I'd go to her myself if I didn't think it would upset her further. Get me a meeting if you want to keep your job." Without waiting for her to respond, I strode toward the elevator and headed back to my room with Eamon close behind.

Almost two hours later, my cell phone buzzed in my pocket. I pulled it out and saw it was Annalise.

"Speak to me." I said, in an irritated tone.

"Maggie has agreed to meet with you, but not in her hotel room or your suite. I've booked another—eleven forty one. It's on the floor above the conference suites and is reserved solely for conference attendees. She's making her way over there if you want to meet me there. Don't worry it's very private. There hasn't been a conference today, so the floor is completely empty."

Relief flooded through me, followed swiftly by apprehension. I was glad for the opportunity to set the record straight, but I also wanted to offer my support personally for what she must have been going through.

My only problem was I wondered how I could convey my condolences and support the family of the girl I never knew. I felt a huge sense of responsibility toward Maggie and her family and I hoped she understood my concern was genuine. I was pulled out of my thoughts when Eamon knocked on the door and I realized Annalise must have alerted him that the meeting was about to take place.

I saw my assistant leaning against the wall further down the corridor when we stepped out of the elevator. She quickly pushed herself off the wall and stood straight when she saw us come into view. Handing Eamon the key card, he opened the door.

When I looked past Eamon into the room, I saw the woman in profile, leaning against a piece of furniture. She was staring out of the window and her presence filled the whole room with sadness.

I moved past Eamon and signaled for him to wait outside. As I closed the door, I cleared my throat and expected her to turn to face me. When she didn't, I knew it was because she blamed me for her sister's demise.

"Thank you for agreeing to meet with me, Maggie. I appreciate you giving me the time to explain. Please accept my heartfelt condolences at this sad time for your family." Maggie eyed me with a guarded expression then looked back out of the window again, so I continued. "I'm very sorry to have met you under these circumstances, and I apologize for the way I approached you downstairs. I genuinely had no idea about Shona's death."

When I called her sister by name Maggie's head jerked in my direction and her eyes searched my face. The sorrow in her eyes pierced my heart. When she didn't reply, I moved closer until I stood directly in front of her.

"I really am so sorry for your loss and I feel pretty inadequate to know what to say to you. I know this is hardly the time either, but be assured I will be supporting all the financial obligations connected with Shona's death. It's the least I can do."

For a few seconds Maggie continued to stare directly at me but I noticed there was no animosity in her expression like there had been before.

"I only learned what happened after you became distressed downstairs and left. No one had told me of the terrible incident involving your sister. It was very wrong of my manager to advise Annalise to keep me in the dark until we were back in the USA."

Standing quietly, I watched as she hugged herself, her fingertips blanching as she squeezed her upper arms. Tears began to stream down her face, and I became aware of the weight of the burden she carried. I wanted to hug her... to comfort her, but I held back and folded my arms, instinctively knowing the move would feel wrong to her.

"Would your family like some support to plan the funeral?"

"I'm angry. So fucking... incredibly angry," she said in a sudden outburst. At first, I wasn't sure if she meant angry at me, then I realized it was a general statement directed at no one in particular.

"I can't begin to imagine—"

"No, you can't," she sobbed, wiping her tears roughly from her face. "My sister was infatuated with you. You have no idea the trouble it caused us. She walked away from her responsibilities at home and flew around the world just to ensure you had a pressed outfit to wear on stage and she had an opportunity to be close to you."

Maggie dropped her arms, shook her head, and waited for my response.

"Responsibilities? I thought Annalise said Shona was single?"

"Yeah, she was single. I mean she had no partner... but she was a *mom*. Now it falls to me to take care of Molly... her daughter. So, if I sound bitter and have no time for you doing your duty here, you'll forgive me."

"Fuck." I muttered in disbelief. The burden of the situation was felt by me, yet I had no understanding what it would feel like to have someone else's child to care for in the wake of their death. Maggie was grieving the loss of her sister and had become a mother figure the moment Shona died.

My heart squeezed at the terrible situation Maggie had found herself in through no fault of her own.

CHAPTER SEVEN

Maggie

*I*t was clear from the genuinely shocked reaction on Noah's face he was affected by what had happened with my sister, and I believed him when he said he wanted to help. I was surprised because the guy appeared so different from how he behaved on stage.

"Right. I want you to know you're not alone. I refuse to let that happen. You're not on your own so long as I'm around. Tell me what you and Molly need and it's yours." His flashy statement made me eye him suspiciously. I didn't want someone who threw money at a problem. No amount of money in the world could bring Shona back.

"Just like that? You think money makes everything better? Makes it go away? Maybe your help will get us through the immediate aftermath of Shona's passing, but what then? I'm more focused on what happens when the dust settles. I'm a schoolteacher of limited means and I have no choice but to accept your assistance to bury my sister due to my lack of savings, but after that I need to work and find my own solutions to this. I won't become dependent on handouts."

"Your sister was employed by my band; therefore, it is our responsibility to ensure her family don't suffer financial hardship."

"Listen, you'll forgive me if I'm not that grateful for your support. I don't really know what I'm going to say or do from one moment to the next right now, but it's Shona that I'm most angry with. Not you. She knew how hard I had to work to keep our heads above water and still... abandoned us."

My voice broke and I couldn't stem the fresh tears, or the lump burning at the back of my throat and I broke down in front of him. I covered my face with my hands and began to sob uncontrollably. Hearing the worries that had been swirling in circles in my mind for days was too much to handle. Noah hurriedly reached out and hugged me. I was so desperate for that human touch that I didn't pull away.

"Will you be able to keep her? I mean will your partner be supportive?" Noah asked, eyeing me with a questioning stare.

"There *is* no partner. Shona already saw to that. Look at me. What guy in his right mind would want a thirty-three-year-old schoolteacher with someone else's child to care for?"

Noah's eyes met mine and I could see him study me. "Most men I imagine," he mumbled almost to himself, "look this isn't the time, but you are one very beautiful wo—"

"Enough with the shit. I can't believe you'd take an opportunity like this to turn on the charm."

"Hey, I'm not lying. I think you're an extremely attractive woman, but I didn't mean it the way it sounded. I just meant any man would be proud to be with you. Having a child, yours or otherwise, doesn't make you any less appealing. But I'm sorry the conversation digressed. I'll set up a trust fund for Shona's child, Molly, is it? Whatever she needs: a monthly allowance, college fees. How old is she? I'm sure we can figure something out, I'll have my legal team draw something up—"

As if he suddenly became aware I was still wrapped in his arms, he dropped his hands and stepped back. He gave me an awkward glance which made me feel self-conscious. I felt the loss of his warmth and crossed my arms again grabbing my upper arms.

"She's only five, but it's okay. I'm okay. We'll get by. Thank you for taking the time to come to speak with me personally."

"Don't push me away, I want to help. Genuinely... I'd like to help you and Molly."

"You don't have to feel guilty. Until Annalise explained you didn't know about Shona, I hated you. I'll admit I was wrong. I've come to my senses on that and realize none of this is your fault. If it hadn't been your band Shona had chosen it would have been another. Looking back at the way she lived her life she never really gave a shit about anyone but herself."

We fell quiet for a minute then he turned and leaned back on the small sideboard, swapping places to where I had been when he had first entered the room. "Believe me, I'm not paying lip service to your loss. Shona was on my team; that makes you and Molly part of the Fr8Load family. We take care of family."

I thought about the press coverage surrounding his domestic issues and raised an eyebrow.

"Don't look so surprised, Maggie. I can guess what you're thinking. Don't believe everything you read about me in the papers. That's not who I am... that's who they want me to be."

"They?"

"The media, my management. I shouldn't have to say this, but I will for your benefit. No matter what you've read or seen about me in the press there's only one thing I can be bothered to defend. And that is, I love my son with my life. I'd die for him. My ex is a difficult woman, but if I thought taking Andrea to task would solve the issues she's created with Rudi, I would. Unfortunately, the world would never believe my side of the story. My only hope is that one day my son will know the truth about me."

I knew what he was talking about. According to the newspapers, Noah was forbidden to have contact with his son, Rudi, on account of his volatile behavior. I eyed him curiously because the man who stood in front of me didn't appear anything like the reputation he'd been given.

"Regardless of what my ex, Andrea, told the papers about me, my relationship with her was never totally serious. When I first met her, I thought she was lovely. I really liked spending time with her. We had a lot of fun and I thought she was good for me. What I didn't know then was she figured she could change me. When it became clear after a couple of months I was still the same person, she began to show her frustration when she couldn't get her own way. Then I guess she became frustrated when I refused to do what she wanted."

51

He stopped for a moment and I saw the hurt in his eyes when he stared back at me. For a few seconds I wondered if he felt he had said too much, then he sighed like it was a relief to tell someone and carried on. "From that moment on she became clingy and argumentative, but she knew me enough to know that being pregnant would be a game changer for her."

"So, she trapped you?"

"The day I drew a line under us as a couple she was understandably upset, but I never knew then it was too late for a clean break because she was already pregnant. After a long discussion, it was agreed I'd pay all her medical bills, set her up in a safe comfortable apartment close to my home, and employ a housekeeper and nanny to move in to support her. I was on the road a lot, but I wanted to see my child as much as possible and I'd have been happy to help bring him up every second that I could."

"It was also where your son would live so it made sense to take care of them both."

"After initially accepting the plan she reneged on the deal and decided if I wanted to help her bring up our son they should move into my home. From a previous incident I witnessed, I already had an understanding of her true character, and figured it was a bad idea. I'd seen how she treated her ex-boyfriend and after that there was no way I'd have allowed that to happen."

I moved over to a chair by the window, sat quietly, and listened with interest to him.

"Emotionally I still was a kid, far too immature to commit to a lasting relationship, but that didn't mean I wasn't willing to take responsibility for the care for my child. However, the way Andrea corrupted the information about the public incident I was involved in ruined any chance of me being involved in my son's life. I have to admit she was smart, the way she got everyone onboard with that. As the story escalated, I knew I'd never get a fair hearing."

Noah's own sad situation distracted me from my mine for a while and I felt bad for him as I watched how his body language reflected the genuine rejection he felt.

"Since Andrea and I split, I've never felt the same about relationships. I thought she was beautiful inside and out. She appeared kind and loving until I learned how manipulative and vindictive she could be. It was my own fault. I was so busy acting up to the self-indulgent arrogant public image people expected, that I must have missed how cunning she was."

"Noah, with the money at your disposal I'm sure you could find a way of reconnecting with your son."

"You'd have thought so, but that hasn't been the case. My parents see him, but not me. No one saw that side of the situation. I cared what happened to her and my baby. When she began defaming my character, I allowed the story to run until it was too late to shut her down. At the time, I was still trying to keep her on side for my baby's sake. By the time I let my legal team act, the damage had already been done."

"And you haven't seen him since? Did I read that somewhere?" I asked, remembering a court case of some kind.

"No, and that's a whole other story. Every spare moment I've had since the day Rudi was born has been occupied by thoughts of him. At first Andrea appeared to accept how we were, and fortunately she gave him my name, but when I was pictured with a female artist during an awards event she suddenly refused my requests to visit with my son. My legal team were on it, but I became depressed at being excluded from his life."

"Envy can have a vicious side," I agreed.

Noah nodded, "Except for the financial side, she cut all ties and I was fighting her on that, but my depression overtook everything. With that came my dependency on alcohol. As my drinking got worse, I didn't care about my work, life... anything except Rudi. Andrea boxed clever, delaying legal moves with a range of excuses. All that changed when Rudi was five months old. I punched a guy who groped me. It was an instant reaction in self-defense, but the dude fell badly and was knocked out. I'll admit I did mean to hit him, but I didn't mean to harm him to that extent. Anyway, as my reputation preceded me that wasn't how the courts saw it, yet I was only drunk because of Andrea's unreasonable behavior in the first place."

"You must have felt like you were your own worst enemy when that happened."

"Exactly, and I suppose from how she made things look it must have appeared like I couldn't give a shit she'd had my kid, but behind the scenes I was a mess. Her behavior has been so unreasonable even when I've tried to do the right thing. Not once have I asked for a DNA test or denied her baby was mine. She was with me and I knew it was. Back then, I may not have been the most stable guy in the world, but that didn't mean I'd have ever turned my back on them."

I couldn't help but feel sympathetic toward him because if what he said happened was true, a court fueled by bias reporting made a judge make a damning decision which kept him from his son just as much as Andrea had.

"One mindless act of defense marked me as a violent man, which Andrea used to obtain a restraining order. It still gets renewed and prevents me from visitation rights with my son. I thought my legal team were good, but she's got one clever motherfucking attorney. Every time it comes up there's been another story about me somewhere that has kept the ball rolling as to me not being a suitable person in Rudi's life. Funny how everyone has recognized my financial capabilities, yet they reserve the right to prevent me from demonstrating my parental ones which would have allowed my son to have a mother and a father."

My heart clenched tightly in my chest when I saw how devastated he was when he relived a painful moment in his mind. No one saw the real crime in the scenario he painted. He was arrested for defending himself. From what he said, Noah reacted in shock to defend himself. However, no matter what the circumstances were, to the establishment in authority he was a lowly wayward rock star and the other guy was the potential Harvard law student with a perfect 4.0 GPA, according to Noah.

"Why in Hell's name do people always equate intelligence with common decency and moral standards?" he rightly asked. "It would never have entered my head to pull a stunt like that on someone for any reason. He wasn't asked to give a reason by the way. However, the papers stated that he had brains and I was essentially, a fucked-up alcoholic musician, so I must be guilty."

Fury gripped my head, forming a band like a tightening vice, and I felt angry by the sense of injustice he'd suffered.

"I'm not going to justify what happened. Revisiting that is pointless. What's done is done, but I swear to anyone who will listen that some day people will know me for who I really am. Sure I drank—way too much in fact, but I don't anymore. I felt helpless. My situation felt helpless... still does. Perhaps that's why I empathize with your situation so deeply. Maybe it takes someone who's been there to see the level of despair in someone else. And believe me, Maggie, when I look at you, I see your distress as clear as if you wore it written on a button and pinned it to your lapel."

Hugging myself tighter, I wandered toward the door of the suite. "Thank you for sharing your story. For what it's worth, I believe you, Noah. As for your offer, Shona didn't have life insurance so I feel I have no choice but to accept your help for the funeral expenses. You'll never know the relief I feel about that, but Molly isn't your responsibility and I refuse to take advantage of your own personal situation to better ours. I'll manage somehow."

CHAPTER EIGHT

Maggie

*C*losing the door on the suite, I eyed the tall Irishman who protected Noah. He nodded at me acknowledging my presence, then I made my way back to the safety of my hotel room. The hatred I'd held for Noah had been replaced completely by sympathy. My perception of Noah Haxby had been totally altered to what I felt before I'd met him personally.

Instead, I'd found him a very intelligent, amenable man who was full of genuine compassion for our loss. The last thing I'd expected was to find a very level-headed, softly spoken man, yet I found that in Noah. His brash rock star persona had irked me from the moment I knew my sister was into him and I was relieved to find he was nothing like that at all.

Even though I was grieving, when Noah wrapped me in his arms and held me the way he did, I was aware of his warmth. It had been a spontaneous and comforting hug. I would never have thought him capable of that from the stories I'd read if I hadn't experienced it first-hand.

Later, when I sat reflecting on our conversation, the thing that struck me the most during it was although he was only a few years older than Shona, it was clear his life had been vastly different. He was worldly and appeared to have a level of maturity I rarely found in men of my own age.

A painful ache returned to my heart and squeezed tight when my thoughts turned to my poor little niece, Molly. I had no idea what the future held now I was all she had. My throat closed with emotion when I realized nothing could prevent the heartache she would feel at the loss of her mother, no matter how lax Shona had been as a parent.

Even after the initial grief of her loss passed, she would still be a small child with so many 'firsts' to face in her lifetime. The natural order of things would have been to share them with her mom, but I knew she'd never get the chance to do that now.

A soft knock on the door pulled my mind from that dark place and when I answered I was surprised to find Noah standing there with his hands in his pockets. "Traveling can be lonely at the best of times and as you're traveling without a companion I wondered if you'd be so kind as to share a bite to eat with me?"

It was the last thing I had expected to happen, but I was amazed by how thankful I was for his thoughtfulness. Nevertheless, I wasn't hungry, and even if I had been, I would have had no intention of walking into a restaurant and being seen in public with him.

"Thank you for your kind offer; however I don't have much of an appetite and I ate a sandwich not that long ago... besides I don't think being seen in a restaurant with you would be a good idea," I answered honestly.

"I'd prefer not to be in the restaurant either, so I was wondering, if I ordered something could we just hang out for a while? I'd like to know more about Shona... that is if you're up to sharing about her with me?"

My gut feeling was Noah felt lonely, and I wondered if he was unsure after sharing all that he'd told me. Weirdly, I felt the need to reassure him on that. "A little company may be nice," I heard myself reply as I fought against the weirdness of sharing an evening with him.

∼

Although the situation felt weird, it didn't feel strange letting Noah into my room because he didn't feel like a stranger after all he'd shared with me. I gestured to the small sofa for him to take a seat and wandered over to the wet bar to get us some drinks. Grabbing a small bottle of white wine, I began to remove it then hesitated when I remembered Noah was in recovery and went to put it back.

"Don't. Drink it, I'm fine. I'll have a soda water with a piece of lime if you're pouring," he said with a relaxed smile. I found myself returning it with a small smile of my own.

We sat side by side on the small sofa like two old friends and the conversation between us came easy. It was appropriate in the circumstance that neither of us appeared to hold back, nor were we afraid to say what was in our hearts about those we loved. And I found it refreshing not to have to pretend I was strong.

Instead of pizza he ordered an eclectic selection of dishes to share, then he sat back, leg crossed at the knee, and listened attentively as I gave an affectionate account of the colorful life Shona had led as he waited for his food.

"She sounds like she was quite a character," he offered once I was done.

"She was. For all her annoying and difficult ways, she's leaving a huge hole in our lives," I replied as tears filled my eyes to the brim. Swallowing roughly, I tried to stem the flow, but the feeling of loss became so overwhelming I had no option but to give in to the new wave of grief that washed over me.

Noah turned to face me, snaking his strong arm around my shoulder and he pulled me into his side. Wrapping his other arm around me, he rubbed my back until my tears were under control. As soon as I felt my strength return I pulled back, but not quick enough before he cupped the sides of my head with his hands and dried my wet cheeks with his thumbs.

No one had ever looked at me the way he did at that moment. His eyes were full of honesty as they stared intensely into mine. "It's okay, Maggie. Let it all out, honey. Just do whatever you need to do to stop the sadness from building so high that it stops you from moving forward."

Only someone who'd experienced despair could have expressed those words. As soon as he'd said them I believed he knew how I felt.

Sometimes you meet a stranger and instantly know they're a good person. Noah Haxby was that stranger to me. I knew instinctively the man beside me was the true version of Noah and nothing like the crazy rock star I'd turned my nose up at whenever I'd heard the media churn out yet another story about him.

After my emotional breakdown, dinner arrived and with a change in the direction of our conversation I felt my strength return. Naturally, I slid into the matter-of-fact mode I used in school to get me through and led Noah into a conversation about himself.

My heart ached when I heard him talk about how difficult life was for him after his son was born and I sympathized with a young dad whose life was changed forever by the will of someone else. Not because he was too young to be a father, but because he wanted to accept the responsibility and had been prevented from doing it out of spite.

Most surprising was how open Noah was when he spoke about his depression and I was touched by how he described his raw feelings toward his son, and how devastated he was about not being able to have a normal relationship with him. If what he told me was true, Andrea's behavior had led to his depression and alcohol dependency.

His story tugged at my heartstrings because I knew how the absence of either parent could affect the emotional wealth and confidence of a child. I saw it every day with children I taught in school. I wondered what Andrea had told Rudi and how that would affect his son as he got older. Would he grow up watching his father on television and think he'd abandoned him?

Two hours later, I had eaten more than I had in days despite my protests of not being hungry and I found myself reassuring Noah the truth would come out in the end. I suggested he keep a journal or something positive to show his son when the time came, to show him that he'd thought about him often.

I saw how uplifting this idea was when Noah became enthusiastic about making a video journal of his feelings toward his son where he'd talk about events that had happened from week to week and it felt good from my point of view to have been able to offer something to comfort him in return.

For five hours in total that day we shared our inner and darkest thoughts, our deepest fears as well as our hopes for the future. His hope was to have a relationship with his son, mine was to find the resources and strength to meet Molly's needs.

When Noah left to go back to his room, I was a fan. Not of the rock star; someone who would never normally have given me the time of day, but of the man, and my gut told me I hadn't seen the last of him and I was thankful for his time.

That night I was distracted long enough to help me get some sleep. Life had dealt me a poor hand but when I looked to Noah—a man almost broken, with a fractured family life behind him before it had even begun—I reasoned at least my life was still full because I had Molly. As I lay staring at the window cloaked in darkness, I drew strength from spending time with him in my hour of need.

Shona and Andrea had shaped Noah's and my fate in ways neither of us could control, but like Noah said, by keeping our sadness to a controllable level hopefully the pain would be bearable enough to keep us moving forward.

The hotel room phone rang loudly, dragging me from my sleep. I pried open my eyes as I grappled around for the phone handset and held it to my ear.

"Good morning, this is your early morning wake up call. The shuttle bus will be leaving for the airport in forty-five minutes. Have a great day." Click. I slumped back into the luxury of the soft pillows and for a second everything seemed fine, then the wave of grief rose like a huge dark shadow and the tragic memory of what had happened to Shona shot back in my mind with force.

I pushed back my grief, showered, and was changing into my

clothes when my cell phone rang. An official from the US embassy in Dubai informed me Shona's body was about to leave a chapel of rest and was being taken to the plane for the final leg of our journey. My throat stung at the never-ending hurt I felt in my heart.

Dressed in black slacks and a black shirt, I wrapped a thin black cardigan around my shoulders then pulled the handle up on my pull along suitcase from the luggage stand. Closing the hotel room door, I made my way downstairs to the shuttle bus. As I left the elevator, I noticed Eamon standing by the door. He intercepted me before I boarded the bus.

"Maggie, Noah was wondering if you'd travel with him to the airport. He's waiting in the car over there," he said and nodded toward the only other vehicle in the parking lot. I was touched and nodded, thankful I didn't have to face everyone on the shuttle. I followed Eamon in silence toward the car and when he opened it I saw Noah slide across the seat to accommodate me next to him.

"Hi, Maggie. How are you doing? Tough morning for you, honey," he acknowledged. "I figured it would be better if you had someone to help you through this. Is that okay?"

I was too choked to speak because I was so touched by his gesture. Until I'd spoken to Noah I had felt alone in my journey. Noah pretended not to notice, turned to look out the window and leaned back in his seat when I became upset. "The sky is fantastic. Not a cloud in sight. Let's hope it's a smooth ride today."

Something in the way he said it meant so much to me. I knew he was distracting me from the pain I held inside. Nothing would have changed the course of events taking place, but at the very least Noah had tried to make it bearable for me.

The short journey to the airport was over too soon and I knew I had to face the sight of my sister's casket being stowed onto a plane. Noah swept past me and jumped out of the vehicle, "Wait here. Eamon will make sure you're taken care of if we can't go through together."

Staring at the back of Eamon's head while he spoke to the VIP host, I felt embarrassed again—like a charity case. I was used to being strong and taking care of my own needs, but I was out of my depth and it felt excruciatingly difficult for me to rely on someone else. I waved the thought aside because getting home was all I cared about by that point.

"All right, Maggie, come on, honey," Noah softly coaxed when Eamon came back. Noah got out of the car and I glanced at the outstretched palm he offered. I hesitated for a second then reached out and accepted it. His fingers curled around mine and I drew comfort from his warm gentle touch.

Stepping out onto the sidewalk, I glanced up at him when he turned and began to pull me along with him toward the airport building. I pulled my fingers slowly from his grasp and adjusted the shoulder strap of my purse as an excuse to break the contact. Noah's brow furrowed, but he acted as if he didn't notice my deliberate separation. "An airline representative is coming to meet you to escort you to the plane."

A young English woman in a flight attendant's uniform joined us less than a minute after we went inside. "My deepest condolences," she murmured, bowing her head as she stepped forward to meet me. "If you'd care to follow me, the car is waiting to transfer Shona to the aircraft." I nodded slowly and Noah squeezed my shoulder, then he turned and walked off with Eamon beside him.

After an exchange of paperwork, I was transported to the plane and shown to my seat in first class—this time in the center isle at the very back near an exit and the restrooms. My cot seat was one of two adjoined and I was surprised when a few minutes later Noah came on board and sat next to me.

"I'm sorry sir, this seat—"

"Is mine. I'm supporting Ms. Dashwood today," he informed the flight attendant who had tried to prevent him sitting down, with an authoritative tone.

"I see, but this seat is assigned."

"Then reassign it... to me. What's the big deal? Everyone's going to bed soon anyway."

The cabin assistant huffed heavily, turned on her heel and strode purposefully toward the cabin manager. We both stared silently at her and I willed her boss to tell her Noah was staying put. Seconds later she turned to look at me with pity in her eyes and I knew he had agreed Noah should stay if I wanted him to. Relief flooded my body, and I was thankful someone familiar to my situation was close by.

"Watched any good movies lately?" Noah asked, distracting me from the attendant.

I turned and watched as he flicked from one page to the next of the inflight media magazine. He stopped at a double page display of a sexy new flick I'd seen being advertised on a loop on TV since the release day was announced.

"I'm sure you'd enjoy that," I teased and wondered what the hell had possessed me to say it.

Glancing down at the page with the scantily clad female he smiled. He didn't try to deny it, and I was glad of his honesty. "Well that's my bedtime entertainment taken care of," he agreed and smirked wickedly.

I was pleased for the moment of normalcy.

"So, what floats your boat? Bridget Jones? The Titanic? Or are you into a little BDSM yourself?"

Something happened in a heartbeat when he asked me that question. I became a woman again, and aware of being older than him. It shouldn't have mattered, but I wondered how he saw me. Then I felt ridiculous because he was only a traveling acquaintance in that moment, but it had mattered.

"The latter, can't you tell?" I said and I felt disgusted with myself given the circumstance, then I quickly put it down to my emotional state.

"Seriously?" he asked, his eyes widening flirtatiously back at me.

Despite the circumstances I found his attention welcome before I dismissed what I thought I'd read in his eyes. I excused my out of character behavior and thought I was reading him that way because of my vulnerabilities.

"No of course not. I'm a single woman with a child to take care of, when would I have time to be tied up?"

Noah burst out laughing attracting the attention of a straight-laced businessman who sat across from him. The affluent looking man gave him a look of disdain and vigorously shook his newspaper as a show of annoyance.

I looked back to Noah who was smiling warmly. He was still facing me and was oblivious to the passenger's reaction. I felt my cheeks warm and his eyes softened before he reached over and took my hand in his. His sudden act of affection made me feel slightly embarrassed, excited, and confused.

"Now, you see that? Finding your sense of humor even in your darkest hour, that's what's going to get you through this, sweetheart." Reality came crashing down, his reminder instantly filling my head with everything I still had to go through, and my heart sank to my stomach because I was foolish to even think in terms of men because my life was governed by Molly the second the call came about Shona.

"It's not a matter of getting through it, it's the 'being amongst it' that bothers me most." I replied honestly.

Noah squeezed my hand like he understood. "Listen, I know how daunting all this is for you, but you'll get through this, eventually. That's not me being glib or minimizing what's happened to Shona. People never know what they can cope with until they stare situations in the face. After our conversation last night, I have no doubt in my mind you'll do an amazing job with Molly."

Noah didn't know me from a hole in the wall, and yet he'd gone out of his way by offering me his company and words of comfort when most other people I'd interacted with since Shona's death had treated me like a hot potato in their hands. His thoughtfulness meant a lot. Unfortunately, the flight attendant interrupted with her cabin safety check before I'd had the opportunity to tell him so.

When he reached out and took my hand it had felt natural given his words of comfort, but when I saw the female cabin crew member notice, his gesture made me feel awkward.

I tried to slip my hand out of Noah's grasp, but as his grip tightened I realized, as a nervous flyer he was worried about the imminent take-off. The chatty conversationalist in him had fallen silent and instead I saw the knuckles of his other hand blanch as he clutched tightly on the arm rest. Knowing this gave me a valid reason to continue to hold his hand.

When the plane gathered speed along the runway, I saw his eyes squeeze shut and his fingers tightened on my hand. My heart clenched in empathy when I was given a glimpse into another layer of a guy who sang to tens of thousands in one hit, suddenly displaying his vulnerability like that.

We sat there for a few minutes while the huge manmade bird climbed to settle into its chosen flight path, then Noah released my hand and stared seriously into my eyes. "Fuck. I don't know why I put myself through this," he muttered.

"I don't know why you're so worried, you only die once, right? And anyway, the size of this thing we'd fall so fast you'd be unconscious by the time we hit the ground." I offered trying to lighten the mood.

Noah's eyes widened, but he offered a smile. "Thanks, and to think I was beginning to like you," he muttered.

My heart flipped over in my chest at his unexpected comment, even if was made in sarcasm. He turned his attention to his small backpack and pulled out a huge pair of expensive headphones. He flashed me another smile and slid them onto his ears. Seconds later he was selecting the raunchy movie we spoke about and settled back into his chair.

If it weren't for Shona, I'd never have thought I had anything in common with someone like Noah, yet after the compassion and consideration he'd shown me he had left me feeling closer to him than I had to anyone for years.

I had always praised myself on being a good judge of character and once I had gotten to know Noah, I'd decided despite his reputation, wealth, and fame, he was one of the most genuine men I'd ever met. He had more vulnerabilities than most would have realized, and I felt glad I had given him the opportunity to set the record straight as to who he was as a person.

Once the cabin staff's duties had settled, and the aircraft fell quiet, I felt my eyes grow heavy due to a couple of sedative pills my doctor had prescribed. I adjusted the chair into a bed and within minutes of closing my eyes I fell into a dreamless deep sleep.

Amazingly enough I slept through most of the journey, but I woke up feeling disorientated and dehydrated less than two hours out from New York City.

To my right, Noah lay facing me, sound asleep, with his blanket tucked up under his chin. He looked beautifully peaceful. Suddenly his eyes opened, and he stared up at me. My heart pounded in my chest and I felt embarrassed he'd caught me watching him. Part of me wanted to make an excuse, but I decided honesty was more important.

"You looked very peaceful lying there," I said, and was rewarded with a sleepy smile.

"I guess I got so tired I could've cared less if we crashed," he answered, making me chuckle.

We landed all too soon for me. Not because of leaving Noah, but facing the final journey to the chapel of rest with Shona. All the time I'd been on the plane I'd been strong, but as soon as the wheels of the plane landed a new wave of grief washed over me.

"Thank you for everything. I appreciate what you did and I'm thankful to you for helping us."

Noah stood and as we were separated by two small shelves between our cabin booth seats he reached over and hugged me.

"Stay strong, Maggie. You got this," he said in a deep voice laced with concern. Another wave of emotion rose in my throat and I swallowed a lump, gathered up my possessions and turned to the flight attendant who came to escort me from the plane. I couldn't look back at Noah again because I knew I'd never make it off the plane without breaking down if I did.

CHAPTER NINE

Noah

*W*atching Maggie leave the plane hit me harder than I expected. Obviously, I was devastated her sister had died while working for me, but at the time I went to see her I had never expected to connect with someone in the way I had with her.

The way I opened my heart to her about Andrea was a first. There was just this... connection, a feeling so familiar I somehow knew I could say what I felt, and she wouldn't judge me. And she hadn't. Instead of being the listening ear I'd intended to provide her with I found myself pouring my own troubles out. Everything I'd been bottling up for years came tumbling out like it would have choked me if I hadn't gotten it off my chest.

Maybe it was my way of empathizing with her hurt. Perhaps I thought she'd be too busy with her own grief to absorb much of what I said, or maybe... it was just time I let it out.

I knew very little about her—still didn't after we parted, yet I felt as if I'd known her all my life. There was an invisible tie between us and I had no idea how that happened so fast, or how it happened at all given the tragic circumstances.

My heart ached as I watched her leave the plane. I stared until she was out of sight then gathered my shit up, stowed it in my bag, and headed for the main terminal where Annalise had a car ready and waiting. Several reporters snapped shots as we walked over the concourse which attracted a small group of women in the pickup zone.

There's nothing like stretching out in your own bed—that comfortably familiar feeling of falling asleep and waking up knowing exactly where you are. Being on the road was tough and leaving my family behind brought loneliness. It was much worse for a guy like me because staying away from booze in those conditions wasn't easy.

My thoughts turned to work. The guys in the band all drank for sport, some dabbled in drugs, one more than dabbled, and everyone spent most of their spare time getting laid. Sometimes it looked like a competition between adolescent boys.

I'd be lying if I said I never indulged with drinking and getting laid. Alcohol had been my drug of choice. But since Andrea and my deep depression, I had picked my social events carefully, and my women with clinical scrutiny.

At my lowest point I woke covered in vomit. Luckily, I always slept on my side or my fate may have been the same as Shona's. I never dreamed alcohol dependency was in my future when I signed up with the band. At seventeen I was athletically fit, and I'd never drunk anything stronger than the occasional beer with friends, until I toured with Fr8Load.

If the same pressure to drink like that was put on me now, I'd never have stayed in the band. Being young and impressionable I'd done as I was told without question and if I had my time again, I would have been stronger. Hindsight is a wonderful thing. During the earlier days, we were four impressionable young teenagers in a rock band and our then manager coerced us to do some outrageous things to attract more publicity. It gained Fr8Load a reputation for being a band of hellraisers.

After a couple of years, we learned it wasn't the stunts we pulled off stage that kept our name up there in the dog-eat-dog environment of the music industry and ditched the guy who managed us. The problem for me was, as the lead singer, most of the focus had been on me, and subsequently I was the one who found it most difficult to shake that reputation.

～

After a marathon jetlag-induced sleep, I woke feeling refreshed and I remembered about Maggie. Rolling onto my side I reached out for my cell and called Annalise. After she informed me of all the arrangements for Shona's funeral, I asked her to text Maggie's number then I headed to the shower while I waited for a reply and thought what I'd say when I called her.

Refreshed, I rang her number and heard it connect on the second ring. "Hey, Maggie, it's Noah."

"Noah?"

"Yeah, I hope you don't mind me calling. I just wanted to check if there was anything else I could do to help?"

"Annalise has helped organize everything, but thank you for taking the time to call."

"Would you like me to come to the service?"

Silence stretched between us and I knew the answer before she spoke.

"I don't think that's such a good idea. Don't get me wrong, it's a lovely thought that you'd take the time to do that, but this is about my sister. I'd hate the last moments we celebrated her life to be marred with the attention you could attract."

Even although her words were honest, it still hurt to hear the rejection.

"I understand. Perhaps I could come and visit with you and Molly after a few days."

"It's okay, Noah, you don't have to do that. I know you feel bad about what happened to Shona, but, really, I don't blame you in any way."

"I know... you said that already. But, I'd still like to visit, if that's okay?" When she said nothing, I felt disappointed. I really wanted to spend time with her and was surprised at how quickly I had formed an attachment to her.

"Listen, I'm sorry, this is all too much when your focus is rightly on your sister. I'm here if you want to speak to me. This is my private number, Maggie, call anytime, I'd like to catch up with you about Molly's future. I really do want to help."

A few more moments of hesitancy passed before she agreed she'd call before she hung up. A pang of regret shot through me when she'd gone. I began to question whether it was because of Rudi I felt so responsible for Molly's future and found it weird that Maggie had such a profound impact on me.

During the morning I'd spoken with George, the bandmate I was close friends with, and arranged to have him over to my place for dinner. It was the way I got by when I was feeling less than a hundred percent. George was one of my biggest supporters since I'd been drink free and I'd utilized his, 'call anytime' plea about a dozen times since I'd been on the wagon. Closing the call out I felt marginally better when my doorbell chimed.

Eamon answered, and I heard Annalise's voice downstairs in the distance. I could hear by her tone there was something I wasn't going to like about her visit. She never came over unless it was something she felt would upset me.

I headed down to meet her and saw her and Eamon standing close and in deep conversation. When they heard me they both stopped and stared up at me as I came down the stairs.

"What is it?" I asked in a hurried tone.

Annalise juggled her large notebook and clipboard under her arm. "Aussie press," she stated.

My brow furrowed, "What about them?"

"They've got wind of the story about Shona's death."

I let out a deep sigh, "I suppose it was gonna happen," I offered and ran my fingers through my hair.

Annalise cringed. "There's more I'm afraid," she added.

"More? What exactly are they saying?"

"I've already spoken to legal and Steve, but it makes you and Maggie look terrible."

"*Maggie?* What the fuck—"

"Someone has obviously had access to a lot of information. There's more than one source because the news agency states sources as plural. We're trying to find out who they are; however we'll get information from the private investigator and PR team as soon as they have any."

"Private Investigator?" I became more confused and frustrated by the minute, "Will you just shut the fuck up about the peripherals and tell me what the fuck they're saying."

"Naturally, they are running the story of Shona's death, how she choked on her vomit, but the reporter has embellished the details saying it was at a drug-ridden after party." Annalise strummed her thumb against her clipboard, "But that's not the worst of it. They're reporting you and Maggie hooked up and spent the night together in Dubai after you hit on her when she came to identify her sister."

"What the fu—. I want an injunction, right now!" I bellowed. My heart rate soared and fueled my adrenaline to the point where I was spoiling for a fight.

"Already in progress. We can't stop what's already out there, but we've managed to prevent it from being published here in the US. We're in the process of taking gagging orders across Europe, but Australia and the Asian countries already have it. There's also a picture of you holding hands outside the car at the airport and one of you sleeping in adjacent cot-beds on the plane back to New York."

"Jesus H. fuckin— Eamon, where were you when this happened?"

"Boss, I swear I watched you all night. I never saw anyone approach you on the plane that wasn't employed by the airline."

"Fuck. How do I tell Maggie about this?"

"Is there anything between you? I mean did you—" Annalise asked.

"What the fuck do you take me for? You really think I'd try to fuck someone at a time like that?"

"Well no, I—"

"You what? You were just asking? If you had to ask, then you think I'm capable of it."

"I'm only asking what others would be thinking, Noah... what Steve is thinking."

"But you aren't 'others' you're my fucking PA for Christ's sake. We don't have secrets, but you are supposed to know me and have my back. By asking, it suggests you've considered I have it in me to stoop so low."

Annalise's gaze fell to the floor in shame with my dressing down; the disappointment I felt at her lack of trust was almost as hard a blow as the fake story itself. I'd come to rely on her honesty and wisdom, but when she questioned me that way it had felt like a stab in the back.

"Get out of my sight. Report back to Felicity in PR. I'll deal with her for now. You've really disappointed me, and I'm not sure how I feel about you right now," I said. Turning to Eamon, I threw a challenge at him. "Do you think me capable—"

"No way, Boss. I have to admit I was a little concerned at how close you appeared to be with her, but that was from the perspective you're too trusting, not that you'd fuck her," he said, holding his hands up in front of him.

My heart rate slowed down with his reassurance. "How do I tell Maggie what's out there?" I asked as my phone rang.

Glancing down I saw an unlisted number, but I knew it belonged to Maggie because I had memorized the last three digits. I felt sick to the pit of my stomach.

"I am so fucking angry right now."

"I guess you've heard. I only found out myself a few minutes ago, so I was just about to call you."

"Don't call me. Don't come near me. Isn't my life difficult enough right now without the press calling me a cougar and asking if I have no shame?"

The shock of her words twisted my heart with pain. "They fucking what? Who's said this? How did they contact you?"

"Some guy turned up at my door offering me money for my story, Noah. I brought my dead sister home and these people think I let you screw me." Maggie sobbed into the phone and my heart ached that I had inadvertently caused her more heartache.

"I'll fix it. My legal team are on it now. Annalise assures me nothing will be posted in this country."

"It's being tweeted for fuck's sake. How naïve are you? You think the press doesn't know how to get around social media?"

"Maggie please, I assure you—"

"Don't assure me. Just stay away from us. Don't help anymore. I'm begging you, please leave us alone."

Before I could say another word, Maggie hung up. My frustration and anger at the press shot up to a whole new level. Stuffing my phone in my pocket, I strode across the room. At that moment there was nothing I wanted more than a neat whiskey.

"Sue the bastards. What do they have? A picture of two people sleeping next to each other in what must surely constitute a public place."

"Noah, they have eyewitnesses from the aircraft that state you insisted you sat next to Maggie."

"Fuck, that was to support her during the journey home."

"That's not how they see it given your past."

"I don't give a fuck about the past, most of what they wrote back then was lies anyway." A text alert distracted me, and I wondered if it was Maggie.

Andrea: I just got a call from a reporter asking for comment about yet another indiscretion. Another reason if I needed one as to why Rudi is better without you in his life.

Fury coursed through my body and I launched my cell at the hallway wall. "Fuck. I am so fucking done with these people," I screamed as I ran both hands through my hair and tugged it in frustration. "I want to sue all of them. Get me legal, I want to talk to them."

Annalise looked shocked. She'd never seen me in such a rage and she looked unsure if she was to do as I said when I had previously said I preferred to deal with PR instead of her a few minutes before.

"Well?" I said, giving her the go ahead. Pulling out her phone she swiped the screen, scrolled for the number, and put the phone to her ear. "Gimme it," I said, grabbing the phone out of her hand as I wandered through to the kitchen while I waited for the call to connect. I knew I wasn't behaving reasonably toward her, but I wasn't feeling reasonable at that time either.

For over an hour we argued legal points back and forth until I concluded the call after they told me the Australian Press Association had printed a retraction, but not before the seed of doubt had been placed in both the public's, but more importantly Andrea's, mind.

CHAPTER TEN

Noah

I decided I had to go public in person to discount the article and dispel the rumors regarding Maggie and asked my PR team to set up a press conference. They argued against it, their feeling being if I protested too much it would give more credence to the story, but I was determined to have my say and put this rumor to bed. As soon as they knew I wasn't backing down they then wanted me to issue a statement instead of facing the press in person.

I didn't feel that was much better than them issuing the denial and refused, telling them if they didn't set it up pronto, I'd do the job myself. Two hours later I had six news crews and various magazine and newspaper reporters assembled in the parking lot of a local hotel. By the time I faced them my blood was pumping with disgust that I'd managed to drag Maggie into something so distasteful.

We arrived before Flick, my PR spokesperson, who only made it to the hotel with less than ten minutes to spare, but she looked super-efficient and calmly collected by the time she stepped up on the steps of the hotel entrance to address them.

"Good afternoon. Thank you all for coming out today. Noah has called this press conference to put the record straight on an inaccurate piece of reporting which was published in the Australian press in the previous twenty-four hours."

Turning to look at me before she looked back at them, she said, "When Noah has made his statement we won't be accepting any questions." Meeting my gaze again she gestured to me. "Thank you, Noah."

I acknowledged her with a nod and took my place on at the center of the steps facing the small group gathered.

"I haven't prepared a statement because I want this to come from my gut so that you can see how disgusted I am about the false reporting that's out there. Yesterday, Australian time, an article was published which was not only libelous to me and the other party, but extremely distressing to an innocent grieving bystander. A few days ago, one of my crew members working in our styling department died. She was not a drug addict, nor was she attending a drug-ridden after party as was sensationally reported by the press.

Shona Dashwood was an ordinary girl, from an ordinary family. A good family. She died after a social get-together with another crew member. According to the extensive toxicology reports there were no illegal substances involved. She was just a girl who threw up as we've all done when we've drunk too much, but tragically Shona asphyxiated when she inhaled her vomit. I believe this happens from time to time... to ordinary people. Now, because Shona worked as part of my crew, the press decided there had to be more to the story. There wasn't.

Had I met Shona? I'm sad to say I never met the girl. I *did* meet her sister, Maggie. Initially, Maggie didn't want to speak to me. She felt I was at least in part responsible for Shona's death, believing if Shona had been home she'd still be alive. I believed that to be true as well. However, Shona did pass in tragic circumstances and Maggie had the arduous journey all the way to Sydney, Australia where we were performing to identify, retrieve, and repatriate her sister's body. That. Is. All."

My eyes roamed the reporters faces as they recorded, scribbling notes or tapping into tablets. At least two film crews were recording live.

"I had no idea that Shona existed as part of the team nor what had happened to her until our plane landed in Dubai, but as soon as I was informed, I asked to meet with Maggie. Obviously, she was very angry and initially refused, but eventually she kindly agreed to hear me out. Did I spend time with her? Of course. Maggie was grieving alone, thousands of miles from home and I felt duty bound to support her. Let's hope none of you ever find yourselves in her shoes and have to endure what she has had too this past few days."

"Is it true you stayed the night in her room?" A short, balding reporter interjected. I shot him a glare then continued as if he hadn't spoken.

"Naturally, I wanted to know about Shona, the girl employed by me, who died before I ever met her. And, I suppose I also felt a strong sense of responsibility to ensure Maggie was taken care of in a strange country. A mutual trust built between us in a very short time and as such Maggie felt more like a friend instead of someone I was doing my duty by. It was because of this I sat beside her during the flight home. When the plane landed, Maggie went her way, and I went mine. There is no other story here except for the tragic death of a young woman.

"Wouldn't you rather sit beside someone who's aware of what you are going through at a time like that, given the length of the journey and the circumstances?"

Even though Flick had said no questions, another reporter, a female with a strong southern accent interrupted.

"Hi, Noah, Alison Digby, PR Celebrity Magazine. Excuse me, but given your reputation we're supposed to believe you suddenly developed a conscience?"

My temper went from naught to a hundred in a heartbeat but

because I thought Andrea may see the statement, I held myself in check.

"So I have a reputation? I'm a performer in a rock band. That's a bit like reading fiction... not everything you see or read is true. Haven't you worked that out yet? And you choose to believe what you've read in the media... the same media that has had to print a retraction of the lies they posted already? Do you all really think you know who I am? If you think I am capable of what they reported why are you even here watching me refute the story the Aussies put out?"

The reporter clutched her microphone a little tighter, the tension showing by the way her fingertips went white.

"Drag my personal life through the gutter all you want. I accept it as an occupational hazard of what I do. Cultivating fame will always cultivate criticism. Fine, do your worst, but don't target the people we come into contact with and create collateral damage for the sake of making a libelous sensationalist snippet for your respective magazine or newspaper at their expense. I urge you to consider the people you pull into those stories who often have no choice about being thrust into the limelight. They don't have a platform of denial like I have. And in this case if you have any sense of decorum left since journalism school you'll leave the Dashwood family alone to grieve in peace."

"We hear you're picking up the tab for Shona's funeral costs."

I scowled because my plea had appeared to have no impact on another younger reporter, who didn't look old enough to be doing the job.

"Naturally, she was employed as one of our crew. In all the time Fr8Load have been an entity we've had two deaths by natural causes and paid for theirs as well. Now if you'll excuse me, I have a private life to be getting on with. The tour finished a couple of days ago and I was looking forward to a quiet spell before these lies were printed. I know this is an impossible task, but I'll say it anyhow. Let's not do this again, shall we?"

The reporters continued to fire questions, some general about the band and a few levied at my lack of contact with Rudi. I ignored them as Eamon held them back as I climbed into the waiting SUV. The first thing I did was try to call Maggie back to tell her I'd held the conference, but her cell went straight to voicemail.

"Hi Maggie, I just want to let you know I've set the record straight in a news conference. My legal team has contacted the social media platforms to have all them remove the posts now that the legal team have been on it. I'm going to sue the publishers of the article on your behalf and ensure a retraction is issued with your name on it." I fell silent for a moment because I wanted to know she was okay and felt hurt to have been put in this position with her.

"Obviously, I'll be staying away from the funeral, but I'd really like to meet up with you as soon after it as you feel is appropriate. All right, I hope you are okay, and Molly is holding up. You have my number. I hope to hear from you soon, honey. Take care."

Three weeks passed with no contact from Maggie and although Annalise went to the funeral and brought me up to speed afterward, I still felt a connection to Maggie. I don't know why, but I had expected her to at least acknowledge the fact I'd fought for the truth with the press.

It was weird how she'd unexpectedly pop into my mind with increasing regularity. I found myself wondering how life had settled down for her and Molly. One morning I couldn't stop thinking about them and decided to try to call her again. She picked up at the fourth ring, right before I thought her voicemail was going to kick in.

"Hey, Maggie. Thanks for taking my call. I've been thinking about you and I hope you don't mind me calling. I wanted to know how you're doing and if you need anything."

"No, I'm glad you called. I want to apologize for the way—" she started in a soft tone.

"You have nothing to be sorry for. I should never have put you in that position," I replied, cutting across her apology.

Maggie gave me a sigh of relief, "Thank you for not being mad at me. I wasn't my usual rational self with everything that was going on."

I decided to move the conversation forward. "How is Molly doing?"

"Life hasn't been easy for her. She asked if she could die then she could visit with Shona."

My heart ached to hear that. "Tough. Even tougher on you when you are the one faced with all the questions. Kids are so innocent, and they have difficulty in understanding a concept like death."

"Loneliness is the hardest part. You know... doing this alone. My Principal has given me compassionate leave, which will take me through to the summer break. I'm fortunate that I work at a private school because I would have struggled to get three days if I worked for the State."

"I've got a lot of time on my hands. Would you be up to a visit from me?"

"Here?" She sounded freaked out by the idea.

"Or you could come here if you preferred?"

Silence stretched between us until she eventually said, "No offence but I don't think visiting your home would be the best idea based on what was reported after you came to my room in Dubai. Did you ever get to the bottom of that?"

"I read a bunch of legal papers they sent me. Apparently, it was a member of the cabin crew who spun the story. I was rude to her during the first leg of the journey home and I remember what she looks like. She saw the paperwork about Shona and saw us leaving the hotel in Dubai for the airport together. She happened to be hitching a lift back to New York with her airline on the same plane as us and saw the opportunity to get back at me. She took and sent the picture to a male friend who worked for the paper in Sydney. He then did some snooping in Australia and at the hotel in Dubai about Shona's death, got info from the receptionist about us meeting and ran the story."

"Jesus. That's insane."

"No, that's normal for my life. I should have protected you better."

"If it has any worth, I believe you about the guy who assaulted you, Noah."

"It's the truth, but thank you. What made your mind up about that?"

"You. The way you are. You're nothing like that shit-for-brains rock star image they've molded for you."

I laughed, "Thanks. Wish the judge had seen past the lies that kid spewed out in court. I may have been able to have a life with my son now if it weren't for him."

"Truth," she agreed. "Yes."

"What?"

"I'd like a visit, but I need to know you're not bringing the media with you."

"Would tomorrow night be good?"

"Tomorrow?"

"Yeah, I visit with my family on Thursdays. It's common knowledge and the media find the routine of it dull as dishwater. Maybe I could have a car bring you over there. They have a pretty private spread inside a wall of dense woodland and it's not accessible once you're inside the gates."

"And you're sure no one goes there? Won't your parents mind? Your family?"

"They love visitors. My dad doesn't get around much after an accident he had while felling trees, so he enjoys having new people around. I've visited there for the past nine years like clockwork when I'm home and the last picture they took of me there was around five years ago. They know there's nothing to see."

"Then Molly and I would love to come."

"Great. I'll have a car pick you—"

"No. I'll get someone I know to drive me. Text me the address."

I was about to argue then thought better of it. If Maggie was going to meet with me, it would have to be on her terms after what she went through with the media. We concluded the call and my chest felt lighter. She appeared to have that effect on me whenever there was any contact between us.

It was dark by the time Eamon pulled off the road and headed down the old dirt track to my parents' house. I was still an hour earlier than usual, but I had wanted to make sure I left the way clear for Maggie. I figured if by some remote chance there was someone lurking and I was already inside, they'd leave knowing I always stayed overnight.

Mom was excited because it had been years since I'd brought a female home—high school in fact—but when I explained I was only taking her there for privacy a light went out in her eyes. Nothing would have given her more pleasure than to see me settled after watching me sink to the depths I had after the restraining order was placed on me against seeing Rudi.

When Maggie texted me five minutes out from the turn off to our place, Eamon went down to the gates to ensure she made it smoothly inside the property. Oddly, when I saw her text, my heartbeat accelerated like it hadn't in a while and I realized I was really excited to see her.

CHAPTER ELEVEN

Noah

"*A*re we in the enchanted forest, Aunt Maggie?" The sweetest little voice asked.

"No, Molly." Maggie chuckled. "We're just having dinner at a friend's place."

"Does he live in the woods?"

I stepped out to where they could see me and smiled warmly at Maggie. My heart sped up when I saw her, and I glanced down at the cutest little girl with waist length blonde hair. I crouched down in front of her. "Hey, I'm your Aunt Maggie's friend, Noah, and no, I don't. But my parents do. Would you like to come with me and meet them?" I said, interrupting before Maggie could respond.

Watching Maggie intently, I saw her cast a glance around the heavy oak paneled walls until her gaze landed on the staircase, then her head turned as she followed the banister upstairs.

"Sorry, I hate to dispel the rags to riches image people expect from musicians. My grandfather was an accountant on Wall Street. This place was his weekend hideaway, hence the name," I explained.

"It's incredible—stunning," she remarked as she continued to look around in appreciation, her head turning this way and that. Molly stood patiently waiting at first, then as if she saw an opportunity she suddenly broke free and did a cartwheel across the floor. Straightening up she threw her hands in the air as if she were competing for gold at the Olympic Games. Maggie's jaw dropped, and she looked adorably embarrassed.

"Molly! What on Earth's name do you think you're doing? We're guests and you must remember to behave when we're invited to someone's home."

Molly frowned, and she stared at the floor for a second then slowly brought her eyes up to meet mine. "Do you still have a mommy," she asked in a tiny sad voice.

"I do, sweetheart," I answered honestly then felt lost for words.

"Mine went to Heaven because God wanted her to be an angel, didn't he Auntie Maggie?"

Pain flashed across Maggie's face and I thought how difficult those questions must be for her when she had her own grief to bear.

"Then she must have been very special because God only takes a few young mommies to be angels." I was concerned at how I had answered in case I'd said the wrong thing. However, I had been brought up to believe death was part of life having lost my grandparents at a young age myself.

"Did you hear that, Aunt Maggie? Noah said God thought my mommy was very special," she asked with pride in her voice.

"I did, darling—and she was," Maggie replied. I saw the silent thank you in the look she gave me for giving Molly a positive thought to replace the worry of not seeing her.

"Shall we go to meet my parents?" I asked holding out a hand out for her.

"Are they wrinkly like Mrs. Richie?" I frowned and looked to Maggie for clarity.

"Our elderly neighbor," Maggie advised me.

"Ah, I haven't met the famous Mrs. Richie so I'm not sure. Why don't you come with me and see, then you can tell me?" I replied and chuckled.

Molly slipped her tiny fragile hand into mine and a pang of hurt struck me like a punch to my gut. *Her hand would be around the same size as Rudi's.* It was almost unbearable to keep hold of it.

My gaze fell to our hands and a lump unexpectedly grew in my throat. I'd never missed Rudi more than I had at that moment.

As if Maggie sensed I was struggling, she distracted me. "Can I use the restroom first?" Guiding her to the bathroom I stood outside and waited patiently for her to come back.

"Do you go to school, sunshine?"

Molly stared up at me with bright crystal blue eyes and they looked surprised. "My mommy always called me that."

It was clear Shona was never far from Molly's mind and she didn't answer my question. I wasn't sure what to say and wondered if I had made a mistake calling her that. Luckily, Maggie came back quickly, and I led them both into the comfortable den my parents had settled in after my siblings and I flew the nest.

My mom was instantly smitten with Molly and Molly with her, then Molly turned to look at me. "Your mom is nowhere nearly as wrinkly as Mrs. Richie."

Maggie was about to tell her off again, but I shook my head and my mom spoke changing the subject. Within minutes Molly had tagged along behind my mom as she went into the kitchen to see what our old housekeeper had made for dinner. When I watched them go, it tugged at my heart and my soul ached for Rudi.

Of my mom's six sons I was the only one who had given her a grandchild, the others all too wrapped up in their careers to be tied down with kids. When the restraining order was granted they were devastated both for me and for themselves. Mom being mom didn't let the grass grow under her feet and sought her rights to visitation, so my parents saw Rudi four times a year.

Each time they brought home pictures for me and tried to keep me involved in his life, I died a little inside. Still, It was more than the authorities did by providing me with two measly update letters and two school photographs per year.

Maggie gave me a rueful smile as she watched Molly go and without thinking I reached out and pulled her into my side, kissed her temple, and squeezed her upper arm. I inhaled the scent of her shampoo, it was pears and something floral and her perfume was highly intoxicating.

"She'll get there. Just keep doing what you're doing, honey. It's early days yet," I offered then realized how spontaneously tactile I was with her. She felt so soft and feminine in my arms and I felt her lean in for a second before she stiffened, like she'd forgotten herself and suddenly realized what had happened.

It made me feel awkward for acting so intimately, especially given the fake news that had previously caused her so much distress, so I dropped my hands to my sides and wandered around the sofa. "Take a seat, Maggie; my father will be joining us in time for dinner.

When I sat next to her, I wondered if I should have given her more space and sat on the other sofa across from her. I'd never been awkward around women, but with Maggie I felt out of my depth because one minute I felt close to her and the next like I had no idea how to act. Another pause in conversation stretched into silence.

Maggie's curious eyes scanned the photographs dotted around the occasional tables and on the huge mantel above the fireplace in the room.

My attention was firmly on her because I couldn't stop looking at her any chance I got. Her beautiful even features, small perfect nose, and full lips, complimented her huge almond shaped, crystal-blue eyes —just like Molly's—and had me transfixed.

Without sounding biased, she was truly one of the most beautiful looking women I had ever seen. She was wasted hidden from the world as an elementary school teacher. She could have been the face of any business, a model, or promoted something very high end and glamorous with the way she looked.

"What is it?"

"Huh?" I asked as her voice dragged me out of my daydream. I turned to see her watching me intently.

"What's wrong?"

"Wrong? Nothing, why?" I asked trying to keep an even tone.

"You're staring?"

Busted.

"Yeah," I said in a thin voice because my throat was dry. I cleared my throat and tried again, "Sorry, yeah, I was. Busted. Forgive me, Maggie, I can't help that I find you fascinating to look at. I was only thinking how beautiful you are." My answer was straight from the heart, but I regretted voicing it when I saw how uncomfortable it had made Maggie feel.

Shifting uncomfortably on the sofa she fiddled with her earing and I could tell she had no idea what to say. I looked away to give her time to recover and felt confused by how unguarded my thoughts were around her.

Since the moment I'd met her I had felt the need to touch her, to comfort her, like words weren't enough. I'd never been a tactile person, but with Maggie I struggled to keep my hands off her.

"Maggie, I'm sorry. I don't know what it is about you, but I act differently toward you than I have with any other female. Perhaps it's the circumstances we met under, or maybe I feel responsible for the situation you're in.

"I don't need your pity, Noah," she said as she sat up straighter and bristled defensively. My father shuffled into the room interrupting another awkward moment. He was a welcome distraction.

"Wow, Noah, when your mom said you were bringing someone to dinner she never warned me how beautiful she was. Kennedy Haxby, my darling, but you can call me Ken, as in Barbie and Ken."

Maggie's eyes brightened with the instant smile that stretched her lips as she reached out to accept the hand my father had offered her. He was hilarious, my father.

"Has anyone told you how gorgeous you look, my dear?" he asked again because he obviously felt he hadn't embarrassed her enough the first time.

"Has anyone told you your directness since falling out of a tree makes people uncomfortable?" I threw back.

Dad chuckled and perched himself on the edge of the antique love seat that sat in the bay window. "Room for one more," he said pointing to the empty space and winked at Maggie. It was an effort to wind me up... and it had worked. I cringed.

Mom heard him and entered the room with a sassy swagger, "I hope it's okay, Maggie. Molly's taken charge of our housekeeper," she informed her with a sweet smile then turned to my father. "And don't be ridiculous, Ken; how could you even begin to think you could compete with our handsome hot rock star over there?"

The smile slipped from Maggie's face and she looked very uncomfortable. I knew I had to put the record straight. Except I didn't know exactly how, so I played it safe and made it about Maggie and diverted attention away from me.

"Cut it out. Both of you. Look at me. I doubt Maggie would ever be interested in what I have to offer with so many sophisticated men out there ready and waiting to sweep her off her feet."

Maggie glanced in surprise for a moment longer than I expected then flicked some imaginary lint off her skirt.

"I don't know about that. You're beyond handsome, Noah. Of all my boys you were the one that had the girls beating down the door since fifth grade," my mom reassured me. Maggie's lips curved up at the edges and she smiled to herself. I pretended not to notice and was about to change the subject when Molly swung by the door looking completely at home.

"Dinner is served," she announced in her cute little voice and curtseyed. We all chuckled but managed to hold it together enough so as not to make her feel self-conscious. I knew my parent's housekeeper had put her up to saying that. She had done the same to my brothers and I growing up, the only difference was we bowed.

Mom was very taken with Maggie and chatted easily to her about her job as a fourth-grade teacher, and my dad became absorbed in chatting to Molly. I sat quietly glad not to be the center of attention for once and waited as Maggie shared the professional side of her life. I'd be hard pushed to tell you what she said because I had been so taken with watching her, rather than hearing what she had to say.

The atmosphere around the table was more relaxed than any meal I'd eaten in a long time and as I couldn't take my eyes off Maggie, I hoped she didn't notice how attracted to her I was. I didn't want the evening to end because I enjoyed Maggie and Molly's company so much I didn't want them to leave.

Molly helped clear the flatware and take it to the kitchen as she helped my mom and our housekeeper to finish clearing up. It was Mom's excuse to keep Molly out of the way because she knew I had wanted to speak to Maggie.

When I suggested showing Maggie around the floodlit gardens at the back of the house, she jumped at the excuse to get out. I showed her around the grounds; the back of the house where my father had created a beautiful private walled garden.

I clicked the black wrought iron latch, opened the small arched gateway, and revealed the plot. Placing my hand on her lower back. I led Maggie inside, down the steps and we stopped side by side at the bottom. She rubbed her upper arms and shivered a little.

"Damn, are you cold? I should have grabbed your coat," I said as my eyes fell to her hardened nipples sticking through her thin top. My cock stirred in my pants at the sight of them and I tried to ignore the urge to pull her into my arms.

"I'm not that bad... there's a tiny little nip in the air," she replied and nursed her arms again.

Reaching over my shoulder, I bunched some wool in my fist and pulled my sweater over my head. I tugged at the hem of my t-shirt and pulled it back into place, but not before I noticed Maggie checking out my bare abs. My heart fluttered erratically when I realized she wasn't entirely immune to me and I bit back a grin.

"Here, let me put this on you," I offered, then rolled the sweater up and pulled it over her head. Again, I was surprised at how passive she was when I did that. She didn't protest or resist and shoved her arms into the sleeves. I continued to help her set it straight and fixed the hem in place, then smoothed my palms down from her shoulders to her wrists.

"There. Is that better?" I enquired still holding her upper arms.

Maggie nodded with a coy smile and without thinking I slid my hands behind her long hair at the neck. Her breath hitched when I touched her soft skin at the nape. I felt her shiver and her eyes darted up to look at mine.

She eyed me with an unsure serious expression and in that split second, we shared a moment until I looked away and broke the connection. I pretended not to notice the questioning look she gave me afterward and freed her long silky blonde hair from inside the sweater.

When Maggie didn't attempt to fix it in place herself, I smoothed it down and held the sides of her head in my hands. Then I noticed again that I touched her all the time.

"I don't know why, Maggie, but I can't stop touching you. Since the first time I saw you I wanted to touch you. I'm not sure if my instinct is to protect you, comfort you, or if my motives are less selfless."

I expected her to pull away from me like she had most other times; however, her gaze fell to my mouth then she looked back up into my eyes and her gaze pierced my heart. Then my pulse raced when she kept our connection going without wavering.

"I so want to kiss you. You wouldn't believe how badly," I confessed.

Her eyes averted to the floor for a second before she looked up and into mine. There was heat in them, but I could also see conflict. "What is this, Noah? This... thing between us? What's going on here?" she asked, eying me with confused suspicion.

"I'm not sure, but I'm so attracted to you. I didn't invite you here to hit on you if that's what you think. Nothing that's happened at any stage since I met you has been planned. Trust me, I'm not usually a very tactile person, but I can't deny the compulsion I feel to touch you, or the swell of pleasure that shoots through my body when I do. I'd be lying if I said I didn't find you attractive—mesmerizing, actually. From the very first moment I saw you on the plane I haven't been able to take my eyes off you."

I studied her carefully and waited for the rejection I felt would come when my words sunk in and was surprised when her gaze dropped to my mouth and lingered there. She swallowed audibly then glanced over my shoulder to look past me as if the connection between us was suddenly too intense. I didn't miss the heated look she gave me before she did that which confirmed she felt something too.

"Does it feel wrong... the way we feel when we're together?" I gently asked and willed her to say, no.

At first she didn't reply, then she glanced back at me through her long dark eyelashes and considered her answer. "Yes—I mean, we're not… together, but you make me feel… excited and scared at the same time. Alive, I suppose. It's been a long time since any man has touched me."

Her honesty made my chest tighten in sadness when I remembered what she'd told me about the guy who ditched her.

"Fuck," I muttered. I hated that she couldn't see how amazing she was, and I wanted to hunt down the guy who left her and hurt him for hurting her. "Do you want me to stop?" I prayed she'd think there was enough between us to let this happen.

"Whatever I say will be the wrong answer," she said in a sad, defeated tone as she shrugged her shoulders helplessly.

"What makes you say that? Why would it be wrong? You're in charge of your own destiny here."

"Think about how we met—what happened to Shona—your history with alcohol. I've been there before with a man who fought his demons through drink and I'll never put Molly through that if I can help it."

Her words stung, and my heart sunk to my stomach. "Shit, and here was I starting to think someone really believed in me. If you never understand anything else about me, understand this. I came through that. I'm a survivor—not a victim. Yes, I'll be a recovering alcoholic for the rest of my days, but my son's life is worth a hell of a lot more than a bottle of bourbon. It took me a while to figure that out during my darkest days, but I'm over those now. I don't want my son to look at me when we finally meet and be disappointed."

A look of shame passed through Maggie's eyes before she replied. "You're right. I'm sorry. You're not my father and unlike him you stopped." She exhaled and her eyes softened when she looked into mine. "I admire you for breaking free from it, that takes strength. I take back that part." I stared pointedly into her eyes, looking for truth in her apology, then decided she was only being rational and if I were in her shoes, I'd probably have felt the same.

"Apology accepted." I said and forced myself to smile even though the after effect of her words still lingered. I took a deep breath and tried again. "Okay. What about this? Forget everything. Clear your mind. We've only met for the first time, tonight. Now consider how you feel."

"I can't, it's too dangerous," her reply told me she liked me... she wouldn't have trusted herself not to go all out if the circumstances had been different. The response lifted my spirits.

"Dangerous? Why would you say that?"

"I'm older, you're a rock star, for Christ's sake. It wouldn't be good for Molly. She's barely dealing with her loss without..."

"Since I met you, Maggie... no, since the first time I ever saw you, I was drawn to you. Even given the circumstances I couldn't stop myself from being attracted to you. You make me feel centered. My thinking has never been as clear as it has been since I met you. And it's been a long time since I felt this grounded. Certainly not since Andrea took Rudi from me. Despite what happened to Shona, you give me hope."

"You don't know how much I'd like to believe that. How much I want for your fame and our ages not to be an issue. Then I think about your past relationship with alcohol, the press intrusion, your ex-girl-friend, and your son, and all I see is a recipe for disaster."

"Not forgetting Molly, your father's relationship with alcohol, your baggage with your ex-boyfriend, or your dead sister," I threw back harshly in frustration. My voice sounded much harsher than I had intended, but it got Maggie's attention. There was no point in hiding how annoyed her comments had made me.

CHAPTER TWELVE
Maggie

*W*hen Noah echoed my issues in response to what I had said about his, it shocked me. My heart clenched tight at the home truths he threw back. All he wanted was a clean slate, and I was putting obstacles in his way. It became clear to me, I had given him hope. He dropped my hands and opened his arms wide. Spinning first to the left then to the right he drew in a deep breath.

"Look around you, sweetheart. What do you see?" he asked with conviction. His family home was enormous with woodland all around and God knows what else because it was dark, and I couldn't get the full impact of their affluence... but I knew his family had very deep pockets from the house alone. *Was he trying to impress me?*

"Now, take a good look at me. What do you see? Try to push past everything you've read. Do you think I needed fame to have a good life? Do you think that's what drove me to make music? Let me tell you I was a kick-ass gaming designer by the age of seventeen, Maggie. I had offers, and I could have had an amazing career. Sometimes I think I made the wrong choice. I think it would have made me happy. Instead of that I joined the band as a favor to George, my bandmate. His life was messy at the time and his family struggled. I wanted the best for him. Plus, I was so young and desperate to make my family proud...

with five brothers who were already successful it made sense to hang in there with Fr8Load. Now? I wish I could go back to being just me."

"You don't mean that," I challenged.

"I swear it's true. What I've been through with Andrea was so gut wrenchingly traumatizing. She screwed with my head until it affected my mental health in ways I can't even describe. I wasn't brought up to be wild, and I never craved attention. I'm the youngest of six; a big tribe of loving, loyal siblings, I had all the attention I could tolerate."

"I get that, but it hasn't stopped you from courting the press."

"You think? My biggest mistake was following the orders I was given when Fr8Load was in its infancy as a band. Our then manager said he'd make us legends. My gut told me what I was told to do wasn't the way to go and I should have followed my instincts with that. No matter what the papers say, I have a good heart, Maggie. My regular life was taken from me and I ended up in this fucked up existence and estranged from my son. If I'd known how much I'd have to give up, I'd never have pursued a career in music."

"If you hate it that much why keep going?"

Noah reached out and held me by my upper arms. "Trust me, I'd do anything to have a second chance with Rudi, but the courts have already decided I'm dangerous and he's a vulnerable kid. What do they think I'd do to him? Believe me, it kills me every day to know strangers who knew nothing about me took my son away and took that pervert who grabbed me, and Andrea's word over mine."

A compelling urge to comfort him consumed me and I stepped closer, wrapping my arms around his waist. He instantly placed a hand on my head and I leaned my cheek against his chest. His heartbeat was strong and steady, then his arms enveloped me and he rested his chin on top of my head.

A deep sigh of contentment escaped his lungs and the warmth and security I had craved for so long was finally met. My heart fluttered in my chest and I knew I'd overstepped the invisible boundaries I'd set by clinging to him the way I was, but the relief of feeling I wasn't alone for a few minutes gave me a settled calm feeling inside.

"I get you. You showed me that by how you supported me during the flight home. I've been listening to you and my heart hurts for the pain you're suffering. I understand how important it is that people believe your side of the events leading up to where you are now."

Noah suddenly pushed me away, staring into my eyes like he couldn't believe I'd said what I had and then he hurriedly pulled me back flush against his chest, but this time his hug felt crushing, possessive, and desperate. Next thing I knew he'd separated our bodies, taken my head in his hands, and kissed me.

I'd never been kissed the way Noah kissed me before. It was an everything kiss, packed with every emotion I figured he'd felt in that moment. Insecurity, anger, frustration, need, pain, sadness... then finally passion.

It was an everything kiss because I felt everything he had too. My heart melted, my knees were weak, and every nerve in my body was alive with desperation, need, and anticipation.

His sudden move was so unexpected I froze at first, thinking he would realize he'd made a mistake, but when he didn't break the kiss and deepened it instead, a hundred thoughts crowded my head at once. I

thought maybe I was the one who should've had the strength to pull away, but at the time what was happening was so inviting and the smell of his manly scent surrounding me was something I'd missed the most since Woody and I broke up.

Caught up in the moment I gave myself over to him, allowing him to lead the way as I enjoyed the feelings that went with it and worry afterward, because who knew if anyone would ever kiss me as thoroughly again? When he pressed our bodies together and held me tighter, deepening the kiss, I thought I would faint from the heady pleasure his tongue made me feel as it dueled with mine.

A low moan of delight unexpectedly escaped from my throat into his mouth as Noah pressed his rock solid cock further into my lower abdomen.

His expert hands wandered up and down my back sending a thrill of desire to my center before they swept sensually around the globes of my butt as his fingertips kneaded my soft flesh at the same pace as his tongue explored my mouth.

My hands instantly migrated to his hair, and I sifted his soft blond locks though my fingers before I clutched a fistful tightly at the back of his head. He groaned loudly, then uttered "Fuck," as he broke the kiss for a second to kiss my neck.

Suddenly we were on the move as his mouth retook mine and I was lifted up onto his hips and I wrapped my legs around his waist. He crashed me abruptly against the garden wall and pushed himself flush against me again.

Rocking his hips from side to side I felt his arousal graze my pubic bone as his need for more grew until he released a low tormented groan, broke the kiss, and buried his face in my neck.

His breathing was heavy and irregular as he fought to control himself. When he kissed me again, his hand groped my breast with urgency as the heat level rose to a new height between us.

I dragged my lips free and dropped my legs to the floor, pushing him back to separate us. Noah stepped back, let out a shuddery breath, and ran his hands through his hair. He looked both frustrated and guilty. "Fuck, sorry, I was getting carried away," he muttered and glanced up at me with the same heat in his eyes.

He stuffed his hands in his jean pockets and stood quietly while I took a minute to gather my thoughts because I had no clue what to say. Then I looked into his eyes, but words still failed me. I stared in an awkward silence and he stared back. The connection I felt when we'd kissed was the deepest I'd ever known and beyond words, yet I felt foolish at the same for almost losing control to him.

Eventually it was Noah who broke our stalemate when he dipped his head and brushed his lips against mine. "What do you say?" I had almost forgotten the question... and barely held back a grin that threatened when I thought his kisses could probably make me forget everything.

"I say I'm scared, Noah."

For a moment he looked disappointed at my answer but the heat I'd seen in his eyes grew darker and he looked more determined as he closed the space between us again. Suddenly it felt like he had something to prove and he took my mouth in another hungry kiss.

His kisses made me feel desired, safe, and needed, and I never wanted them to end. This time Noah wasn't satisfied to feel my breast through my clothing and I felt his hand when it slid under the sweater he gave me as he fondled my breast through my top. His thumb strummed over my nipple through my lacy bra and thin top.

"Do you know how much I want to wrap my lips around this?" he mumbled around my mouth before his tongue sunk deeply back into it again. He pulled my top free of my pants and slid his cold wandering hand inside my bra. My breath hitched sharply at the cold sensation when his hand touched my skin and he broke the kiss and smiled against my lips.

Suddenly we grabbed at each other as our need grew with every passing second and the labored sound of Noah's ragged breaths made me squeeze my thighs together. I moaned loudly when pleasure turned to frustration and I slid my hand to rest over his jeans. Feeling the outline of his hard cock through them.

My fingertips grazed his length as Noah broke the kiss, stepped away and gave me an agonized smile. Once again, he mussed my hair when he ran his fingers through it and the intense look in his eyes made me melt as he cleared his throat and touched his swollen lips with his fingertips.

"Jesus, I almost took you right here, against the wall."

"No, you didn't. I'd have stopped you," I replied with a hint of uncertainty in my voice. In all honesty, I wasn't that confident I could have.

"I guess my threshold is lower than yours then because that last kiss was getting pretty fucking hot."

"Maybe... geez, this is awkward. We shouldn't have gone that far. For God's sake look at you, you're a hot young rock star, Noah. You can have most women. Why me? Do you feel sorry for me because of what's happened?

"Is that what you think this is?" he asked and scowled, "Did that feel like it would have been a pity fuck if we hadn't stopped?"

"No but I'm feeling pretty vulnerable right now. I don't know much about anything."

"I can understand that especially given everything you've probably ever read about me. God, that sounded arrogant, but that's not the real me."

"I knew what you meant. You're not arrogant. Okay, I'm going to bite... say we went ahead with this? What happens when the media get a hold of it?"

"Fuck them. Why do you care what they say? They don't matter... so long as we always focus on our relationship they can all go to Hell. I'm tired of letting them ruin my happiness; it's time they learned I have a real life, not the one they prefer to write about."

"I feel old."

"You are old."

I frowned feeling hurt, "Thanks," I mumbled, and my heart suddenly felt heavy.

"No, sweetheart, that's not what I meant. What I mean is the story of us is old news. I've gone to great lengths to ensure people know the truth—nothing happened—so this time they'll be less keen to report it."

I considered his comments while he watched me intently and I never saw any sign of doubt.

"To be honest, my head has been turned by you. I can't believe someone like you would be interested in someone like me. I'm nothing special," I said in all honestly.

"Someone like you? You're the hottest woman I've ever known, Maggie. Look at you... you're incredibly beautiful. Don't you have any idea how amazing you are?" he asked as he caught my chin between his thumb and forefinger. He looked again into my eyes, his stare piercing my soul, then he leaned in and brushed his lips over mine like it was his new favorite pastime.

"Can we keep things low key between us for now?" I asked, giving into my want of him without saying as much.

"Because?"

"Because I want to know if this is a flash in the pan or is it leading somewhere? Molly needs stability and other than those reasons, being with you could affect my work," I stated. My mind flitted back to some of the parents I had dealt with. How would they feel to know I was responsible for their children while I was fucking a rock star? To a lot of people rock stars equal no morals.

"I can tell you now, Maggie, there's plenty of spark but I'm not doing this lightly. Low key it is. You can dictate the terms.. I'm home for a good year because we're making an album, so we won't be touring during that time. It should give you enough time to decide if I'm worth it or not."

My heart flipped over in my chest at how serious his tone was and the time he was offering me to know if we clicked. The thought of spending more time with him excited me beyond measure, but I was worried. What if I got too attached to someone who would leave to pursue his fame elsewhere? I'd still be left behind and more importantly, so would Molly.

"We best head back to the house. I don't want to leave Molly for too long. She's been with too many people lately." I mumbled, changing the subject. Noah didn't react to my switch and began to lead the way back.

When we began walking, Noah took my hand and spoke about the logistics of how we could meet privately and the precautions he'd put in place to keep our time together away from the press. His plan appeared bulletproof, and it made me wonder for a moment if he'd used it often.

It transpired that Noah used a lodge house owned by his family as a private retreat. It was situated on the same estate about a mile from the main house. He told me it was his bolt-hole whenever he needed solitude and that his parents weren't intrusive people so we'd be able to relax there. Then he added we'd probably need his mom's help from time to time with Molly. I reminded him we came as a package and I was surprised when he didn't blink about that.

Everything he said sounded as if he was serious about getting to know me better. I was reserved but had to admit I felt the same. The only thing that nagged me was whether I was making a sensible decision, especially as Molly was part of the package.

~

We had only been gone from the house for around forty minutes but when we arrived back Molly was sound asleep, curled up on the rug in front of the fire. "I took her out to the barn with Eamon and she exhausted herself by climbing over all the stacks. She's tuckered out. Afterward I gave her some hot chocolate with roasted marshmallows and she flaked right out on the floor five minutes later."

I glanced at my watch and saw it was an hour past her bedtime. "I better get her home. It's late, and it's a school night, Noah."

Nodding, he pulled out his phone and texted. "Eamon will come around to the front in five minutes. I'm sorry I can't see you safely home, Maggie, but Eamon is a good substitute. He left the room and returned with a soft blanket.

Kneeling by Molly he spread it over his legs and tucked his arms under Molly's shoulders and knees. Next, he scooped her up onto his thighs and wrapped the blanket firmly around her. He rose to his feet slowly and looked down at her face like she was precious to him already and my heart fluttered in my chest at the way he had taken care of her. After that I liked him even more.

Molly stirred in his arms, "Shh, it's okay, cutie. We're just going to put you into the car with your Aunt Maggie so she can take you home to bed," he said then kissed her temple. It was such a natural act a father would do that a lump formed in my throat. I thought how difficult it must have been for him to be without his son all this time and a pang of sympathy burst in my chest

Affectionately he smiled at his mom and said, "Thanks for taking care of Molly for a while."

"It was my pleasure to be able to see that beautiful wide smile on your face right now. Maggie's company obviously agrees with you," she replied and winked at me.

I felt myself turn red because I was both embarrassed and endeared. I was quite a bit older than Noah and I wasn't sure if I'd have wanted any son of mine tied up with a woman approaching her mid-thirties.

Fortunately, I never got the chance to dwell on that last thought as Eamon turned up. Noah carried Molly to the car and suggested I got in the back seat with her. Eamon added it would perhaps be a good idea if I pulled the blanket over the both of us until we reached the Freeway, just in case there was a lone camera out there.

Noah didn't kiss me again, and I was torn but I knew he was only being extra careful not to overstep with me. I guess he sensed he'd push me away if I wasn't ready. The only outward sign of affection he showed was when he closed the door and he pressed his hand on the window and looked deep into my eyes.

"I'll call you tomorrow, Maggie. Sleep well, beautiful," he added. Shoving his hands deep into his pockets he stood and watched as we drove away. I watched him until I could no longer see him in the distance and Eamon's voice brought my attention back to the journey.

"You may want to slip that blanket over your head now, Maggie, we're only half a mile from the main road."

I did as he suggested and wondered how my ever-changing life was going to pan out and whether I was a fool to even try to love someone like Noah Haxby.

CHAPTER THIRTEEN

Maggie

*R*ight up to summer break, Noah kept his word and allowed me to move our relationship along at a slow pace. We Face-timed, called each other, and talked for hours during the day when Molly was at school to get to know more about each other, and then again in a more Molly friendly call so he and Molly could get to know each other as well.

During our time, Noah told me some truths that I hated, like how it was for him in the early days. From how he spoke I knew he was a little ashamed of the way he was back then, but he wanted there to be no secrets between us, which suited me fine. I'd have hated to go the distance only to find some piece of his history I couldn't get past.

Our dates were less than conventional for most ordinary people, let alone a rock star who had seen and done most things, but Noah showed me how serious he was by persevering with my pace. When he told me about his life, mine had felt dull in comparison, but the Face-time calls were a great way to build on the relationship we'd started in such strange circumstances.

Thursdays became *our* routine visit to his parents instead of just his. It was a safe, private place where we could spend private time together away from prying eyes, and although it had felt a bit weird to begin with, Noah argued nothing was weird after how we got together in the first place.

The first time his mom offered to keep Molly occupied because we, "Had things to do away from little ears and eyes" I almost fell through the floor at her blunt explanation and I felt like an awkward teenager again.

After picking up Molly, she pulled the door closed, and I moved sideways to the small window and watched them get smaller as they walked away. I was lost in thought as Molly skipped her way toward the trees when I felt Noah's heavy breath on my shoulder. Placing his strong hands either side of the window frame, he kept me in place. Leaning forward he inhaled deeply into my hair.

"God, you smell good," he muttered and took one hand away, sweeping my hair to one side. Bending his head, he placed his soft lips on the sweet spot on my neck and my head rolled automatically to the side giving him greater access.

"Damn, so responsive, baby, I love that," he mumbled in a low voice and continued his ministrations around my neck and shoulders after he'd placed his hand back against the wood on the other side of me. The fact that his lips were the only part of him that was touching me made what he did feel more erotic.

Continuing to pepper kisses on my skin, I couldn't hold back the soft sighs and weak moans that escaped because it took every ounce of free will to resist turning around to face him. His mouth worshiped such a small area of my body, but it aroused me so much and made me ache with anticipation of his touch.

"Do you like how I make you feel, Maggie?" he whispered, in a voice that sounded sinful.

"Uh-huh," I replied, licking my dry lips as my entrance squeezed tight.

"Do you want me to touch you, baby?" he teased, and he ran his tongue from my collar bone to my ear. A shiver tore down my back as my nipples crimped and my whole body shook slightly with need.

"Yes," I whimpered in a weak, soft voice as my addiction to Noah grew.

"Like this?" he taunted again as his hands left the window frame and traced down my sides. He dragged his wet tongue quickly from my neck to my ear again and stuck it inside. Fresh gooseflesh erupted over every inch of me. Another long shiver made my skin feel electric and my heart pumped like crazy.

His warm arms curled around my waist from behind and pulled me roughly against him. My breath hitched, and he chuckled softly into my ear.

"Am I turning you on, Maggie?"

"A little," I answered afraid to admit to how he made me feel. He laughed louder because he saw through my lie by how much my body was responding to his touch.

Noah inhaled deeply then let out a slow shuddery breath, "Fuck, you smell so delicate, yet I don't think you will be once I'm inside you." His remark hinted at the sexual power he possessed, and it took me off guard, making my heartbeat treble. I held my breath in anticipation of what he'd do next.

Grabbing the hem of my top he lifted it up. He stopped when I tried to turn and placed his hands on my hips, keeping me in place.

"Stay right where you are; I'm enjoying unveiling you by the fading light," he whispered close to my ear. I sighed and felt in awe that someone as amazing as Noah would think like that, even for one minute in relation to me. His words sent a shiver of need down my spine because the combination of his hot breath as it fanned my skin and his words laced with intent made me breathless.

"I'm in no hurry to take you yet, this is enough... for now," he informed me softly as his gentle hands explored more of me. "I aim to please my woman by taking her slowly," he whispered again, except this time in a sexy mock French accent. I smiled at that, but it was a short distraction because the combination of his hot breath on my skin and his playful tone had ignited the fire within me.

Staring out the window at the twilight I became conscious of each breath I inhaled and exhaled. They sounded raged and uneven. From the way Noah took control it was clear he knew what he was doing, and I was glad one of us did. I was amazed by the way he deliberately targeted only one erogenous zone but had still managed to gain total control of all of my senses. His unhurried dominance sent thrills of desire through my body and my trust in him grew greater with every minute that passed.

"You make me feel weak, Maggie," he murmured, in a low seductive tone as he stripped my top from my body then discarded it on the floor. I closed my eyes and felt glad I was facing away from him because my figure wasn't slender and lean like the women he was normally seen with.

Noah's hands slid around my hips again, one snapping open the button on my jeans. His hands slid up to my breasts, and he held each one firmly in his hands as he pulled me back to lean against him.

"So fucking beautiful, baby," he muttered near my ear. I felt his erect cock poking into my back as he did this. Separating from me he slid his hands back down to my hips and his fingertips grazed my skin next to the rough denim waistband. A sharp jolt of electricity coursed through my body making my core clench tighter. My breath hitched again, and a small vibration of need rocked deep within me.

Crouching down, he tugged my jeans down my legs to the floor and made short work of removing those too. He added them to the growing pile of clothes on the floor as the silence between us weighed heavily in the air as I tried to contain the feelings of lust that swirled all around me. "Relax," he whispered, placing a gentle feather-light kiss from behind on one thigh then the other. My heart raced frantically as the nerves in my stomach balled tightly at the sound of that single word.

Palming my calves, he slid his strong warm hands from them up to my thighs. Fresh wetness pulled at my entrance as my knees almost buckled.

"Steady, sweetheart," he murmured in a low sensual tone, then a soft chuckle escaped his throat. "Your skin is exquisite... like porcelain. Has anyone ever told you that?" he asked in a serious tone as he lifted one foot and spread my legs wider. In a long sweeping movement his warm gentle hands glided up my smooth legs, around and over my thighs to the front and trailed back around until he slid them over my butt cheeks. "Stunning," he said through a breath.

"Not really," I replied in a barely there voice as I quivered with anticipation again.

"Have you any idea how hard it is to touch you this slowly when all I want to do is to flatten your beautiful firm tits against this window and fuck you as hard as you can take it?"

I wondered if I could get any wetter between my thighs when I heard his admission and a new bout of self-consciousness washed over me. I never imagined anything like what was happening right then, to happen to me—ever.

Standing in front of a window in a vulnerable undressed state was so far removed from who I was. My cheeks were on fire and I felt like an unsure teenager for a moment, but I was soon distracted from that thought when Noah suddenly knelt, lifted one leg over his shoulder, and repositioned his head between my open legs. My heart did a somersault in my chest. I ran my dry tongue over my lips.

"Stunning," he said again, as a finger gently slid past the lace of my thong and circled lightly around my folds. "Even in the dim light I can see how I've affected you. God can you feel how wet you are?" he asked, "You're soaked." It was clear from the lower gravelly pitch his voice had, Noah was definitely turned on. I heard him swallow, right before he pressed his closed lips firmly against the lace of my thong.

He stilled then I heard and felt him inhale deeply. "Damn, Maggie," he cussed as he tugged my thong to the side. His hot wet tongue explored my folds, his tender strokes once again slow and deliberate. Giving me a teasing nudge he almost breached my entrance then slid back up my slit to circle my clitoris over and over.

Suddenly he sucked vigorously, his rhythmic suction so strong I could hardly bear the sensation. My hands fisted the drape on the window and I twisted it in a desperate bid to stay in control. For a second I thought I would come, and he abruptly pulled away, just enough and blew cool air against the wet swollen lips of my entrance.

Pulses of pleasure shocked my body, and I knew it wouldn't take much to make me come. I hadn't been with a man in over five years. When I thought about that I suddenly felt inadequate beside him.

"Noah..."

"Shh... it's okay. I know," he said breaking his ministrations to answer.

My brows bunched.

"What do you know?"

"I'm gonna have to go easy, right?" He asked, placing his mouth back on my pussy where he continued his foreplay.

My heart squeezed with affection for his consideration and I stood in wonder about how intuitive he was. I knew my body's reactions were stiff because both it and I felt unsure about how to react to someone as incredible as Noah.

I felt choked up that I was so easy to read, and I felt less than desirable at admitting I'd been alone for so long.

"You can either be yourself or be what everyone expects you to be, Maggie. It's up to you," he suggested, his finger replaced his mouth and circled my clit again.

"I don't know how to be anyone else," I replied, honestly.

"Is the correct answer, darlin'," he agreed and replaced his finger once again with his mouth.

Standing on one leg made it weak. Especially with a man like Noah, it buckled that time. Noah caught me from falling and swiftly jumped to his feet. Scooping me up like I weighed nothing he carried me through to a bedroom at the end of the hallway and tossed me play-fully onto the bed.

Before I could draw a breath, he placed one knee on the bed then snuck up beside me, fully clothed. He turned on his side and propped his head up on his hand.

"Maybe it would be better if you did me the first time," he said. A wicked smile played on his lips.

"Huh?" I asked not sure if I heard what he said for sure.

"You know... take charge.... feel empowered," he said with a small sexy smile as he wiggled his eyebrows.

"You want me to fuck you?" I asked in shock and felt even less confident than I had before.

"I want you to do what you want to me."

God, I wouldn't know where to start.

"Seriously?" I asked and chuckled. What I really wanted was what he wanted to do to me.

"How about I tell you what to do to me until you decide what you really want to do?" he asked with a persuasive smile.

I gave him a coy smile in return and didn't miss the amusement in his eyes.

"Maybe you could start by taking me out of these threads," he suggested gesturing at his clothing.

Doing my best to hide my nerves I crawled up onto my knees and sat back on my calves as he rolled onto his back to give me access to his shirt and jeans.

One by one I undid each button unveiling his beautiful hard smooth body. I marveled at his flawless skin and I couldn't resist reaching out to touch his torso. Exploring further, I traced each ridge of his six abdominal muscles and watched as a slight shiver ran through him. Leaning toward him I placed a kiss over his heart and saw his skin react in goosebumps the same way mine had reacted to him.

My long silky hair trailed over his bare skin as my hands moved to the belt threaded through his jeans. I glanced up a little unsure and was met by a sexy smirk which creased the skin around his eyes, but they shone down at me with genuine affection.

Even if this doesn't last between us I know I'll never have the attention of a man the way Noah pays attention.

Slowly I unzipped his zipper and my eyes darted from his undone jeans to his face because he wasn't wearing any underwear. I should have been prepared for that. As soon as I saw his thick veiny shaft my mouth watered, my core clenched and my heart rate doubled. I was excited and petrified at the thought of what came next. My confidence and nerves began to wane.

Fuck, Maggie, you're not a child. Pull yourself together.

Noah was a rock star and women had done all kinds of dirty deeds to him, and once I had that thought I contemplated what I knew and figured I could barely leave a smudge, let alone give him a dirty memory. My heart sank to the pit of my stomach and I felt sure he'd be disappointed in me. The thought almost made me grab my clothes and run. I looked up for any sign of doubt in his eyes and saw none. What

I saw instead was a man who wanted me. The desire in his eyes was unmistakable, and it gave me the confidence to continue.

Noah had tucked his forearms behind his head, his sexy confidence radiating from his eyes. I slid from the end of the bed and leaned over to remove his jeans. Grabbing the material, I tapped his hips in signal for him to lift his butt and his smile spread wider. He complied effortlessly, and I yanked them down to his ankles. He decided to help me at that point and kick them off his feet. I had tried to concentrate my eyes on the blue denim as he did this, but they had other ideas and kept flitting back and forth to his beautiful thick cock.

Once he lay naked, and I'd had the full Noah effect, I inhaled deeply, taking in as much oxygen as I could. He was incredibly fit, toned, and oozed sex appeal. I felt speechless as to what to say and my lack of speech caused my cheeks to flame. I looked down at myself and my blush had reached my chest and it made me feel even more inadequate.

Noah saw my reaction and began to laugh, then reached up and extended a hand which I took. Giving him a weak smile, I was about to climb back on the bed when he suddenly grabbed me, flipped me over onto my back, then crawled over me. He hovered above me on all four limbs and smiled affectionately again.

"Did you honestly expect that I'd leave it all up to you?" he asked, grinning a little wickedly as he dipped down and rested his forehead on mine.

"I was wondering if you'd forgotten what to do," I replied as I tried to hide my nerves. My heart rate galloped when I gazed into his eyes, so near to mine, and my voice sounded a tad shaky.

Noah snickered and sat back on his heels, then his eyes turned serious as he studied me carefully. Placing his hands on my ribs he slid them up my skin to my bra and delicately lifted the cups over my breasts with his thumbs.

"Beautiful," he whispered as if talking to himself before he bent his head and took one of my nipples in his mouth. A quick jolt of electricity coursed through me again and I shuddered in pleasure at the sensation as he sucked and rolled his tongue around the hard bud.

Rubbing my other nipple between his thumb and forefinger he

repeated the action again, then peppered kisses down my body leaving my flesh vibrating just under the layer of goose bumps on my skin.

"Let me look at you," he demanded in a low voice. His hands grabbed my calves from underneath when he sat up on his heels again. Cautiously, he spread my legs wide and bent them at the knee, abducting them outward before placing his palms on my inner thighs, gently pushing them wider still. When I saw the look of pure desire he gave me, my doubts momentarily left me. *This beautiful man really wants me.*

My mind struggled to compute the way he focused on my center when he suddenly grabbed my thong I wore and tore it apart at one side, leaving it hanging over my thigh. From that point every act that Noah did was laced with intent.

Watching his first taste of me as I lay naked beneath him will stay with me forever. His touch felt feather-light, yet it had almost made me come. The mere thought of him between my legs sent adrenaline flowing through my body.

I abandoned all thoughts, to concentrate on the sensations he evoked in me and it took nothing to get me off. I hadn't been with anyone in so long, but after that first time, Noah was more forceful, more demanding in extracting pleasure from me.

I'd never had a man who took so long and such delight in going down on me the way Noah did, and I feared if it didn't work out between us I'd never feel the way he made me feel when he had.

Before I could even consider reciprocating the favor for him, his thick cock was in his hand, his even strokes steadily tugging himself to full girth and length before he swept his thick smooth head against my pussy. I felt lightheaded at the thought of the pleasure he may bring me if his foreplay was anything to go by.

"I think you're about ready for me, what do you think? he asked in a serious tone. The way he looked at me was overpowering. I felt choked after all I'd been through in the previous couple of months and my throat closed with the emotion of it all. I closed my eyes for a second because I thought I may cry, but as if Noah knew he dipped his head toward me. Brushing his lips across mine he stayed silent and let me gather my feelings together.

"It's okay, Maggie, I get that you're overwhelmed. I'm not that far behind you myself," he said. I doubted that, but I thought it was a lovely thing to say to make me feel less of an idiot.

Swallowing hard, I licked my lips, and I heard him say, "Open your eyes for me, Maggie." I did as he asked. As I stared into his deep blue eyes, suddenly all my fears disintegrated. I focused on the intensity we built between us in that moment until the connection was so strong,

I'd have trusted him to do anything. I knew instinctively he'd never have done anything to hurt me. I nodded slowly, and Noah gave me a slow sexy smile.

Tilting his hips, he slapped my swollen clit with his tip then held it firmly as he slid it down to my entrance. I felt him exert some pressure and push himself forward. As soon as the head of his cock breached my entrance, both hands cradled my head as he slowly stretched my pussy walls and sunk deep inside me. He sucked in a deep breath and uttered only one word. "Fuck."

My breath caught in my throat when he pushed past his own feelings and whispered words of encouragement as he told me how good I felt around him. I winced as he settled deep inside and thought he'd split me in half he felt so big. At first having him inside me hurt like a bitch—it had been a long time and he wasn't a small man—but after a couple of minutes with Noah moving slowly within me I became accustomed to his size and began to relax.

"Damn... so tight. Maggie, fuck... are you okay?" He exhaled, "I think I've wanted this since the moment I saw you. Not that I knew that at the time, but it feels like I was made to do this with you."

It sounded corny but after the pain subsided, I knew what he meant for I felt like that too.

In the hour that followed Noah showed me things I never knew I'd been missing and eventually as if he knew I couldn't take any more he finished, his body suddenly stiffened and he came, pulsing inside me in slow rhythmic bursts.

I'd been on the pill for years and with Noah's history, I should have insisted on protection, but he'd made me feel like a woman for the first time in years and I wanted to be reckless. During one of our Facetime calls he'd disclosed he was tested regularly, and he'd never had unprotected sex since Andrea. And despite his public reputation I believed him.

Drenched in sweat and soaked in cum, I lay and relished in the damn feel and manly smell of the raw experience we'd shared together. My limbs tangled in Noah's and his strong arms wrapped around me tight as my head rested on his chest listening to his strong steady heartbeat. I must have dozed off until I was suddenly startled awake when the alarm went off on my cell phone.

No matter what else was happening in my life or how I felt, Molly was waiting. Sliding out of bed I found the shower and cleaned myself off, went back to the room and pulled on my clothing. Noah stirred as I was dropping my thong in his garbage bin. Perching up on his elbows he looked over at me.

Noah groaned and stretched his sleepy sexy body and I took delight in staring for a second. "Damn, is that the time already? I don't want you to go. Can't you stay, Maggie... please?"

"No... I can't," I replied. I couldn't hide my own sadness in my voice. "Molly has school tomorrow, Noah. It's already 9pm. We're going to have to figure something else out because I don't want her to suffer at school because of late nights."

He sighed heavily in disappointment and flopped back onto his pillow. He ran a hand though his hair and sighed in resignation. "I know. Let me think about it. I'll call you in the morning. I'll get dressed and come over to the house with you," he offered.

"No, stay where you are. Relax, I'm already dressed. I'll be heading straight out anyway. I'll talk to you tomorrow," I promised.

"Come here. You're not leaving without a goodbye kiss," he said, extending one hand, patting the bed with the other.

I leaned over and gave him a quick peck on the cheek and he tried to grab me. I was too quick for him and laughed because he never expected me to do that. As I made my way to the door, leaving, he called out, and I turned to look at him. He stood naked and scratched the back of his head before rubbing his hand down his abdomen.

"Thank you for tonight, Maggie. I know we didn't have much time, but I thought it was pretty special... right?" he said in what was both a statement and a question at the same time.

My heart flipped over at his words and I nodded. My eyes scanned his beautiful body, and I almost groaned because I felt tortured because I had to leave. "Yes, Noah, it was special," I confirmed and closed the door.

As I walked back alone to pick up Molly, my head was in turmoil because I knew that day, even before we had sex together, I had fallen in love with him. My worry of knowing that, was the insecurity of wondering when he'd hurt me.

CHAPTER FOURTEEN
Noah

*B*eing with Maggie was everything I thought it would be. It was agony holding back, but I had no choice because it was clear from the way her body reacted she was overwhelmed. It had been a long time since I'd considered the woman I was inside and in Maggie's case I most definitely never fucked her. It was gentle, intense sex, instead of the fuck-with-abandon kind of lay.

She was clearly very nervous, so I played around a little to take the edge off those nerves and it proved worthwhile. I could feel she was worried, but watching how her ass arched off the bed to meet my mouth when I ate her out, had my cock stretched to breaking point as I ached to take her.

Maggie was no virgin, but I never expected her to be quite as tight as she was, and when I first entered her I had to go slow... so slow it almost killed me. My whole body shook with the level of restraint it took.

When I slid inside her, I felt every muscle within tense and clench against me. I stilled because I knew from the way she was breathing; I was hurting her. The fit was exquisitely tight, and I almost lost control of myself. Moving gingerly, I spoke softly, persuading her to relax, and even though I'd been waiting patiently for weeks to be inside her, once I was it was still a slow, tentative process.

Sensual and gentle was how I played it. I wanted Maggie more than I'd ever wanted anyone, so I felt at pains to show her how considerate a lover I could be. I believe she really needed me to do that, and I was glad I did because I cherished every moment inside her. She felt incredible beneath me and I figured once we'd been there a few times we'd be amazing together between the sheets.

Several times I had a compelling urge to tell her I loved her, which was a surprise to me as much as it would have been to her, but I swallowed those words back because I felt Maggie wasn't ready to hear that from me.

I wanted her so much, and I didn't want to do anything to scare her away. I sensed when I was inside her that her feelings toward me could be the same but I couldn't be sure, so I kept my thoughts to myself and instead I tried to put the words I couldn't say into giving her feelings instead.

After I had sex all I usually wanted was to be by myself, but I felt crushed with disappointment when I had drifted off for a few minutes after my first time with Maggie and saw her dressing to leave. I wasn't prepared for the ache of loss that settled in my chest as soon as she'd gone, and I realized I didn't want to be without her.

Time isn't a rock star's friend. The pace was fast and the life we lived transient. We don't get to do a nine-to-five Monday-to-Friday gig like regular people, and the thought of having to walk away from Maggie at some point was already playing on my mind. I missed her, and she'd only just left my bed. If our feelings got any deeper, and I went to work away, I figured I'd be on the phone every spare minute of the day. I had it bad for her. Worse than any high school crush I'd ever harbored. *Damn.*

A couple of hours later, when I was still thinking about Maggie, I called my best friend George, to gain some perspective of my feelings.

"You didn't even know this chick existed a couple of months ago, Noah."

"Well I'm pretty sure I do now. Inside and out."

George snickered, and I realized what I'd said. "No, man. I didn't mean it like that. Well... I guess I do, but that's not what I meant. We just... connect. It's like... it's intuitive between us. We're on the same level and for the first time in my life I'm not scared of commitment."

"It's one hell of a commitment," George added.

"True, but I feel I really want to spend my life with her."

"And what does she say to that?"

"She's scared... she voiced that, so I haven't even expressed my true feelings for her yet."

"For Christ's sake, Noah, she's got a kid."

"Correction, she's got a kid, and that happened to her because of me."

"You think you're responsible, is that it? Is that what all this is?"

"Not at all. I'm saying Maggie has Molly because her sister got drunk and died on my watch. And let me tell you, Maggie's not in the least bit star-struck like everyone else. She hated me before she knew the real me. I'm saying the child is hers by default. That wasn't a decision Maggie was in control of. I don't care that she's part of the package. I'm happy to be in Molly's life. She's a very sweet kid."

"Damn, Noah, you've got it real bad. There's nothing I can say that will make you feel different, huh?"

"Nope. The reason I rang was to ask if you had any advice about how I should try to manage this? Like I said, Maggie's scared. And the media isn't my friend."

"Then fuck them. Put her right out there. Tell her she's got to face the press head on. Fuck... tell her to thank them for throwing you together with their accusations."

"She's worried about her job if being with me causes a shit storm."

"Tell her she'll be fine. You know how hard it is to get good teachers these days? It's in the news every day about schools failing targets."

"How the fuck would you know that?"

"What, you think because I like getting stoned most days I don't know what's going on in the world?" I laughed because he was right, most days he was so chilled and laid back he was almost horizontal. It surprised me he paid attention to anything.

Our conversation shifted to another bandmate, Vinny, our drummer. His drug problem had begun to affect his ability to keep time. Annalise and Steve had already expressed their concerns, and we had been considering an intervention. George had pushed for us put it to Vinny to see if he could get his shit together during our hiatus. But according to Steve when he'd visited Vinny twice, both times he was living in squalor and was off his face high.

I agreed the time had long past for us to call a meeting with the remaining band member and arrange to confront Vinny about his habit. We were all concerned and decided if he agreed to go to rehab we were prepared to postpone the start of our new album until he got his shit under control. None of us wanted to consider our options if Vinny wouldn't agree because we knew he'd be hard to replace.

The following morning, I could still smell Maggie's scent in my bed and the smell of sex lingered in the air. I wanted to see her again that day and Facetimed her as soon as I knew she'd be free. When she answered I felt breathless at the sight of her. She was make-up free and even though she was older, there was a purity about her that I had rarely seen in any other woman. Her gorgeous blonde locks were tied up in one of those messy buns and the tie had already slipped from it because her hair was so silky it couldn't grip properly.

"G'morning, gorgeous. You look so fucking appealing I could eat you. Wish I was there," I confessed and leaned closer to the screen. Her eyes lit up when a slow smile spread on her lips and she looked down like she was slightly embarrassed at the compliment. "God, I love that you blush," I said. She glanced at the screen and rewarded me with a coy smile and my heart ached because instead of talking through a machine I wanted to be with her.

"Will you let me come over there?" I asked and was disappointed when she shook her head.

"I really need to see you face to face, Maggie. I have something to tell you."

Her expression was concerned before but after I said that she looked outright worried.

"Don't worry it's nothing bad." I said quickly in reassurance and saw her visibly relax.

"Why can't you tell me here?" she asked, tucking a loose strand of hair behind her ear.

"What I have to say isn't the kind of thing you tell someone like this." She fell silent and stared at the screen.

"So... may I come over?"

"I thought we agreed—"

"We did, and there's slow and habitually slow. It's been weeks and after what happened last night we need to talk." I was done with the slow courtship. I could see by the look she gave me she thought I was blowing her out, and I was quick to add, "I mean I'd like to talk about how we move things forward between us."

She relaxed again and looked pleased even though she tried to hide that and sat further back in her chair. She wasn't as good at self-awareness as she thought because her face registered her surprise.

"Listen, we can't do this in a Facetime call. Please let me come to see you."

Maggie glanced to her watch then back to the screen. "How can I come there without being seen?"

Mom met Maggie in the parking lot of a diner about three miles from their home and drove her back to the house. I watched her clamber out of the back seat. My heart squeezed because it felt insulting that we had been reduced to secret tactics to protect our flourishing relationship.

I shook my head because I felt bad that she'd had to make the journey and I scrambled down the stairs to meet her. My heart beat faster with every step nearer I got to her. I had almost reached the door when it opened, and Mom moved past me.

When Mom moved out of the way Maggie stood in front of me wearing a nervous smile. When our eyes met her lips curved up further, and she looked more reassured. Dressed adorably in a cropped, pink mohair sweater and tight-fitting skinny jeans it was hard to believe she was in her thirties.

Moving toward her, I slid my warm hands around her cool skin at the waist and felt her shiver in my arms. Her breath hitched, and she glanced up into my eyes. "Good to know I've still got the touch," I joked and bent to kiss her softly on the mouth. Maggie pulled away and looked past me. "They already know, remember?" I teased because of the anxious look on her face. "We're not ten years old, Maggie."

"What did you want to talk to me about?" she asked in a worried tone.

"Hello to you too, sweetheart," I said, in a voice laced with sarcasm.

"Sorry, I feel like a crazy teenager sneaking around like this."

"That's exactly what I wanted to talk to you about. Come into the den and sit down. Dad's at physical therapy and Mom's ordering supplies with the housekeeper from the sounds of things," I replied and led her out the hallway to gain some privacy.

When she sat down, I sat close and slung my arm around the back of the sofa behind her head. "All right, Maggie. I didn't want to do this in a Facetime call so now that you're here I have something to say."

Maggie stared at her hands for a second then looked up with her piercing blue eyes into mine. "This shouldn't come as a surprise to you, but here goes. The last six weeks have been the happiest I've felt in years." I took her delicate hand in mine and kissed her knuckles. "I've never been a patient man, yet I've had to learn to be that with you. I wondered why at first, then it dawned on me less than a day ago that you were worth the wait. What I'm trying to say, Maggie, is I'm in love with you... actually, I'm all in and I don't really give a fuck who knows it."

Maggie sat and listened intently as she chewed the inside of her cheek. Her eyes searched my face for the truth. I'd never been more serious in my life about anything.

"You're asking me to throw myself and Molly wide open. I'd be ridiculed. I'm not as strong as you are—"

"No you won't," I scowled. "If you feel anything for me, then we should do this properly. Fuck the press. I give them two weeks max and they'll forget all about us. Let's show them we can't be shaken. I really want you in my life, Maggie. If you decided you wanted me, then you'd have to be prepared for us to go public at some point. What I'm saying is if you feel... this too, then we should get that out of the way." I stared intently into her eyes and drew in a sharp breath. "Do you feel how I feel or am I a fling?"

Maggie's head reeled back, a look of disbelief in her eyes. "A fling? God, no. You think I'd have snuck around with you at all if that's what I wanted? I'll admit that first kiss... I gave into it because it had been so long since I'd been kissed by any man. Then I realized I was kidding myself. It was because it was *you* kissing me. What we did yesterday? I can still feel your touch on my body. I remember how you felt inside me. My heart burned with pain when I had to go home. Then afterwards... I admitted to myself that I'd fallen for you."

The grin on my face felt a mile wide, and I dipped my head to kiss her. Instead of my lips meeting hers, her fingers pressed against them to stop me.

"Once I'd accepted I loved you, do you know what my immediate afterthought was?" I shook my head, smiling warmly. "I wondered how long it would be before you hurt me."

My smile froze on my lips. "Never. I'd never knowingly hurt you, baby. I know the risk you'd take with me. And I'm aware of how difficult I am to love, given what's happened to me in the past. All I ask is for this one chance. I promise it's all I'll need, and I'll show you how serious I am about us."

For a few seconds she sat staring down at her hands and from how I'd gotten to know her I knew she'd never be rushed into something. I gave her the time she needed to gather her thoughts and waited patiently for her to reply. When she shifted to the edge of the sofa and turned her eyes to mine, I held my breath.

"Shona is barely in her grave, Noah. I feel like I've done something wrong by being with you when she was the one besotted with you in the first place."

"Shona was a fan, Maggie. None of that stuff is real. She followed a rock star. She didn't know me for who I was. How can you feel like that when I never even met her?"

I took her hands in mine and brushed my thumbs over her knuckles. "I get your loyalty, but we're here and I was a fantasy to Shona. This is a time for new beginnings for both of us, baby." I prayed she wouldn't place any more obstacles in our way as she thought about my comment.

"Then what? What happens now?"

"Now we fuck everyone who gets in our way and learn to live our lives the way we want."

"And when you tour?"

"I'll do it when Molly is on school break. We'll hire a decent nanny, someone with incredible qualifications for the nights when I'm playing and the rest of the time we'll be like any other regular family."

"What about school... the parents... my career?"

"Like I said, I respect your work, but they're part of the fuck you club if they can't see how amazing you are. If they judge you for being with me I don't want you around them, but that's your call, Maggie. You can either keep doing what you do and ride it out, or you can flip them the bird and move on."

For a few seconds she pondered what I said and I willed her to take that leap of faith with me because there was nothing I wanted more in life than to be with her. Every second I spent with her I fell in love a little more and I had yet to find some way of making her understand that.

"All right, Noah. But... I'm petrified. For some reason I feel as if I'm going to be obliterated by the media, but I guess I'm more afraid of not jumping in with both feet and taking a chance on what I feel could be an incredible life with you."

CHAPTER FIFTEEN
Maggie

*I*t was one thing agreeing to be Noah Haxby's girlfriend in the sanctuary of his parent's house, and quite another when he shrugged himself into his brown leather jacket and insisted on picking Molly up from school with me.

My heart pounded in my chest as his mom drove us back to my car closely followed by Eamon his bodyguard in the car behind. I felt ill prepared for what I imagined would be a public onslaught of my personal life by the press. And I wasn't wrong.

Arriving at Molly's school, Noah slid out the passenger seat and jogged around the bonnet, pulling my door open for me. Extending his strong hand to me I slipped mine into it. He escorted me out then tugged me into his chest. "Don't worry, sweetheart, the more confident you look the less people will stare." He kissed my temple, slid the keys from my hand, and locked the doors with the fob.

Eamon had followed behind in another car and strolled toward us, "Hang back, bud, I got this, it's only school moms," he told him and released me from his hold to grab my hand. "Lead the way, baby, I can't wait to see Molly again." I was pleased because how he and Molly would be together was one of my biggest concerns.

"School moms can be vicious," I warned him, but he smiled warmly and squeezed my hand in a silent we-got-this gesture. "So can Noah Haxby, Maggie. No one fucks with my girl. I got you, honey," he said with protective conviction. His words gave me butterflies. I hadn't been anyone's girl for a very long time and I felt he had meant every word.

As we walked up to the waiting area, head after head turned in our direction before I heard excited stage whispers as the moms at Molly's school began to gossip. Jealous stares and snarky comments tore through the crowd like wildfire and the consensus was that Noah could do much better.

"Good on her, he's a lucky man. I've had a few fantasies myself of what I could do to that woman," one of the dads told another. Noah's body stiffened, and he turned to look the dad directly in the eye.

"That's my woman you're talking about. Shut your mouth," he said, and followed up with a small frustrated growl. "People need to learn to mind their own business and keep their noses out of other people's," he added.

Adrenaline ran through my body as multiple emotions engulfed me all at once and I knew there and then if a relationship was going to work between us I had to be much stronger and less self-conscious than I'd been.

Turning to look at Noah, I smiled affectionately, and he bent his head placing a soft kiss on my mouth. "That's it baby, don't let them get to you. Jealousy is a bitch," he mumbled against my lips.

I squeezed his hand, grateful for his support and turned toward the door to watch for Molly coming out. The urgent gossip continued around us and both Noah and I allowed it to go over our heads until we heard a comment neither of us could ignore.

"I heard from my friend she's supposed to be on compassionate leave from her school. What's he doing, fucking her grief away?"

Noah swung around to face the woman, but kept a firm hold of my hand. His grip tightened in anger and I became worried at how he'd respond.

"Have you nothing better to do? Yes, Maggie's grieving, but we're also in love. We didn't choose the timing of this. When you lose someone like she has, it brings life into perspective, or perhaps you've yet to experience that feeling?" The young woman looked awkwardly first to Noah then to me, shame staining her face at being singled out by him.

"Losing someone close teaches you what you may never have understood before. Life is short. If you find love, don't deny it. Grab it with your whole heart. Love deeply. Love with passion and never be afraid to go all in because we never know when our time will come to lose that person."

My heart swelled and squeezed at how eloquent his words were and at how confidently he'd delivered them. His words were straight from the heart and packed with emotion and I was in awe of his maturity and emotional understanding.

The waiting area fell silent, but I saw a few women recording us on their cells and cringed. "Now if you've nothing constructive to say to Maggie, I'll say this to you, but it's for everyone here. Do us a solid. Quit recording us. Maggie and I think what we have is the real deal. We're finding our feet as a couple and Maggie could do with some support from her community right now, not catty remarks and jealousy or selling a minute's worth of video for the press to tear us apart."

The tension was broken by the sound of children bursting through the door at the end of the school day and I welcomed the distraction. Parents greeted their kids and slipped into their normal home-time routines. Molly's eyes were as wide as saucers when she saw who I'd brought with me to meet her.

"Noah," she shrieked and ran full pelt at him. Her arms went around his hips and she hugged him tightly, with her cheek resting on his jeans. Noah smirked. "Why are you here?" she asked excitedly then pulled her head away to look up at him. It was clear that in the short time she'd known him he'd wormed his way into her affections as much as he had into mine.

"Hmm... let me see... maybe it was because I wanted to spend time with my two beautiful girls," he stated. Molly clapped her hands, jumping up and down with excitement. She was obviously delighted by his answer. Relief ran through me and I felt encouraged by her response because the last thing she needed was even more change to contend with. Then I reminded myself that children were far more adaptable than adults.

⌖

Neither of us could believe our luck when nothing was mentioned in the press and as time passed, I was amazed that we'd been cut a break and none of the people that were at Molly's school had said anything publicly. Then began to wonder if perhaps Shona's death was the real story after all.

Either way, we were delighted by the lack of intrusion and once Molly broke up for summer break, we felt the pressure was off. For months we'd maintained our privacy while Molly enjoyed sharing her time between us and Noah's parent's place.

⌖

As time moved on, so did our relationship and Noah and I became closer with every day that passed. The summer was slow and relaxing which had been great from Molly's perspective, as it gave her some security to spend most of her time with myself and Noah or with Noah's parents. By the time the summer came to a close it had been more than half a year since Shona's death, and with fall right around the corner it came time for me to go back to work.

We'd spent almost all of our time at Noah's place and we'd shared a lot of happy times; however when I suggested it was time to go home, he looked depressed. I could understand that in a way because by that time we had practically been living there. It was then that Noah pushed the boundaries of our relationship again and asked us to move in with him permanently.

Making the move official made me nervous. It was a huge step for us, but Noah was obviously very keen to make it happen because it became a nightly topic for discussion.

To him it made sense because Molly and I had only spent two days at home in the previous five weeks and he pleaded with me to trust him. From my perspective it was no time at all since Shona's death and

I wasn't sure I had made many rational decisions since she had passed. Living with a rock star wasn't something the old Maggie would ever have entertained, and part of me felt I had changed so much since what happened to Shona that I barely recognized myself.

Noah argued it had been six whole months since our first kiss and if I wasn't ready to be with him by that time would I ever be. His point concerned me, and I realized where I was the one feeling insecure, he was the one offering me his commitment.

Add to that the intensity of our relationship where we felt like we'd known each other forever. We had laughed, loved, and supported each other when each of us felt it beyond us to feel comforted, yet we had found comfort, passion and everything in between in our relationship.

If I wasn't with him, even if it was only for an hour, I missed him. He had openly told me the same. Then I reminded myself about how he'd defended me that day in the waiting area at Molly's school, and my doubts dispersed like dust. It was at that point I went with my gut and I agreed.

Noah was ecstatic, his parents and brothers were too, and that sealed the deal for me because I knew Molly would be surrounded by protective men, a kick ass grandma figure and a secure future whatever happened between Noah and me.

The following day I headed home and began to deal with the home I was leaving behind. For most of the week I cleared house until I only had one room left. Packing up Shona's things was the most harrowing task besides identifying and burying her. Noah offered to help, but that felt weird given Shona's obsession with him. It was because of Shona's memory I'd never invited him to our home.

Cracking open her bedroom door took all my mental strength. A faint smell lingered in the room. It smelled of Shona's perfume and the first thing I focused on once I had stepped inside was four, three-foot framed posters of Noah... my Noah, hanging on her walls. Feeling guilty, I tried to ignore them at first, but my mind flitted back to how angry they used to make me feel every time I opened the door of her room.

Now, I couldn't bear to look at them. I turned my attention to her dresser drawers and began emptying her folded clothes into boxes for the thrift store. Noticing one of her favorite hoodies hanging on the back of her chair, I stopped what I was doing then and there and reached out toward it. I grabbed it, held it to my nose and inhaled deeply.

A huge lump grew in my throat and I struggled to breathe as a fresh wave of grief crashed in and hit me hard. Despite all our issues, I missed her so much. It had been weeks since I'd cried for her by then, but to know all that was left of her on this earth was the slightest scent of her, a small child, and a few personal possessions, crippled me.

For an hour all I had done was sat on her bedroom floor and cried. Memories of better times intermingled with the times when I'd almost had to drag Shona from her bed to take care of Molly when I had to leave for work. After a while anger crept into my emotions again when I remembered how selfish she'd been when she left Molly behind. I wiped away my tears when aggression replaced sorrow.

When I recommenced what I set out to do, I reached for her shelves full of vinyl albums. Taking a handful at a time I shoved them into one of the larger cardboard boxes bound for the charity shop. Noah and his band suddenly smiled up from one. I closed my eyes as another pang of guilt hit me before I shoved it in with the rest and tried to forget he was my sister's fantasy crush, not mine.

Four hours after I started the task my work was done, and Shona's life footprint was almost erased. I didn't keep anything except a small silver picture frame for Molly that sat by Shona's bed. In it was the smiling face of two of most beautiful girls in the world, Shona and Molly.

I was fortunate because the thrift store was only four blocks away and when they offered to send a small truck to collect everything I felt relieved that I wouldn't have to walk away seeing all her things being set out for sale for bargain hunters to rummage through. Once I had made up my mind that Molly, and I were starting afresh I also donated most of my parent's possessions as well.

Initially, I considered keeping the house going just in case we didn't work out, but then decided if it would be an admission that I never expected it to. If Noah was all in, then so was I, and scary as it was, I had to show the same level of commitment to the new life we would build together.

What did give me confidence was that Noah's intentions were completely on point, but my one nagging doubt was his history with alcohol. I believed what he said about his son being worth more than slipping back to drinking, and by moving in with him I had also accepted I had a responsibility to help make sure nothing changed his point of view.

Then the way Noah took to Molly was incredible. He doted on her every word and after a very short time they appeared to be joined at the hip. She idolized him but in a different way to her mother. Molly copied him incessantly, nagged for his attention and followed him around. Noah, instead of being annoyed, appeared to revel in her affection for him. I knew I'd be hard pushed to find anyone else like Noah... and I didn't want to anyway, so as scary as it was, I had to have faith in us.

The delight on Noah's face when I agreed wiped any nagging doubt from my mind. Oh how he wanted us there. His beaming smile and obvious joy was an image that would stay in my mind. It was the one that got me through as I discarded my family possessions that held painful memories of the past. And as soon as the truck full of my history disappeared, instead of the sadness I'd expected to feel I was suddenly free to breathe.

Glancing around the empty house I took one last look around. I scanned the walls in the hall, noting I had missed one small picture that hung above a doorway. It was a family snap of my parents with me and Shona the day after she was born. I wondered how I missed it when I had taken down everything else.

Sliding it off the wall, I wrapped it carefully in the last piece of padding I had and placed it in the trunk of my car. Closing the door for the last time I was surprised to realize I felt no deep attachment to the place, perhaps that was because I'd experienced so much pain when we all lived there.

I climbed into the car and reversed past the 'For Sale' sign at the end of the driveway. Glancing one last time at the house I put the stick into drive. Pulling away from the street, I took a deep breath and sighed in relief then I prayed I was headed for happier times in the next part of my life's journey.

With one part of my plan complete, the next was to face my colleagues at work, and just as I suspected there were more than a few who frowned upon my relationship with Noah. His reputation preceded him and it was decided in my absence among my peers that I must have had some kind of breakdown to even think of being with Noah. From the way they demonized him I grew worried about their constant questioning about how he was with Molly. I knew what it felt like to be guilty by association during that time.

Maybe I wasn't thinking straight, but I hadn't figured it would be a problem with him. It wasn't like he was any threat to her. He loved Molly almost as much as I did. I never for a second worried about him being with her, and legally, I was her guardian, not Noah, and ultimately, I made any decisions regarding her welfare. That wasn't how they saw it and I knew from those questions they thought I had moved a vulnerable child into the home of a man who was forbidden to have contact with his own child.

At the end of a trying week, I left work and drove home feeling far less confident about the interference of others than I had that first night we'd moved in for good. Noah noticed how withdrawn I was and after Molly was settled in bed, he pulled me onto his lap on the sofa.

"All right, out with it," he coaxed as he rubbed his hand possessively up and down my thigh.

"It's nothing," I replied shaking my head.

"If you're telling me it's nothing, then it's something. Come on, what's got you so preoccupied?"

I stared longingly into his eyes and felt angry that I was being made to voice the concerns of some who judged him wrongly.

"Remember I told you how concerned I was about work?"

"Right... and?"

"Most of the shit I can handle but there are a couple who have now taken the mantle about Molly."

"Molly?"

"Yeah… they want to know if she's safe around you," I said quietly and cringed when I said it out loud.

"Yeah?" he asked in a defeated tone. His hand stilled on my leg.

I nodded and wrapped my arms around his neck. His head drooped in thought.

"Fuckers," he muttered and glanced up at my face. "You know I'd—"

"I've never doubted Molly's safety for one second so don't even think about that part. What's worrying me is they've mentioned there could be safeguarding issues because of the restraining order against you."

I felt his whole body sag further into the sofa before he glanced up at me. "Tell me what to do and I'll do it," Noah stated. He sounded desperate to do the right thing.

"There's only one way I can think of to curb their thirst and that would be to contact welfare myself, but it would be an intrusive process, Noah."

"Do it."

"Are you sure? I thought if I make it open house then they'll see how you are with Molly and that you pose no threat. It may even help to re-establish contact with Rudi."

Noah leaned back into the back of the sofa taking me with him.

"What the fuck has the world come to?" he asked, sounding as sad as I'd ever heard him. "Call them."

"Okay. If you're sure. We'll just have to make them see you're a great influence in Molly's life and then they'll leave us in peace."

CHAPTER SIXTEEN

Noah

There were times in my life when I thought I could sink no lower and then there were visits from Child Welfare. There aren't many men who would open their home for inspection but that's exactly what I did to protect my relationship with Maggie. I couldn't help feeling like we were being punished by people because they had nothing better to do.

Not one, but two social workers visited, traveling in pairs because they deemed me a high risk of violence, according to Maggie. If that were the case how could two middle-aged women defend each other against me unless they were carrying concealed weapons. I'd only ever hit one person in my life and that was in self-defense—yet this was the result.

When I opened the door the shorter, heavier built of the two women looked past me. "Anyone at home?" *Is she blind? I'm right in front of her.*

"Maggie and Molly should be home any minute," I replied when I looked at my wristwatch. "Please, come inside. I put fresh coffee on a few minutes ago." Standing clear of the door I gestured by sweeping my hand toward the sitting room and waited for them to enter. The same woman looked dismayed when I had asked her inside like I was some kind of serial killer and stayed put stuffing her hands into her pockets, the second stepped over the threshold.

"Thank you, Noah."

I watched her move further into the hallway and glanced back at the first again. It was clear she thought she was in charge but was confused about what to do since her colleague had undermined her. Deciding to ignore her I turned away and walked in front of the first leaving her in the doorway. I wasn't going to be the one to coax her to come in. I didn't want her there in the first place.

"You have a beautiful home. Clara Simmons," she advised as she began unbuttoning her coat. Seconds later the one from the door wandered into the room. She still had a wary look on her face.

"It's very... homey," she offered warily as I watched her scanning the room. Probably for knives and gun since I was such a threat.

"How long have you lived here, Mr. Haxby?" the hostile one asked in an indignant tone.

"I'm sorry, I didn't catch your name," I replied, reminding her of her manners.

"Jean Thompson," she replied dispensing with civility.

"Well Jean, and Clara," I added, careful to address both women, "I've had this house for just four years.

"Don't you have a place in New York?"

"No. That was when Fr8Load were first starting out. I shared that place with my bandmate, George. He lives there alone now."

"And you don't miss the excitement of New York?" Jean asked.

"When I was a teenager everything was exciting, Jean. These days spending time with Maggie and Molly is what I live for. I enjoy the sedate life I have now and I'm glad I had the opportunity to live in New York, because it's taught me to recognize what I really want out of life, and that Noah Haxby the rock star isn't in fact anything like who I am at home."

"Good answer, Mr. Haxby," Jean replied, like I'd anticipated her question and had an answer ready.

"I didn't realize I was being quizzed, Jean. What I've said is the truth."

Before she could react again to what I said the front door burst open, and I heard the small footsteps of Molly scurrying down the polished wooden hallway. "Noah, Noah, look what I got at school today," she said before she was even in my sights.

When she entered the room she hesitated, glanced from one woman to the other than back to the small shield she held in her hands. Her need to show me what she had in her hand overtook any shyness she may have felt about the strangers in the room and she hurried to my side.

Taking the small silver award from her hand I read what it said with interest as Molly kicked off her shoes right where she stood and climbed up on the sofa beside me. 'Most considerate student in class,' it read.

"Wow, Molly, I am so proud of you, baby girl. What did you do that your teacher was so impressed about?"

"Jonny Dinks wet his pants during morning recess. All the boys saw it and made fun of him. I told them to think how they would feel. I felt bad for him, so I took my coat off, told him to hide his wet pants then I took him to the school office and they fixed him up with clean ones. Auntie Maggie, my coat is in the blue bag. Mrs. Lane said it needs to go in the wash as it has pee-pee on it," she shouted out to Maggie who still hadn't shown her face.

"I'm very proud of you for helping Jonny, Molly. It shows how grown up you've become, and I hope those boys have learned a valu-able lesson from you today," I replied.

Molly's face beamed brightly a wide smile making her face shine. She climbed up onto her knees and took both sides of my face in her hands, "I knew you'd say that," she offered and planted a kiss on my cheek. "Can I have a cookie?" she asked, quickly moving the conversa-tion forward to the next thing that interested her.

"I think Auntie Maggie will be doing dinner in a little while and I'm not agreeing to anything unless she says so, but before you ask her there are some ladies I'd like you to meet."

Molly snapped her head around to face the two women who had been sitting quietly observing.

"Hello," she said and gave a small wave that was much more in keeping with the five-year-old she was.

"Hello, Molly, I've been looking forward to meeting you. It looks like we've picked a great day to do that what with your award and everything," Clara told her.

"Who are you?" Molly asked, and I smirked because she had picked up on the fact they hadn't introduced themselves to her.

"My name is Clara and I've come to visit with you because I heard you and your Aunt Maggie recently moved in to live here with Noah."

"Oh," she replied like Clara's explanation was all she needed.

"How do you feel about having moved home, Molly?" Jean enquired.

"Good."

"Good? Do you miss your old house?"

"Nope. I like it much better here."

"Why is that, Molly?"

Molly shrugged her shoulders and looked at me. I knew she wanted me to help her with that, but I also knew she had to say what was in her heart. Then I wondered if she felt comfortable talking about her feelings in front of me.

"Do you want me to go get your Aunt Maggie, sweetheart?"

"No, it's okay. What was the question again?"

"You said it's better here than your old house. Can you tell us why?"

"Sure. Because Noah is fun, and he plays with me at board games when Auntie Maggie is making dinner, and he's good at Math... and he tells me the funniest stories with silly voices."

"Is there anything else?" Jean prompted.

"There's hundreds and tens of things," she replied in an exacerbated tone, "I just can't think when you're putting me on the spot," she said flicking her bangs from her eyes like she was tired of the question.

"Sounds like Noah really likes you, Molly."

"Well, duh. He wouldn't do all that if he didn't. He loves me. He told me... and I love him right back," she said with a shrug.

Maggie came into the room and placed a tray on the coffee table. It had Molly's small plastic mug full of milk, cookies, a pot of coffee, cups, sugar, and a small jug of milk. As soon as Molly saw it she hurried to get off the sofa.

"Careful, Molly, the pot is full of hot coffee," I called out urgently. I looked over to Jean and noticed she was making notes on a small pad and wondered what she had written.

When Maggie sat down, Clara and Jean asked me if I would take Molly out of the room to give them some privacy. I felt a little on trial being ejected from my own living room when they did that, but was determined not to allow my lack of confidence to show. I asked Molly if she'd like to help me start dinner and she jumped at the chance. "Can I piggy back, Noah?"

"Of course, Princess, your chariot awaits," I replied and bent down. She climbed on my back and I carried her out of the room. I tried not to think too much about what was being said, but my heartbeat raced every time I thought of something that may stop us being together.

A lot was riding on their visit and as I chopped the shallots and threw them in the pan, I wondered where my 'fuck you' attitude could possibly fit in when the authorities came calling. I never found one scenario where I could have had the remotest chance of winning.

After fifteen minutes in the kitchen with me Molly had gotten bored, done her phonetics, and gotten bored again. She asked if she could play with her dollies and that suited me just fine. I wasn't used to preparing dinner with a tiny whirlwind at my feet. I agreed as it was straight across the hallway from the kitchen and I could watch her from there.

I was straining some green beans when Maggie came into the kitchen. She hugged me tightly and offered me reassurance. "They want to talk to you now." I guess the worry must have shown on my face because Maggie was quick to reassure me, "You'll be fine, Noah. You've got this, there's nothing for them to know. You're great with Molly, and I'm sure they saw how fond she is of you. A kid like her wouldn't be all over you if you weren't a good person."

"True." I smiled and gave her a soft kiss on her lips then pointed at the oven, "Only ten minutes more for the chicken," I advised and wandered toward the sitting room again. Right before I entered I heard Molly call after me.

"Are you done making dinner? Can we play a board game now?"

"Not tonight, sweetheart, we have visitors remember? But I

promise we'll play two board games tomorrow night, okay?" Molly pouted, the look of dejection clear as her tiny shoulders slumped.

"All right," she replied and sloped off toward Maggie in the kitchen.

Turning back, I made my way into the sitting room became aware the atmosphere had softened since the last time I was there.

"Thanks for coming back, Noah. We only have a few more questions for you today, then we'll get out of your hair," Clara informed me

"Fire away," I said as I sat back in the sofa in a relaxed pose opposite them. I was used to thousands of women looking at me for hours at a time, but I'd never felt under scrutiny in the way I had with those two watching my every move.

"We both feel Molly has a genuine affection for you and that appears to be reciprocated by you."

"No appearance about it. It's fact," I replied unable to stop myself from being defensive at that.

"Quite, but there is obviously some history around your capacity to parent that both Clara and I need to address," Jean advised me in a commanding tone.

"Can I just say something here? There has never been an assessment of my ability to parent. I've never been judged on my parenting skills. I have an injunction against me for being violent against another adult who assaulted me first. It had nothing to do with my capacity as a father."

"Exactly, Mr. Haxby," Jean drawled. "You have a violent past and you are a recovering alcoholic, I believe."

"Correct on both accounts. I'm not going to deny either of those issues; however, I'd like a fair hearing as to exactly why those issues exist at all."

Jean looked to Clara and was about to speak when Clara got in first. "I'd be interested in hearing what you have to say, Noah, as it would help us to form our final decision about Molly's safety since she's living in your home.

～

Half an hour later I drew in a deep breath and ran my fingers roughly through my hair. I'd poured my heart out without embellishing the facts nor smoothing over the parts that were damning to their decision. I sat forward placing my hands between my knees, rubbed my hands together, then clasped them before I glanced back to them.

"And you've never challenged that decision in court since, Mr. Haxby?" Jean asked. The softness in her tone surprised me because she was obviously the henchman of the pair.

"I was told I'd never get it removed because I was found guilty of a violent crime."

"I see," Jean replied and communicated something with a look to her colleague before turning back to me.

"Well I think that concludes our session for today, Mr. Haxby. I'm happy that Molly is safe for now and that you and Maggie have her welfare at the fore. We will be back in the form of some unannounced visits in the future... just to get a bird's-eye view of your lives together, but in the meantime if there are any illnesses or injuries, Maggie has been asked to contact us so we can document the cause." I frowned and was about to challenge her when she added, "It's standard practice when we are considering placing a child on the at-risk register. I'm happy to keep Molly off that list for now. At this present time, I see no problem with Molly remaining here with you and Maggie."

How I kept my temper I have no idea. My tolerance levels were waning at the prospect of yet more invasions of our privacy, and the things that she'd said. However, I kept telling myself that Maggie and Molly should never have been in this position in the first place. It was the only reason that kept me from losing my shit with both women.

I held it together and thanked them for their assistance in ensuring Molly's safety and I swear Jean Thompson almost fell over. Molly came out the kitchen as they were leaving and raised her arms for me to lift her up into mine. Clara noted this and the way I held her before she turned and walked to her car.

"Thank you for your cooperation this afternoon, Noah. I know it must have been difficult for you," she acknowledged.

"I wouldn't describe it as difficult, just a little tiresome having to disprove an image I was encouraged to cultivate by my band manager at a young age. That person doesn't exist in real life, Clara... what you see here is what you get—the real me in all my domestic normalcy," I replied. She stared deep in thought then nodded her head in a slow and deliberate manner.

"We'll be in touch," she said as she slid behind the wheel of her car and closed the door. A short exchange took place between the two women then Clara drove away.

CHAPTER SEVENTEEN

Maggie

I fought the urge to say goodbye to the social workers because I had wanted them to see how normal our lives were. Deep down I knew our routine would change and wondered how Noah would change when he went back to work.

Our relationship had yet to come under that pressure and I hoped we'd continue like we had been doing as much as possible. I hadn't even met any of his band members. They had all flown back to New York together the day before Noah as he had a photo shoot to do. Hence the reason why Noah was on the same plane as me.

When I overheard Noah reply at the door as they left I could have punched the air with joy at the answer he gave Clara. It was honest and straight from his soul. My heart squeezed because I knew how hurt he was at having to face such a degrading process to prove himself.

He wandered into the kitchen with his hands stuffed deep in his pockets; the serious expression he wore said we weren't out of the woods yet. He silently nodded in Molly's direction but said nothing in front of her.

Taking a seat beside her he suddenly scooped her out of the chair and swiftly tilted her upside down. The quiet kitchen was instantly filled with the sound of her infectious giggle.

"You're crazy, Noah," she shouted then screamed in a high-pitched shrill of delight.

"I am, baby girl. Haven't you heard? I'm a freaky rock star, we're supposed to be crazy," he replied as he set her back down on the chair next to him again and began setting the table for dinner.

"Noah, will you sing to me after we've eaten?" she asked, hopefully. Noah stopped what he was doing straight away and sat opposite her. "Why wait until then? We can do that now if you want," he said with a shrug and a wink.

Leaning over toward the utensil pot he plucked out two small wooden spoons, gave them to Molly, and began to tap out a beat on the table with his hands. Nodding his head, he encouraged Molly to join in and she began to hit the table with them, trying to copy the beat. Noah began to sing "Don't Worry Be Happy" by Bobby McFerrin.

I had begun plating up the food and stopped when I became enthralled watching him engage Molly by singing the song. He chuckled when she mumbled incoherently at the parts she had no clue about and at others when she suddenly became loud and sang with incredible clarity, which was mainly during the chorus.

Noah's face broke into a grin often but he kept on nodding to keep her attention and my heart swelled with love for the man that most on the outside would never know the way I did.

I turned away with a lump in my throat and swallowed with determination because the last thing I wanted to do when they were having such fun was become emotional. Molly had seen me do that too many times in the previous months.

Once I had composed myself enough, and they had finished the song I placed the food in front of them. Sliding into my seat, I turned to look at Noah who hurriedly placed his hand on the back of my head and pulled me closer. "I love your Aunt Maggie to infinity, Molly... is that okay with you?"

Molly stuffed a green bean into her mouth then threw her hands in the air. "Hmm. I'm not sure because I don't know where infinity is," she replied in all innocence.

"What he means Molly is Noah will love me until the end of time... I mean forever," I said quickly correcting myself when I anticipated the 'when is the end of time' question that would have been inevitable if I'd left it there.

"That's fine by me... but you know I'm part of that package, right?" she added and scooped some mashed potato into her mouth.

Noah and I chuckled because she'd obviously heard me say that to him and it had stuck in her mind. "Of course. I'd never dream of loving Maggie without loving you as well. Except I love you in a different way from the way I love your auntie."

"How?"

"My love for her is like when my heart bleeds because she's not in the room beside me."

"Yuck," Molly replied and screwed up her face. My eyes met Noah's, and I knew he spoke the truth because I knew exactly what he meant. I hated being apart from him.

"How do you love me?"

"Ah, that's a special kind of love. It's the kind of love that makes me want to wrap you up in a big comforter and keep you safe on the sofa for the rest of your life."

"Well I don't mind you loving me, but I think that would get a bit boring after a while."

Noah and I laughed again, then he leaned over and took her little hand in his.

"What I'm trying to say is if you and your Aunt Maggie are happy then my heart is happy too. If you hurt, I hurt because I know I'd be crazy not to love you."

"Are you saying you don't have a choice to love me?" Noah looked at her like she'd solved a Rubik's Cube puzzle all by herself and nodded.

"Got it in one," he replied and high-fived her.

She dropped her fork and stared directly at him. "You're like a dad then. They don't get a choice to love, they just get whatever comes out of the mommy's tummy," she replied oversimplifying the love a father should have for his child.

I watched the sharp intake of breath he took and saw the way he swallowed like what she'd said hit a raw nerve. He was too choked to speak and nodded slowly.

"All right, now we've established that Noah loves us, let's eat up before our food gets cold." Molly picked up her fork again and tucked in without another word, but it took Noah a minute to collect himself before he attempted his.

~

After Molly went to bed, we both felt drained and opted for an early night. It had been an emotional day, and I knew Noah hadn't slept well the night before. I noticed when he spent a long time in the shower that night, but I didn't go in after him because I sensed he needed some space to reflect and left him to come to bed when he was ready.

It was almost forty minutes before he came to bed and when I saw the red rims around his eyes my heart was in pain.

"Are you, okay?"

"No... but I'm getting there. Those women just got to me earlier, you know?"

"You were fabulous today, Noah."

"Yeah?"

"Yeah. I don't know many men who could have taken that in their stride with what you've had hanging over your head all these years."

"Difference is I had no choice except to cope. It was either that or lose you and Molly, and I'm damned if I'm gonna let that happen."

"You won't lose us, honey. Let them do their job and see for themselves who you are. I won't ask more of you than that."

Noah reached out and scooted down the bed with me, pulling me tightly to him in a spooning position. He kissed my shoulder and smoothed my hair.

"I've gone through this once before with Rudi. I don't think I could live if I lost you both." He hugged me tighter until I stretched to free myself and turned toward him.

"You made a mistake, Noah. One mistake like you said. Those women that were here today aren't stupid. They've seen it all... the good, the bad, and the liars of this world who relish in their actions of hurting innocent children or women. They'd have to be insane not to know you're not like them after today."

Noah dipped his head and took my mouth in a gentle kiss, "You're so good for me, sweetheart. I can't believe how lucky I am."

"You need to stop saying that like this is all on you. It's not. I need you more than you know. My life felt over before us."

He began to stroke my hair softly then pulled back to look at me, "We were made for each other. We're a force together and two broken people apart." I agreed with his statement but didn't say anything, then he leaned in and kissed me again this time sliding his tongue into my mouth as his hand slid to my butt.

Pressing me closer my hand moved to his cock, and I felt it stir. I stroked him gently and felt my hand open as his shaft extended in arousal to full length. I broke the kiss and rolled him onto his back, then worshipped his hard body by peppering kisses down his torso until I was level with his groin. Without a moment's hesitation there I took him into my mouth.

A sharp gasp of pleasure escaped his lips as his legs fell wider apart and he adjusted his butt. I rolled my tongue around the head and sucked him deeply into my mouth taking pleasure from the storm brewing in his eyes as I watched him fall under my control.

His hands swept up my hair, and he held it tightly then rocked at the pace to fulfil his need.

"Fuck, Maggie, you wreck me," he murmured in a raspy voice laced with lust.

When he thrust deeper, I gagged and my pussy clenched at the salty taste of pre-cum coating my mouth. When he became more animated and fucked my mouth, I thought he was going to come, but he pulled out and flipped me onto my back.

Dragging me to the edge of the bed his tongue glided between my spread legs; a low groan escaped from his throat then he stood lifting me high above him. I wrapped my legs around his waist and he slid me down spearing me steadily with his cock and bit my neck as I took him inside me.

I moaned softly in ecstasy as his expert hands, the speed of his penetration and rhythm he set for us made me wild with desire. As he gathered pace, I became so excited I rode him almost as fast as he moved deep inside me.

His smooth hard hands appeared to know exactly where they were needed and within a few minutes I could feel the familiar tightening only he had ever achieved with me with penetrative sex. In a few more heartbeats my legs began to tremble, in another they shook violently as I clung to him for safety while I lost control when I came.

Tight arms embraced me, keeping me safe as his pace continued relentlessly and white heat scorched behind my eyes as the pleasure he gave me rained down on every cell in my body. My heart pounded in my chest and a scream of pure ecstasy tore from my mouth, I barely recognized it was me, until he covered my mouth and muffled the noise coming out of me.

Seconds later Noah stopped and became rigid. He groaned again and bit into my shoulder as his cock pulsated deep inside and I hugged it deep in my core as his warm seed pumped in short spasms. Noah looked up briefly then dipped his head down and buried his face in the crook of my neck. "Tell me you're mine always, Maggie."

I swallowed roughly at the torture in his voice, "I'm yours."

As soon as we'd both cleaned up and climbed into bed, Noah resumed his favorite position of spooning against me. He slid one hand under my ribs and cupped a breast and wrapped the other around my waist. Nothing was said until we were both almost asleep then Noah said, "If... and it's a big if, they leave us alone, do you think we could adopt Molly?"

My chest swelled with love for him. It was one thing to be a father but quite another to want to be a father to someone else's child.

"I don't know. I've never thought about it. Shona was her mom."

"Where is her dad? We've never spoken about him and I've wondered when you were going to bring the subject up, but you never have."

"Shona would never discuss it with us. She took that knowledge to her grave," I said, saddened for Molly about that. "When she left to catch up with your tour, I went through her room with a fine-tooth comb. None of her friends knew either or if they did, they've never said. I tried again after she died, but they gave me the same answer, so I guess they really never knew."

Letting out a deep sigh, Noah snuggled his head against his pillow, kissed me softly on the back of the head and fell silent. I lay thinking about what he said and knew he was right. Molly deserved parents, not to grow up an orphan with an elderly aunt as guardian by the time she had kids, and I promised Noah I'd look into the legalities of it when I got home from work the following day.

CHAPTER EIGHTEEN
Maggie

A few weeks later Noah's band came to town and I finally got to know some of them a little when his manager called a meeting. I knew Noah had been concerned about their drummer, Vinny, but I wasn't sure of the details. When Noah told me about Vinny's drug issues I asked him not to bring him to our home. Noah stated he had never been to any of the places he had lived in because his reputation was bad enough without being classed as a junkie by association as well.

I couldn't even imagine how that would have gone down with the welfare services. The first time Noah left us to do some band stuff they showed up again. I was following Molly's evening routine and had only just taken her out of the bath as the gate buzzer sounded from the entrance security gates. Molly ran downstairs to the monitor room to see who was there and when I went in after her I recognized the car as that of Clara Simmons, the social worker.

I glanced at Molly and looked at the time on the monitor, it was 6:15 pm. It annoyed me that someone from children and family services felt it was okay to call so late when a child's routine was important. I pressed the intercom and invited her inside the gates, fired off a text to Noah giving him a heads up about the unannounced visit and waited for her to arrive. I felt it was inappropriate to visit during quiet time. In my view they hadn't considered Molly when they'd decided to spring a surprise visit on us.

Tasking Molly to put her pajamas on, I went to the kitchen and began to make a new pot of coffee and as Molly came back downstairs the doorbell chimed. I picked Molly up and answered the door.

"Hi, Maggie. I was on my way back from a visit to one of my regular children and figured I'd kill two birds with one stone and carry out a visit. It's not too late, is it?" Clara Simmons was alone, smiling hopefully.

"Come in, it is a little late. I had just gotten Molly out of the tub when the buzzer sounded."

"Is Noah home?"

"No, he had a meeting this afternoon with his band and their manager."

"When are you expecting him back?" she asked as I walked her through to the kitchen.

"To be honest, I'm not sure. Today is the first time he's not been here," I answered honestly.

I had only finished speaking when my cell vibrated with a text alert. I picked it up and saw it was Noah.

Noah: Only ten minutes out, remember to breathe, baby.

I felt relieved he was going to be here and smiled at the text. "Talk of the devil. It's Noah. He'll be home in ten minutes."

Molly grinned and clapped her hands, "I knew he'd be back. He said he'd be home by story time."

Glancing at Clara, I could see her pull out a notepad and jot something down.

"Molly, go and put on a movie and wait for Noah."

Molly ran through to her playroom and switched on the TV with her remote control. From her own movie app she chose what she wanted to watch and I checked she was settled.

"Does Molly spend much time watching movies?" Clara enquired.

"Not at all. She's usually only allowed a movie at the weekend; both Noah and I believe too much television stunts a child's natural imagination, but I don't want her to be concerned by anything we may say so I've had to change her routine."

Clara shifted uneasily in her chair and wrote another note. "I'm not the enemy, Maggie," she said, and placed the writing materials on the countertop. "I'm following process, and you may see that as a disruption of your lifestyle, but this is in Noah's interests as much as yours and Molly's."

"How can you say that? You don't know how worried this makes him. What happened in the past affected him greatly. Noah's incredible with Molly and she adores him."

"Yes, but your relationship is new, Maggie. Your niece has been through a hugely traumatic event and needs very careful handling."

"And may I remind you I'm a schoolteacher quite used to helping children through their time of loss. There's no one better to help Molly through this than I am. I've parented Molly her whole life. My sister wasn't interested in what was best for Molly. It was what was best for herself."

"She went to join Noah's crew abroad, yes?"

"Yes, but her death had nothing to do with Noah."

"I accept that, but I'm also aware of what the official documents say about your boyfriend."

"Maggie knows everything I know, so if there's something else perhaps I need to submit a Subject Access Request to see those papers." I turned to see Noah standing in the doorway. I hadn't heard him arrive and Clara was clearly stunned by his sudden appearance. She shouldn't have been—after all it was his home.

Noah came toward me and kissed my cheek, "I'm going to read to Molly. I promised her earlier I'd be home in time." He left the room dismissing himself without any further challenge and Clara was once again writing in her notebook. When she had finished she placed her pen on the pad.

"Shall we start again?"

"That depends if you're going to insult my partner. I think he's suffered enough at the hands of the authorities. If I thought he'd be better off without us, I'd have thrown in the towel rather than put him through this. But unfortunately for him, he's deeply in love with me and he loves Molly as well."

"That much is clear," she replied.

"What I was trying to say was this... if we deem Noah fit for Molly as a parental figure, he could reapply to see his son. When we came here for our initial visit I will admit I had a biased idea of what Jean and I faced. I was very wrong. Instead of a loud-mouthed, drunken hell-raiser, I found a dedicated, hands-on family man.

It was refreshing to hear how candid he was about his past, and personally I think he was misrepresented when he faced charges about the assault incident he was involved with. The law clearly states every citizen has a right to protect themselves in self-defense and I think if the student was questioned alone under formal interview he may have been more honest in admitting his offence."

I stared straight at her, my mind still adapting to what she'd told me then my heartbeat raced, "You believe him?"

"I do but if I don't complete the process and document it in the correct way it won't do either of you any good. And I *will* do this properly. Any resistance to the process will be documented, Maggie. You know that... it's the reason you contacted us in the first place.

Clara continued to observe the evening routine and once Molly was in bed she thanked us for our cooperation and left.

I was scared to tell Noah what she had said to me in the event it never transpired. Instead I told him she viewed us positively so far and they would reach their final decision in the coming weeks.

It wasn't a lie as such because she had told me those things as well. It was mainly because of the depression and subsequent consequences that I held back. The way I saw it, it wasn't my story to tell and if I built his hopes up about Rudi and that didn't happen I'd destroy him.

Keeping the status quo would help Noah to remain the man he was in front of the authorities, and as soon as it was documented that he was safe to parent Molly I knew any judge worth his reputation would have difficulty in denying him access to his own son.

≈

Another two weeks passed and Noah still wasn't back to work with his band because the manager and George had staged an intervention with Vinny, who had agreed and was in rehab. We'd only had a third visit the day before from Clara and Jean, during which they documented the practicalities of Noah's working life and how that would impact on Molly. They appeared satisfied with the arrangements we had made, and we sighed with relief when they left.

Noah flopped on the sofa and ran his hand sexily through his hair then smirked wickedly. "You're definitely sucking my dick later after all the praise I just gave you," he joked in a low voice when Molly was out of earshot. I loved that he had attempted to lighten the mood. I dropped down onto the sofa beside him and ran my fingers across his tight abs over his t-shirt and he shuddered.

"Mm... do that again my cock twitched," he said and gave me a lopsided smile. When I didn't respond and placed my head on his shoulder he pushed me back to look at him. "What? What's the matter?"

I closed my eyes for a second because I was scared to tell him. I had a secret and I was shit scared of what it would mean for us and Molly and I was worried about how it would affect our future.

"Maggie? What is it?"

Forcing myself to look at him I bit my lip and was afraid to say it aloud. My heartbeat pounded in my chest because I had no idea how he'd respond. I had no idea how to respond myself, because it was yet another complication.

"I'm pregnant," I blurted out. I had no worries about Noah taking care of us, it was the timing that worried me.

Noah's body stiffened, and he pushed me away. Rising to his feet he walked nervously away from me his fingers threading through his head. Turning to look at me he held a fistful in his hands and stared down at me.

"Seriously?"

My anxiety had made my breathing erratic and l felt afraid when I watched his initial response. "Yeah. About five weeks... only just."

Noah rushed at me and pulled me to my feet. "This is fantastic news, Maggie. You're pleased aren't you? Tell me you're happy. I thought you were on the pill?" he said, looking puzzled as he pushed me to arms-length to stare bright eyed at me. I felt relieved he appeared happy about it.

"I don't know how I feel. With everything we're going through... and Molly, it's a lot to take in."

Noah slumped down on the sofa and put his head in his hands. "You don't want our kid?

"I do... of course I do. I'm just a bit stunned right now. Give me a little time."

"You kept this from child welfare."

"I did because once they say the case is closed it's none of their business. We've been through enough shit without someone sullying this baby's start in life."

Noah gave me a sideward glance full of concern and nodded. "I'm really happy, Maggie. If we have this child I'll have almost everything I could ever want in life, and if I live it right then one day, Rudi may come to find me. I want him to find a solid man. Not a broken one like I was for the first few years of his life."

"For the record, I do want your baby, Noah. *Our* baby. But I want to wait until I'm in my second trimester before we announce it to anyone. God knows what the media are going to make of it. Are you okay with that?"

"How long is that?"

"After twelve weeks."

"I can live with that," he agreed and scooped me into his arms. "Fuck. I can't believe how my life has changed so quickly, and it's all because of you. You've made me the happiest man alive."

I stared into his gorgeous deep blue eyes and felt a huge swell of love for the man who was everything to me. *Who would have thought this time last year my life would have changed this much?*

At the back of my mind I figured everything would be okay with the authorities because I couldn't afford to think otherwise. It was Molly's reaction I worried about the most. How would she take to a new baby? How would she feel growing up not being completely ours when our child began to call us Mom and Dad?

Noah had loosely talked about adoption for Molly, but that was several weeks before. I'll admit I had kind of let it slide again because we were new. It was a massive step for me to give someone parental responsibility for Molly, and I wondered if the courts would have even given him legal ties to her with his past record of assault?

For the rest of that night Noah talked animatedly about how we'd reconfigure the house to accommodate our new addition and the thing that struck me about how he spoke was how considerate he was about upsetting Molly's routines and environment. He was a natural parent and his enthusiasm for the role was so far removed from his stage image as part of Fr8Load.

That night after we'd gone to sleep I woke to an empty bed. Confused about where he was. I slid from between the sheets and went downstairs. Noah cut an appealing figure dressed in boxer briefs sitting in a relaxed pose with both arms behind his head on the sofa, his ripped and toned torso bare. Glancing over when I came into view I noted the sadness in his eyes.

"Are you okay?"

"Yeah, I couldn't sleep... too many thoughts going on in my mind."

"About?"

"Molly...the new baby... Rudi... the fucking mess I've found myself in but don't appear to be able to do anything about."

I'd never seen Noah in as low of a mood before and worried he was close to a bout of depression. I sat down beside him, and I slid my hand around his waist. He pulled me close, placing my head on his warm chest and I listened to his slow steady heartbeat.

"Honey, I've never seen anyone try to be what everyone needs them to be more than you have. You do it so effortlessly as well. You're amazing, Noah, and I truly believe everything is going to be okay." He turned his head to look at me and a look of desperation passed through his eyes. He barely managed to control his frustration.

"I hope to Hell you're right, Maggie, because there's no alternative to this."

I didn't protest because I felt the same—the consequences for us of a negative result from Child Welfare didn't bear thinking about. We stayed there on the sofa for most of the night, and I had a new worry to think about—Noah's mental state and how that could affect him.

CHAPTER NINETEEN

Noah

*N*o one knows what it's like to wait when you have an addiction—unless they're an addict. Only someone in the same position as I was could understand what it felt like to have their life ripped apart and not even be able to have a drink to temporarily make it go away.

I'd never been so happy, sad, or frustrated since I'd met Maggie, but she had definitely saved me. She was my angel on Earth and made me a much better version compared to the man I used to be before I knew her.

She surprised the Hell out of me when she told me she was pregnant, and I think she surprised herself as well. As far as I was concerned it was a very happy accident. My chest tightened with excitement, like my heart was a beat away from bursting out of my chest and it was a different feeling from the suffocating way my chest tightened when I heard I was forbidden to see my son.

Happiness was within my grasp, I could feel it, the only downside was how everything hinged on two women from Child Welfare Services who only really knew what I told them and the reports they'd read.

During their assessment, I prayed harder than I had ever prayed in my life, in the hope that the authorities would sanction our home as the best place for Molly to live. If they'd decided it wasn't I figured I'd lose Maggie in a heartbeat. Molly came first... as she should.

In the meantime, Maggie drove Molly to school while I stayed home and tried to occupy my time by writing some new material. That was the one good thing to come out of this so far, the songs I'd written since I'd known Maggie contained a level of angst I'd never produced before. Writing was the only activity that kept me sane when she was out during the day.

Night after night Maggie came home and I waited expectantly thinking that day was the day she'd have the answer we needed to crack on and make our family plans, but each time she came back and shook her head it lowered my mood.

For most of the time I kept it together for all our sakes and I had no choice to do anything else. No matter how strong the craving got to drive to the nearest liquor store and buy the largest bottle of bourbon I never let it get the better of me. Anxiety almost ate me alive, but I was determined I'd never sink that low again, no matter what. Even without Maggie and Molly, I still had Rudi as the focus for my continued sobriety.

Eleven days after the third visit by Clara and Jean to our home my cell rang. Clara told me she was coming over, and that in itself was unusual because they'd already told us the deal was for them to make unannounced visits. My defenses rose and I wondered if she'd found something that made the rest of their reports null and void as to giving us permission as a family.

A sick feeling settled in the pit of my stomach and I can't describe the feeling of impending doom that washed over me. Announcing her visit made me an emotional wreck and brought me close to tears because the right answer meant so much.

Before I suffered from depression I'd never felt the impact of someone saying no to me. It happened in life and there was usually a reason for it. That was until I heard the word no in relation to Rudi... and there was no valid reason for that.

For a moment I considered calling Maggie to tell her what was going on, but I decided against it because I didn't want to worry her. It wasn't good to be anxious in her condition, and it wouldn't have changed the outcome if she knew, so I decided to brave it out on my own and tell her when there was the whole story to tell.

It was almost a whole hour later that the buzzer on the gates alerted me to her arrival. I let her in and waited nervously as she drove up to my door. My palms were sweaty, and my nerves jangled inside. It was a familiar feeling like I had a hangover and the only thing that would fix it was if she told me everything was going to be okay.

Clara was looking at her feet when I opened the door and I immediately thought she'd brought me bad news, but then her head snapped up and she looked directly at me then flashed me a beaming smile.

"Afternoon, Noah. Thank you for seeing me," she said in a cheerful voice as she stepped over the threshold without waiting for an invitation. I closed the door slowly watching for signs of what her visit meant, but I couldn't read her.

"I guess you're wondering why I'm here?" she said pulling her driving gloves off one finger at a time before she placed them on the countertop in the kitchen we'd entered. Sitting down on one of the breakfast bar chairs, she smiled again.

"We had a team meeting this morning where we discussed your case and I wanted to come over personally to deliver our findings." A shock jolted my heart, temporarily stunning me, before it raced to the point where I felt electrical aftereffects tingling in my mouth. I swallowed roughly and leaned back to grab a stool from the breakfast bar while retaining eye contact with her and slid myself on it slowly.

"And?" I asked as I tried to keep the hostility out of my voice.

"Noah, I had a gut feeling the first time I met you, but we had to follow all the processes to protect everyone. You're no more a risk to Molly than I am. I've looked over the court papers from your assault and in my opinion, you've been badly advised by your legal team. There were several processes that weren't followed, in particular a home study assessment where your environment, interaction with the child and your ability to parent were omitted entirely. I've made my findings and we've recommended this case be closed. I wish you, Maggie, and Molly, a great future together."

For a few seconds I felt numb then a rush of overwhelming feelings swamped me. A large lump grew rapidly in my throat and tears welled in my eyes despite my best efforts to hang in there with my emotions until she'd gone.

I felt it was high time I had a reprieve from the worries that plagued my crazy life. Inappropriate or not I grabbed her off her stool and swung her around in a huge circle. If I could have bottled the stunned look she gave me, I'd have made a fortune from it at horror events.

"Seriously? I may get access to Rudi?" My voice was gruff with emotion. I set her back on her feet and I ran my hands through my hair in disbelief as I continually swallowed back the tears that burned in my throat.

"Obviously that isn't my decision. The family judge reading your appeal would decide on that." I felt as if my guts were going to burst out of my belly with excitement. It was the news I'd prayed for but never thought would ever come. Clara smiled widely and looked shocked that my reaction was as strong as it was. I guessed she still had remnants of issues from the public perception of me.

I was long overdue a little sweetness in my life and I made a defining decision then and there. I was done doing what everyone else expected me to do. If I got a second chance to be part of Rudi's life, then Maggie and I would be extremely busy and as far as I was concerned music took second place to spending time with those who mattered the most to me.

Clara wished me luck as she packed her paperwork back into her briefcase, left me a file around five inches thick to read, and extended a hand to me. "I'd just like to say you're one Hell of an actor, Noah. You're nothing like that asshole you are on TV."

I chuckled and led her to the door.

"Let me know if I can help when you submit your paperwork regarding your son, or if you and Maggie do decide to adopt Molly."

"Decision has already been decided as of today. It's time that little girl truly belonged to someone again."

"You're a good man, but don't worry I won't tell anyone. My client's information is confidential" she commented with a small chuckle.

"So I've been told many times by my beautiful woman."

"She's a good judge of character," Clara said, pressing the fob to unlock her car door.

"Or she's insane. Either way, I think I'll keep her."

Clara laughed, opened the car door, and slid behind the wheel.

"The driver's door window glided into the metal as it opened, and she turned again to look at me. "As I'm not directly involved with your case anymore I'm sure I could persuade my manager to let me accept an invitation to the wedding," she teased, then headed down the driveway. I chuckled softly, but she gave me something else to think about.

When I stepped back inside the house I checked the time on my wristwatch and noticed it was lunchtime at Maggie's school. I was excited to call her and ran to grab my cell from the kitchen. When I called her phone, Maggie picked up on the first ring.

"That was spooky, I was just about to call you," she said sounding playful.

"Telepathy, baby. We're connected on another level."

"Or you knew it was my lunchtime," she said with a smile in her voice.

"Or that," I replied chuckling, "I know you said no calls during the school day; however, I have something you may want to hear."

"All right, get on with it then," she teased.

"I've just spent the last hour at home with a lone female... Clara."

"And?" Maggie's prompt sounded urgent.

"And... case closed. I'm apparently no threat to Molly... unless Clara is, because she said, 'I was no more of a risk to Molly than she was'."

"Oh! Thank God." The relief was clear in her voice.

"There's something else. After reviewing all the paperwork from the trial her team believed I was poorly advised... and she reckons I could file an appeal petition to get access to Rudi."

"Oh, Noah. I'm so happy for you," she said. She sounded relieved which was a great sign for how she'd be if Rudi came into our family.

"For us... all of us. We can be a family, Maggie. No more shit from anyone. Will you let me adopt Molly with you?" Maggie fell quiet for a few moments then she replied. Her hesitancy stung, but I understood she was part of Shona and that made me less impatient.

"Can we discuss this at home, Noah? Right now on the phone, isn't the time."

"Sure. I'll order in tonight, see you at 4:30 pm."

~

Adoption was a big commitment. I knew that. It was a 'rest of your life' commitment, but I was ready. Before that, I set about figuring out a bulletproof master plan to get someone to grant me permission to build a relationship with my son.

For the rest of that afternoon I trawled Google for a kick ass Family Law firm and after a couple of duds, I found Lester Crossly, an attorney with thirty years of experience under his belt.

Within five minutes of getting to talk to the man he'd cut through the bullshit and advised me of the processes I had to follow. Clara had left me copies of the paperwork from Molly's investigation, so I sent Eamon straight over with those and had Annalise chase the guys in legal who held all the relevant documents from the court case and restraining order.

I was relieved when Lester advised me Maggie and I wouldn't have to have another home study report as it was only completed the day before and then advised me of his intention to file the petition as soon as he and his juniors had sifted through the paperwork. By the time I closed the call out I felt like Hell had frozen over and I had finally caught a break. *Now all I have to do is convince Maggie about Molly.*

From how she avoided the subject the last time I brought it up, I knew Maggie needed a little persuasion to see the benefits of adopting Molly... and I got that. She was sole guardian and it was a huge decision to trust someone else with that role.

I explained I understood her reserve and how difficult it was for her to put that much trust in me. She hugged me. Then I asked her to think about Molly's sense of belonging now that we were about to have a child between us and Rudi may come back into the frame. I watched the dilemma and confusion in her eyes clear as she considered my explanation.

Everything I had said was true, but the real reason was I had grown to love Molly as if she were my own.

"You're right." She stated after a while and my heart pounded in my chest with excitement when she agreed.

"I'm always right... what am I right about now?" I teased, lightening the heavy atmosphere.

"Molly deserves a Mom and Dad."

"Didn't we get to this point before and then... nothing?"

"No... I mean yes we did, but with all the intrusion I guess I got a little worried if their decision went the other way... that, and I felt Shona was barely in the ground."

I nodded with a serious expression on my face, and looked for any doubt in her expression. I found none. "You're sure?"

"I am. She'll be excited."

"I know, but we won't tell her until it is absolutely certain it is going to happen."

"Agreed," I replied and pulled Maggie into my chest. I wrapped my arms tightly around her and kissed her cheek. "We're finally free to do what we want and I'm definitely gonna pull out that fuck you ticket whenever the occasion demands it," I mumbled then kissed her slow and tenderly.

Breaking the kiss, I leaned away and asked, "One more thing... have you given any thought to quitting your job? I'd prefer you to be here with the kids rather than a nanny. It's important to Molly's recovery. I'm up for the challenge of course and I'm not being sexist, but you'll be home for at least a year either way once you have the baby. And I don't want you under any pressure while you are carrying our baby and getting to know him after the birth."

"Him? You think?"

"My family only do boys. Check out my mom and dad. Six boys. Not a hairclip in sight."

"And mine only do girls... we'll see," she replied with a smirk. "As for my work, I love my independence. I hate my job and I wouldn't miss the politics of it for sure, but I love the kids. Let me think on it. I have a while yet before I have to decide what I want to do."

That fiercely independent streak in Maggie told me not to push—

she would do exactly what she wanted. I knew subtle persuasion would be my only tool to convince her to be a stay-at-home mom. It was a little selfish of me, but I didn't want her to be too tired to give us some time as well and working full time with a family would eat into that time.

We'd been living in a bubble since she'd moved in with me. Our extended hiatus due to Vinny being in rehab had helped us stay out of the public eye. I was surprised my rant at Molly's school never made the press, but I guess my words about supporting Maggie had struck a chord with the people that were there.

It was never far from my mind that Maggie had only had the slightest taste of what the media could do, and I had tried my best to protect her from all the fake news that got published. Trust was the most important thing for dealing with that. As for the crazy assed fans Fr8Load had out there, what they were capable of was anyone's guess.

CHAPTER TWENTY
Maggie

*a*fter Child Welfare bowed out the pressure was off. Noah and Molly's relationship continued to flourish, and I knew Molly would have been heartbroken if Noah wasn't in her life anymore. I'd made up my mind to agree to the both of us adopting Molly and once I had I was determined to make that happen before any decision was made about Rudi and the arrival of the child Noah and I had made together.

Every morning when I woke, I'd stare at Noah lying next to me. He was so handsome it was hard not to. Occasionally he'd get that feeling someone was watching him and would suddenly open his eyes.

A lazy smile would grace his lips then he always pulled me close and tell me he loved me. I couldn't remember a time when I'd felt happier and so one morning like the one I described, I made up my mind to give in to his wishes.

I went to the store to grab some supplies on the way home. I was planning a special dinner to surprise him with the news. By the time I arrived home with Molly I was a little put out because the table was already set, and a caterer had been to deliver dinner.

Somehow, I managed to hide my disappointment and focused on

Molly's evening routine, after all it was only dinner, and the preamble to what I had to share with Noah.

Time had passed since the home assessment to the point where I could barely hide my swollen belly and I had decided it was time to tell Molly about the new baby.

I was nervous of her reaction to the news because she'd already been through so much change in her little life during the previous months and I was fearful of adding another level of stress to that.

Noah was great at keeping things even for her and was busy playing a board game with her as I changed from my day clothes into something more comfortable. When I went back to the playroom he and Molly were in deep conversation and when they heard me approach their conversation abruptly stopped.

As I came into their sights Molly turned to look at me, both hands flew to cover her mouth and Noah chuckled. "All right. What's going on with you two?" I asked and stared at Molly who still sat with her hands over her mouth. She shook her head with a guilty look on her face. "You're not going to tell me?" I asked.

My voice was a little sharp because I didn't want Molly to keep secrets from me and thought if Noah had told her to, I would have had to have words about that.

"You'll see," was all she replied. I was not about to argue especially when Noah had a sly smirk on his face, so I turned and left the room pretending not to care. My stomach felt a little tight as I wandered into the kitchen and Noah swiftly followed. Sliding his hands around my waist from behind he swept my hair to the side and kissed my neck. Despite being annoyed I felt the sharp jolt of electricity when his lips connected with my skin.

"Don't be mad, Maggie. Even though that pissed look makes your eyes full with fire I hate you being upset."

"Then don't tell Molly to keep things from me."

"Ouch. Sorry. Please don't be pissed it's not good for the baby. I promise I'll never do that again."

His voice sounded full of remorse and the tension I had felt left my body.

"Come on, sit. I ordered dinner because I wanted to suggest something to you and I didn't want to give you any reason to hate it, so I had someone else do the cooking." When I heard how playful he sounded my anger completely dissolved and I smiled.

"What suggestion?"

"Ah... after dinner, okay?" he added. Without waiting for me to reply he released his hold and moved past me, then began taking the food out of the oven.

"Chicken Parmigiana—your favorite, right?" It was the meal I was going to make. *It's like he read my mind.*

"I was going to make that for dinner," I said surprised by his choice.

"Then I've saved you the effort," he replied and gestured with his head for me to sit, "Molly, dinner's ready, sweetheart. Go wash your hands and get here before Aunt Maggie eats everything."

Molly scurried down the hall and was back in less than a minute. "Let me feel your hands," he ordered, checking she'd done what he asked, and my heart squeezed because I knew what I had to tell him would make him deliriously happy.

Dinner was delicious, and I was just about to break my news to both him and Molly about the adoption when he suddenly stood, stepped back, and dropped down on one knee. "I'm sure there are a million more romantic ways of doing this, but I think you'd prefer it if I didn't attract attention through grand gestures. I figured I'd focus this more on the people who matter to me. Maggie, since you came into my life it's as if I've emerged from a long spell under water. I know its cliché to say, but since the second I saw you I knew you were... significant. I don't know how else to explain it. But it wasn't until I got to know you I learned how hugely important you were to me."

My eyes darted over to Molly who was clapping her hands and bouncing up and down in her seat with excitement because she'd obviously been in on his surprise. Suddenly her response earlier made much more sense. I tried not to smile and focus on her too much because this was my moment... and Noah's for that matter, to declare what we meant to each other.

"During the past few years there were many days when I felt I'd had enough. Life was dark and depressing because no matter how hard I tried I couldn't see any other purpose apart from playing music for the pleasure of others. Personally, I even lost the joy in that."

Reaching up he took my hand in his and placed a soft kiss on the back of it. "I was going through the motions of living without really involving myself in it. Then I found you... and then you, Molly," he said involving her in his speech. He made a fist with his hand and held it over his heart, thumping it twice. "Both of you fill my days with laughter; your smiles are like rays of sunshine that constantly beam down on me and every second since I've met you both I've never been able to have enough of you. Maggie Dashwood, what I'm trying to say is, will you marry me? Will you and Molly have me for keeps?"

Molly jumped down from her chair and threw her arms around Noah's neck. "You did it. You did great, Noah," she said singing his praises before glancing up at me. Clinging tightly to his neck she said, "Well? Tell him, yes, Auntie Maggie."

Looking at his face I saw honesty, warmth, love, and the deepest affection for me I'd ever read from anyone's expression toward me. I had no doubts about spending the rest of my life with him, even if I was still worried about the rock star lifestyle and any other influences on Noah.

"Yes. Yes, I'd be proud to be your wife," I replied as my heart pounded in my chest with happiness and excitement.

Noah stood up straight, lifted Molly into his arms and scooped me up in a hug. "You've just made me the happiest man alive."

"I thought I'd done that already when we agreed to move in?" I asked.

"Exactly and now I'm even happier," he said and smiled. The way he squeezed my hand emphasized that. "You'll notice there's no ring yet. I hope you don't mind, and I know it's selfish, but I wanted you for myself a little longer if that's okay? If I start shopping for rings it makes things much more complicated. We can do that together then you'll have exactly what you want and what fits."

I glanced up at him, "I don't need a ring. I'd rather have you."

"Is the correct answer," he replied and gave me a smug smile and placed Molly back on her feet.

"By the way, thanks for hijacking my surprise tonight." I said changing the subject because I knew my decision to adopt would mean even more to him after his proposal."

"Surprise? What surprise? I had no idea you were planning anything."

"Well, duh. That's the whole point of a surprise, Noah."

"Can I have it now?" he asked tentatively.

"Another surprise?" Molly shouted, then whooped and did a little dance.

"Yep, and this one involves you too, Molly."

"Is it a puppy?" she asked clasping her hands and pulling them to her chest in hope.

"No puppy, but I think what I have to tell you, is even better."

"Oh my. Is it a giraffe? Where will we keep it?" Both Noah and I chuckled, and I stared in wonder at the innocence of a child's mind.

"It isn't an animal, Molly, now sit back down because what I have to say is quite important."

Noah lifted Molly and sat her back at the table, then sat in his chair and took my hand.

"All right. What an exciting night this is. My turn. A while ago Noah and I were talking about you, Molly, and us big people sometimes think about what's best for the little people we care about."

"That's me, isn't it?"

"Yes, Molly, that's you."

Molly straightened up in her chair, placed her elbows on the table and placed her chin in her hands.

"When your mom went to Heaven to be with the angels I became responsible for your care." Molly looked sad and nodded.

"Well, Noah and I had some long conversations about that and we don't think it's fair for you to grow up without a daddy or a mommy. Noah's head turned to stare at me and swallowed roughly because he had anticipated what came next.

"Are you giving me away?" Molly asked, her voice was full of alarm and tears had started to well in her eyes.

"Gosh. No. What we were thinking was... if it's okay with you... that we could be your new mommy and daddy?"

Molly burst into tears, her lungs exhaling so hard she didn't breathe until she changed color. Noah stood in distress, his chair scraping roughly along the floor in his panic as he made to grab her from her seat.

"Yes...yeah... please," she cried through her tears. My throat closed down with emotion and I also stood from my chair and caught a breath. Tears streamed down my face from her reaction and my chest felt tight with sadness and happiness in equal measure. No small child should ever have had to go through what Molly had.

"Then it's settled, Molly. I'll file the papers and we'll celebrate as soon as the people who make decisions let us know we are."

Noah dried Molly's tears and swung her around making her giggle and with the distraction Molly regained her composure in a heartbeat.

"You're right, Mom, this is better than a giraffe. I've never had a daddy before." Her words stopped me in my tracks. What she had said was true; I'd thought it myself, but to hear her say it so soon after I'd explained the plan told me Molly herself had already noticed her difference from some of the other children at school.

It was then I decided to break our other piece of news to Molly and told her about the baby. I had been worried about how she would take it, but she almost burst with excitement again. There had been a huge amount of information for a small child to take in; however, I reassured myself Molly would cope. She had two loving people around her who had her back and I felt with our continued patience and guidance she'd be fine.

That night as we lay in bed Noah pulled the cotton sheet down my belly. I was fifteen weeks pregnant and although I hadn't felt any movement yet, I'd read not to expect anything until mid-second trimester. Even though I had explained this to Noah he was impatient and lay talking to my bump most nights, waiting for a sign the baby was really in there. It was endearing to see how caught up he was in our life changing event.

His strong warm palm swept back and forth over my taut belly, "Can you hear me, son?" he asked and looked at me a little sheepishly. "Me and your mom can't wait to meet you," he murmured softly. Noah continued to stare at my bump like it was going to magically spring into action and lay as still as I'd ever seen him. That night he was deep in thought.

"What are you thinking?" I asked after a few minutes.

"How lucky I am. How I don't want to go back to work. How I don't want to miss a single second of this precious little baby's life. This is never going to happen, but if a meteor struck this Earth and I did something wrong, please promise me you'd never keep my children away from me."

My heart almost broke that he had to think like that. "I hope we're never in that position, Noah, but believe me when I say a child has the right to keep in touch with their parents... that is unless that parent compromises their physical or emotional wellbeing."

Noah moved closer and placed his cheek next to our baby bump. "Believe me when I say I will always love you, Maggie... no matter what. I hate the thought of going back to the band and the longer Vinny stays in rehab the less enthusiastic I am about the whole deal. Nine years is a long time to be stuck inside a revolving wheel, you get me? This is the longest time I've ever had off since we started."

Clutching a clump of his hair, I tugged it gently for him to look up at me. He shifted his head on my bump to glance up and I saw a tortured soul in his eyes.

"We'll make it work, Noah. There are very few fathers in life that get the opportunity to do what you do and can take an extended break like this. Most are lucky to spend a few weeks a year with their children and they spend the rest of their time bringing home the bread to feed them. You only feel this way because of Rudi. I hate Andrea for the way she's kept you from your son and I don't even know her. Focus on the positive parts of what's happening, and the rest will take care of itself."

He leaned over and took my hand in his and gave it a small squeeze, then lifted it to his lips. He kissed my fingers and let his mouth linger there before he glanced back again. "You're right as usual.

I'm so fucking lucky. Blessed. I have a job where I can at least control when I tour and to that end I think we should consider putting a nanny in place before this little man is born. I want Molly to be second nature to her and her to Molly before our new arrival. It will give us both peace of mind to know we have someone who's familiar with Molly's routines."

I shuffled myself up the bed and leaned back, "I can't get my head around the way you're always thinking ahead. You're a deep man and you have incredible insight, Noah. You amaze me at times, you know that?" He sat up quickly and carefully slid me back down onto my back then hovered above me surrounding me with all four limbs like he often did.

"I know... that's why you find me so irresistible," he mocked in a seductive way and buried his face in my neck. His soft warm lips connected with my skin and goose bumps riddled my body as tiny wired tingles radiated through me. Noah thought he was lucky, but he had no idea how lucky I thought I was to have him in my life.

CHAPTER TWENTY-ONE

Noah

*B*y the time the band finally ventured into the studio, Maggie was almost eight months pregnant. I was reluctant to leave her so close to her due date, but by then we'd hired a sweet southern girl called Kathleen to help with Molly, so I knew she had some help at home.

Fresh out of college, Kathleen had a mature, quiet attitude and at twenty-one years old, she was the oldest sibling of a large Southern family. Despite her tender age she was a natural care-giver and had a wealth of personal experience from taking care of her siblings and cousins.

Maggie took to her straight away, and I figured if she was okay by Maggie's standards then she passed the test for mine. Saying that I still found myself watching her like a hawk and waiting for her to put a foot wrong—then again, what parent wouldn't?

For the first time, I knew what it felt like to hate leaving home to go to work. Vinny, was out of rehab and clean for the first time in years, so there was nothing keeping us at home anymore. However, he lacked stamina and strength, so recording was slow.

George, and Mel—the remaining member of the band—became short-tempered with him because unlike me they'd been eager to get the album going and were frustrated by all the setbacks. Personally, I had more empathy with Vinny because at one time I was an addict myself.

On the other hand, Steve, our manager; and the guys, were stoked with all the new material I'd written in my downtime. Uncertainty in my private life obviously brought out my inspirational angsty side.

Five songs made it onto our album, but not before I'd taken a huge amount of stick from my bandmates for being whipped by Maggie in the process. *Jealousy is ugly*. Then again, they were all still single guys, wandering aimlessly from place to place looking for the next pussy to dip their dick in—and they were welcome to that.

George called time when Vinny had fucked up for the fifth time during the last track of the day, his arms too fatigued to keep the pace of the beat through lack of practice. One by one we gradually finished stowing our instruments on the stands and filed back into the studio office. I was about done packing up when my cell vibrated in my bag. It was Annalise.

"Good news. Lester Crossly called regarding your court hearing about Rudi. A judge has been appointed to your case, and the date is set for Tuesday. Lester thinks with the evidence his team have and the omissions to follow due process from your original case, dispensing with the restraining order should only be a formality."

Thoughts that I may finally get to see my son made my heart pound and I could barely speak. Tears welled faster than I could swallow them back. "Call you back," was all I could manage because I was choked with emotion. Eamon covered for me with the guys and I hastily made my way to our ride, then he drove me home in silence because I couldn't even think let alone talk about my conversation with my assistant.

Everything appeared to be happening at once. Maggie had given up work the week before. Apart from our baby being due, she figured the adoption board would move things along quicker if they knew there was a parent who was always at home. She had been right on that count because after informing them, her adoption application was finalized and approved a couple of weeks later.

As Maggie was already Molly's legal guardian and her sole surviving relative it had sped up the proceedings. All the paperwork, her background checks as a teacher, and the fact that Molly had lived with her since she was born helped tremendously.

My application was far more complicated, and I continued to wait for the court's final decision. It had been a while since I'd submitted the paperwork along with my medical records. That part had worried me the most because during my medical I was questioned at length about my bouts of depression and misuse of alcohol. I was honest, and I'll admit the interrogation got me down inside; however I had to accept they'd do the same to anyone with a history of problems like I had. I only prayed they weren't swayed by the shit the media had put out about me and assessed me fairly.

The one area that was the most difficult to comply with were the sessions I was supposed to attend as part of the pre-adoption process. Fans and publicity made it impossible for me to do this in a group setting. Eventually a case worker was appointed to work with me at home to ensure I met the criteria necessary for safeguarding Molly.

There were times when I felt it was never going to happen, doubting how people would view me. Maggie, the voice of reason was right behind me when I almost lost my shit a couple of times, particularly after the discussions about my alcoholism and depression.

"They couldn't take the baby we're having away because of your past and you're not that guy anymore, so why would they refuse Molly the opportunity to have two doting parents?"

I only wished I shared her confidence.

After Annalise's call, I was preoccupied all the way home as I turned over every negative issue I could think of that would prevent a judge from granting me permission to see my son. My anxiety at those thoughts caused a pain in my gut. My heart was split right down the middle. One side felt light—blissful at being with the woman and child I loved who held that half in their hands. The other half was barely recognizable as part of the same one beating inside my chest. It had been battered and bruised; crushed, broken, and splintered by the despair I felt at not knowing my son.

Lost in thought, I hadn't realized we'd arrived home until Eamon turned off the engine and looked at me with concern.

"You okay?"

"Yeah, Annalise told me the hearing about Rudi is set for Tuesday."

"Let's hope you have a judge that plays fair this time," he muttered as he got out of the car. "I'm here if you need to get anything off your chest," he added.

~

Molly's enthusiastic chatter greeted me as I turned the handle and stepped into the hallway. It lightened my mood a little to hear it. The pitter patter of her flip-flops quickly followed as she ran out of the playroom to meet me, lifting my temperament a little more.

"Noah," she shouted excitedly, as she ran toward me with a delighted wide smile on her face. Jumping up into my open arms I wrapped them around her and spun her in a circle. I cradled her head in my hand and felt love radiate from her. "How's my baby girl today?" I asked, trying to sound cheerful.

"I'm six, Noah. I'm not a baby," she chastised me with a scolding expression on her face. It made me smile no matter how I'd felt before I stepped into our home.

"You'll always be my baby, no matter how old you get," I replied and tickled her ribs. "Where's that gorgeous mom of yours?" At first her brow creased, then she remembered I was talking about Maggie who was legally her mom by then and as if a little lightbulb went off she scrubbed my chin and said, "She's lying down upstairs. Our baby is tiring her out," Molly replied. I loved that she referred to our unborn baby as 'ours'.

I walked us into the kitchen to find Kathleen. "Is Maggie okay?"

"She's been having some mild contractions this afternoon and refused to let me call you," Kathleen replied. My whole being filled with concern.

Setting Molly down, I took the stairs two and three at a time in my haste to get to our bedroom.

"Maggie, baby?" I said with a question in my voice.

Her eyelids fluttered open, and she gave me a reassuring smile. She rubbed her round belly and replied, "I'm fine, Noah. It's only been a few hours. The contractions are bearable but they're getting a little stronger. We've got time to get Molly to bed before I have to leave for the hospital."

"Have you called your OB guy?"

"My Obstetrician is happy for me to stay home a little longer. If the contractions get closer or my waters break, he said I'd have to go in straight away."

I ran my hands roughly through my hair then stuffed them in my pockets to hide my nerves. I knew she needed me to hold my shit together and be calm.

"You put your bag in the trunk, right?" Maggie nodded, and I pulled out my cell to tell Eamon what was happening by text—he responded to say he was ready when we were.

~

George: Are you planning on putting in an appearance today?

After a long emotional night at the hospital I'd clean forgotten to inform the band of our news.

Me: Shit, sorry. We have a boy. George Oliver Stephen Haxby.

George: Congratulations. Well fuck... George—after me? I'm honored, mate. Did you know your kid's initials are GOSH? LOL.

I grinned widely because no one could piss on my strawberries now Maggie had delivered our beautiful son.

Me: Ha! Yeah... that was my reaction when I saw his head appear. I added a shocked emoticon.

George: LOL. Congrats to you both. Give Maggie our love and tell her she's a saint to give birth to the devil's spawn.

Me: Oy. Thanks. She's the best damned thing about me.

I put my cell back in my pocket with a happy smile on my face as I sat down on the chair. My mind replayed the emotional scene of Maggie grimacing with determination as she pushed George into this world. Watching anxiously as his still little body slid between her legs, his chest still and his skin pale. And I glanced to Maggie with the utmost respect for all she'd been through to bring him into the world.

Within seconds, I saw his lifeless color change from gray to pink as his chest expanded when he took his first breath, and as his lungs filled with air, then he cried. It was the sweetest and the worst sound all at the same time. Then the full impact of emotion of the wonder I'd witnessed caught me square in the chest and I cried with him. I was officially a wimp.

Reluctantly, I took the scissors the doctor gave me, scared to use them but privileged to be offered. My hands shook as he directed me to cut the cord and I nervously severed the tie that attached him to Maggie's body. As I stared down at his tiny naked body, the sudden recognition of what George meant to me kicked in and my heart opened instantly to him.

Next thing I knew he was lifted onto Maggie's chest and I stared fascinated as she breast-fed our tiny son.

"I never expected him to be that small," I mused, mesmerized by the fact he knew exactly what to do.

"That's not what my undercarriage is thinking."

"Undercarriage? You mean your pussy? Does it hurt?"

Maggie drew me a look that said if she didn't need me I'd have been dead and chewed on her mouth as she thought for a second. "Think razor blades, taser shocks, rope burn, and being whipped with a nylon rope... then you'll have the beginnings of an idea what that felt like."

"Ouch," I frowned hating that she was in pain and I was partly to blame.

Despite my protests Maggie insisted I slept at home and by the time I arrived back there, Molly had left for class. I lay on the bed intending to have a couple of hours then go back to the hospital, but I never slept a wink. My mind whirred like a revolving door from one child to the next as thoughts of my responsibilities took hold.

Focusing on one at a time was difficult because all three little ones had needs and as they were all equally my responsibility I had wanted to ensure I considered each one in any decisions that were made. One thought did enter my head which made me smile. Who had time to be depressed or drunk with three kids to take care of?

On the way back to the hospital later that morning I had a call from my welfare key worker regarding Molly's adoption application. Due to someone passing away, case had been bumped, and the judge wanted me to be present due to the previous issues with Rudi. *Why is it that everything happens at once?*

When I told her about the case Lester was progressing and the court date for that, she took the information and wondered if the same judge could preside over both at the same time. It would mean he'd make a ruling not only with Molly but for Rudi as well.

By the time she'd concluded the call my anxiety levels were insanely high again. What should have been the best day of my life was filled with worry and self-doubt. My concerns were if he said no to Rudi he'd say no to both and where would that leave Maggie and I and our family? Then I felt we should never have told Molly until the deal was sealed.

I considered if I should tell Maggie I was due in court at the end of that week and quickly dismissed that thought. It was a special day for us, we were bringing our son home and although the call had taken the shine off *my* day, I was damned if I would do anything to take it off hers.

As Eamon had been privy to the conversation I'd sworn him to silence about mentioning anything to Maggie, then my conversation was cut short as Eamon drove into the hospital parking lot because my heart sank when I saw a group of reporters milling around by the door.

"How the fuck?" I cussed, "Today of all days," I said, angry they'd found out about Maggie and our boy. "Here we go," I said in frustration and shook my head in disbelief. Thoughts about how my appearance in court may be affected by anything they printed made me worried.

"It was great while it lasted, Noah. I'm surprised you and Maggie kept them at bay for so long. Stay calm and don't say anything to piss them off."

Eamon pulled the car as near to the entrance as he could and got out. Opening the door for me, I stepped out behaving like I didn't have a care in the world. "Beautiful morning, everyone." I said believing it was the only comment they were getting from me.

"Noah, we hear congratulations are in order. Can we confirm by your presence here this morning, you're confirming you're the father of Maggie Dashwood's baby?" shouted one reporter.

"You previously denied you were in a relationship with Maggie. Can you tell us why now our sources are saying she delivered a baby son to you here last night?" Asked another.

"Andrea tells us you are trying to overturn the restraining order on your son, Rudi... is that the case?" another called out.

Ignoring their questions, I pushed past them and headed up to the floor Maggie was on. "We need another car and a back way out of this place. I'm not throwing Maggie and my son to that pack of wolves down there," I said to Eamon. Nodding he quickly pulled out his cell, made a call then put it on loudspeaker.

"Yes, Eamon?" Annalise asked.

I answered instead of him.

"Annalise, we need backup at the hospital. The paparazzi know about Maggie."

"I heard she'd had the baby through the calls I've been getting, they're all over this. Congratulations. The office lines have been jammed for the past forty-five minutes, so it's still breaking. I hadn't heard a peep before that. Are you in the hospital now? Are there many reporters? Do you need assistance at your home as well?"

"Quit with the twenty questions. Yes, we're here already. I need a car to get us out quietly. I want Maggie and my son home safely with no fuss, and you better get someone over to Molly's school. I'll have Maggie call them in a few minutes when I get to her room—"

"Wait, there's a change of plan. I'm not taking them home, we're going to Noah's parent's place. Call me back with the details for the car and send extra security to the house. I want them to think we're going back there. You'd better update Kathleen about Molly and they can meet us there," Eamon said.

"All right, you heard the man and Annalise make sure the driver is discreet," I added, leaving Eamon holding the phone and I marched down the hall to Maggie's room.

My tone was harsh with Annalise, but I was under stress. The media could do their worst with me, but I was determined to protect my family and do all I could to keep them out of the limelight. Someone in a position of trust at the hospital had obviously broken our confidence and sold the information to the media. In my head I cursed whoever it was to Hell for being so fucking greedy as I opened the door of Maggie's room with a relaxed smile on my face.

"Good God, could you look any more beautiful?" I asked as I moved over beside her. Bending down I gave her upturned mouth a soft kiss. I held the side of her head in my hand as she looked down at our son and she leaned into my palm. "You're adorable together," I added.

"You just missed George having his first test. He passed with flying colors," she said, looking up into my eyes and smiling affectionately. Hers shone with happiness and my heart swelled because I'd helped put that smile on her face.

"Test?" I frowned, with a note of concern and slid my hand from her cheek to cradle his head. Maggie gestured to me to take him and I slid my other hand under his body, lifting him free of her and held him close to my chest. Pressing my nose to his soft downy hair I inhaled his scent and my heart squeezed with love for them both.

"Yeah, his hearing check—he passed," she added with a slight chuckle.

"You listening to your mommy, son? You're a genius already, rock star," I told him and peppered kisses on his head. George nuzzled close to my body and the way he snuggled... well I had no words to describe what it meant to me to hold him in that moment.

"We're all set. I have my paperwork, signed the insurance forms again, and I have my physical therapy sheet of exercises."

"Pelvic floor?"

"Yeah... I need to work on those to prevent myself from peeing the sofa when I'm old," she answered with grin.

"Oh, honey. You don't need to worry on my account. I have enough money to check you into an elderly care residence if that happens then it won't be my problem."

Maggie belly laughed, stopped sharply, and winced. "Are you okay?"

"Yeah, who knew how much pressure is put on your tushie when you laugh." She replied and snickered and stood gathering up her purse.

Then came the moment I dreaded because I had to tell her about the press and decided it had to be done like ripping off a band-aid.

"How much do you like surprises?"

"Depends what you've got in mind. I'm pretty tired, I didn't get much sleep last night."

"This is... a ten-minute surprise."

"Alright, I can manage that," she replied nodding.

"Here's the thing. The media's found out about us... and George." Her sweet smile froze on her lips and her eyes darkened with worry.

"They have? How?"

"We'll talk about that later; right this minute we've got a posse of photographers hanging around the front door waiting to ambush us when we leave. Annalise is organizing another car and Eamon is going to walk back to our car as if he's going to grab something from the trunk while we sneak out from the back of the building somehow. He's figuring it out right now with the security staff."

Maggie took George from me when he'd begun to fret and shushed him on her shoulder. It was as if he'd picked up on my anxiety.

"We're not going home either; Eamon's taking us to my parents. First, I need you to contact Molly's school and tell them one of my team and Kathleen will be picking her up early and they'll bring her to us." Tension rolled off Maggie but I tried my best to stay calm for the sake of her and George.

An hour later we pulled through the gates to my parent's place and I exhaled loudly because we'd made it there without incident. The relief on Maggie's face caused an overwhelming urge within me to protect her and the kids and my chest tightened. *This is all my fault.*

Maggie remained anxious for Molly even after she'd been assured Molly was already out of school and on her way home to my parents with Kathleen and a bodyguard. It wasn't until Molly came bursting through the door at my parents that she visibly relaxed.

Molly ran over to Maggie but stopped short, hesitant about being around the baby, and peered over at him on tiptoe from where she stood.

"Is this my... brother?" She whispered like it was a secret and looked to Maggie for clarification.

"Yes, it is, Molly. Do you want to hold him?" Maggie asked with a smile in her voice and looked over to me to see if I was watching. I smiled back at her to let her know I was paying attention.

Molly squealed and clasped her hands under her chin. "Can I?" she asked in disbelief then ran on the spot with excitement.

I watched how carefully she cradled his tiny head in her little hand and looked at Maggie because it was an emotional moment for us. I felt my heart swell in my chest and for a second I felt sad because Rudi had missed this event. Then I reminded myself we were almost there as a family and I prayed the judge would be reasonable and see me for the man that I had become and not the foolish teenager I'd been in the past.

CHAPTER TWENTY-TWO
Maggie

*N*othing could have prepared me for the difficult onslaught of media news that followed baby George's birth. Noah was worried for our security for a while because some of his fans hadn't taken the news too well. The press coverage was relentless and by the time we went back home I had a much better understanding of how difficult our lives could be because he was famous.

Annalise kept Noah up to date with the news. When I heard some of the things they were saying I got quite distressed. They had once again implied our relationship had begun when I went to recover Shona's body from Australia.

Many hurtful untruths had been written and after several bouts of tears I decided I didn't want to know what was being reported anymore, preferring to live in blissful ignorance and focus on my children. I figured Noah had the right idea when he told me to ignore them and eventually they'd target their attention on someone else.

Instead of dwelling on the thing I couldn't change, I threw myself into a life of domesticity and insisted that Noah went back into the recording studio. He hated the thought of leaving us but reluctantly agreed when the producers they'd hired became tired of all the delays and threatened to walk away. Therefore, when George was only six days old, his dad kissed his head, pouted at having to leave us behind, and headed off to work.

My life was a little isolated living the way Noah had to and because I hadn't cultivated friends for quite a long time due to keeping Shona, Molly and myself afloat, my only source of company most days was Kathleen. Apart from one of my work colleagues, Gill, I'd hadn't invited anyone over to my home before I lived with Noah and she was the only person I spoke to regularly. I had just finished making a note to myself to call her that evening when Annalise called my cell phone.

"Hi, Maggie. I couldn't get hold of Noah because he's in session in the studio right now. This can't wait so I'm bringing it to you. Do you know a friend of Shona's called Vivian Reed?" I racked my brain and came up with nothing.

"Can't say that I do, why?"

"There was a call from a reporter trying to verify a connection between her and Shona. These people have no decorum at all. From his account she's a hippy type who's been hiking in Tibet and Nepal for a number of years. Anyway, she read the papers and contacted this reporter after reading about you and Noah. It appears she has some sensational exclusive, and he's trying to verify it through people who know you. Sounds like there's no love lost between him and Noah and he took delight in saying if what the girl told him was true then it would rock Noah to the core."

My first thoughts were that there was another baby somewhere. I wasn't sure if my heart would have been able to handle that. It didn't matter how strong we were together, Annalise's call set alarm bells ringing in my head as small seeds of doubt about what Vivian Reed knew still managed to creep in. *What does a rock star what do they do when no one else is around? Who have they known? God alone knew what secrets Noah may have in his past.* I shook the thought away and cursed myself for even thinking that way of him. The man I had given a son to had done me no wrong... and as far as I knew he never would.

Before I hung up, I asked Annalise to message Noah and forewarn him, then I closed the call out and went upstairs to breastfeed George. My cell rang again less than half an hour later and it was Gill, which was weird given that I had been thinking about her that day. I almost ignored to concentrate on George but after the call with Annalise a nagging doubt made me pick up.

"Thank goodness I caught you, Maggie. I'm sorry to disturb you but I think there's something you'll want to hear from someone you know and not hear it for the first time in the press. I rolled my eyes at her dramatic tone and wondered what she could possibly know that would make me anything other than angry that the media were involved again. *It's probably another fabricated bullshit story.*

"Fire away, let's hear it," I replied, placing her on speakerphone as I adjusted George from one breast to the other.

"I have no idea how to make this less worse than it sounds so I'm just going to say it. I'm not saying it's true I'm only—"

"I get it. I won't shoot the messenger, Gill, tell me."

"So... a reporter showed up here this morning... right before school began. He asked me if I was an ex-colleague of yours and I could hardly say no because—"

"For Heaven's sake, Gill, just get to the story," I barked from my frustration and the anxiety building.

"He had a picture of your sister and another girl and asked me to point Shona out."

"And it was her... in the picture I mean?"

"It was, and it looked like she was backstage at a Fr8Load concert. I could make out Noah and that other one... George is it?... from the band. In the picture they were a lot younger than they are now, and they were holding up beers like they were saluting your sister and her friend with their tongues stuck out in a crude gesture around the bottles behind the girls' backs."

My heart almost stopped. Pain shot through me as it struggled to find its rhythm, and it took me a moment to gather my thoughts. *Has Noah been lying to me all this time? Did he know Shona?*

"And you're sure it was Shona?" I asked even though I knew if Gill was calling me she had no doubts that it was. Disbelief and dismay kept me still in my chair as I listened to my workmate's confirmation.

"Yes. Remember that silly phase she went through when she dyed that beautiful long blonde hair black on top and purple at the ends?"

It was exactly how Shona's hair was during the period when she disappeared to go to his concerts. But none of it made sense because I felt sure Shona wouldn't have been able to contain herself from telling me if she had met Noah.

"Did you tell him it was her?"

"Of course I didn't. What kind of friend would that make me? Although, I think it's only a matter of time before he confirms it. Perhaps you should speak to Noah about it because I don't think this guy is going to go away empty handed."

I thanked her for her friendship and the heads up, concluded the call, then looked at my son and my heart sunk to my belly. Thinking Noah had been with Shona and then with me made me feel sick.

The family we'd made between us was already unconventional. By this time, it had been over a year since Shona's death and in that time my life as I knew it wasn't in any way recognizable from the one that I'd had.

~

An hour passed, and Noah came rushing into the house calling out for me. The urgency in his voice made me jump and filled me with a sense of foreboding. I had been lying on our bed resting because George wasn't even a week old and I already felt drained and wondered if I had the strength to deal with any more distressing news.

"Maggie, Maggie! Where are you, honey?" he shouted, his urgent voice gave away his excitement.

"Up here. What's wrong?" I asked from the top of the stairs and began to walk down toward him. Kathleen came around the corner from her room to check that everything was okay.

Noah rushed toward me and scooped me into his arms. "Through here, I have something to tell you," he said, placing a hand around my waist when I reached the bottom step and ushered me into the den. "Sit here," he ordered and instead of sitting beside me he wandered in a circle before turning sharply to look at me.

"I didn't want to spoil your week any further but the day after George was born I had a call to say my court hearing about Molly had been moved up. Lester, the guy who's been working on my appeal for

Rudi handed over the revised files for the judge to read... Never mind," he said changing tack. "I went to present my case to the judge with him today and he's overturned my restraining order. It won't be renewed and I'm going to begin visitation with Rudi as soon as the welfare key worker has prepared him."

Noah stood with his wide arms open with delight as he radiated pure joy at the judge's decision. I was both relieved for him and wanted to know about the decision regarding Molly. I stood up and walked into his arms and he wrapped them firmly around me and picked me up off the floor. "I'm so happy," he admitted.

"What about Molly?"

Noah slid me down his body and I swear the light in his eyes dimmed. "Instead of a restraining order there is a supervision order. It stays in place for three months for the welfare department to monitor the contact between me and Rudi. Until that's dispensed with, the judge thinks it reasonable to wait until I've settled Rudi into a routine without taking on another child."

"Taking on another child? She fucking lives here, Noah," I shrieked, angry with the stupidity of that decision. "What part of that doesn't he understand? How do you think his caution is going to go down with Molly? The poor kid asks every day if you're her dad yet. No offense... and this is going to sound selfish, but I need look out for Molly. Rudi isn't setting foot in our home until Molly's adoption is resolved."

"Are you serious? You know I've been tortured for years about this. And now that I have a chance to be a father to my own child you're telling me he's not welcome here? Fuck you, Maggie. This is my son. My son. My flesh and blood."

"As is George and you're really quick to discard Molly, who isn't *flesh and blood*, in favor of Rudi."

"That's below the belt, Maggie."

"Is it?"

"I didn't make the fucking rules. But I *have* to follow them."

"Then it'll be a first," I snapped. It was the biggest argument we'd had in our whole time together, but there was no competition who's corner I was in. Molly had one advocate in her life and that was me.

Noah scowled darkly and turned on his heel. "No woman tells me I can't have a relationship with my child. No one. I love Molly like she is my own. However, she already knows me; Rudi needs that same chance."

I shook my head and stormed out the room. "Come back here," he demanded.

"Go to Hell," I countered. When I reached our bedroom, I banged the door much harder than I intended to and wept. George began to cry, and I opened my door. Kathleen stood hesitantly on the landing.

"It's okay, Maggie. I've got him," she replied and turned heading quickly into the nursery. Without arguing, I closed my door again and lay on the bed. The day had started out with an air of optimism and Noah and I had been reduced to this, based on the decision of someone who didn't know any of us.

Noah knew me well enough to give me space. He waited an hour before he came to the bedroom and slowly opened the door. Stepping inside he stood at a distance and ran his hands through his hair. "I'm sorry Maggie. Today is the day I've waited almost five long years for. I didn't handle the way I told you very well downstairs."

When I didn't reply he walked over to the bed and sat on the edge facing me. He placed his hand on my hip and rubbed gently on my thigh.

"I love Molly like she's mine. She already feels like she's carved from me. Rudi needs to have the same opportunity. Obviously, I felt devastated when the judge put the condition on Molly, but I could see his reasoning. Deep down I think you do too, but you're right to challenge me the way you did. I wouldn't expect any less. It tells me that no matter what I say, you will insist I do the right thing for our kids. You ground me and its part of the reason you hold my heart in your hands."

"You didn't handle the news badly, Noah; that was a fucking car crash, and I want you to know I'll fight for Molly to the last. She was here first. Our life as a family started with her. I'll never allow you to show preference for any child that lives under this roof," I replied. I was sure he heard the hurt in my response because I saw the way he winced and I forgave what he'd said and how he said it before because

I knew he loved Molly and it was said in a moment of desperation to know his son.

"I can't remember whether it was you or I who said, "*Everything will be okay*," that has become my mantra in life. It doesn't matter who said it, but I need to believe it. We've come this far, Maggie, there's not much further to go. We just have to hang in there a little longer."

"We have no choice, the judge saw to that," I replied.

Noah stood and toed off his shoes, shrugged himself out of his jacket and loosened his belt. He pulled it clear of the loops and dropped it on the floor.

"Budge up," he said, nudging me over to my side of the bed as he lay down beside me. "This week hasn't turned out anything like we imagined, Maggie. I want to apologize for that. Most new moms get pampered and cosseted but my stupid job has dragged us down. I'm so sorry, honey. When things calm down a little, I'll make it up to you." I stared into his serious eyes and had no doubt about how much he loved me. "And I'll have a Hell of a lot of fun doing it," he added, and winked when he saw the beginning of my smile.

Our fight had thrown me, and I had forgotten about the calls from Gill and Annalise. I moved with a start and he tensed. "Have you spoken to Annalise this afternoon?"

"No. I was in court remember? Why... something else to piss me off?"

"Maybe," I said and studied his face carefully for a reaction to what I was about to say.

"Someone has been to a reporter with a sensational exclusive. The reporter called Annalise in his effort to verify the source's connection to my sister, Shona."

"What does that have to do with anything? The coroner in Australia closed the case on Shona. There's nothing to know, honey."

"That was one of the things I dismissed; however, the same journalist visited my old school and questioned Gill, my ex-colleague, before she went into class. He had a picture of Shona and this girl who's stirring things up. From the picture, they're at one of your Fr8Load concerts."

Noah shrugged, "That isn't news, they already reported Shona was a fan and went to our gigs."

"Yeah, according to Gill, my sister and this girl are backstage. You and George are behind them holding up a beer with your tongues hanging out or something, she said it looked crude."

Noah sat up quickly and swung his legs off the bed, then he turned back to look at me, "You're saying I met Shona?"

"It's what the picture implies as far as Gill was concerned. My workmate never confirmed it was Shona to the reporter, but it's only a matter of time until someone does. Shona didn't look anything like the photograph the papers ran with when she died. Her ash blonde hair was dyed black, with purple ends, and she used a lot of heavy makeup and kohl eyeliner around her eyes in those days. Plus, she was a lot skinnier before she had Molly."

"Sweetheart, you've described half my female following. You knew what I was like, I won't deny how I was. However, this girl with the story is probably one of a hundred girls we spoke to during that one particular tour."

"Don't say that, Noah. My sister died because she followed you." It was the first time I sounded like I apportioned blame directly at him.

Noah pushed off the bed, picked his shoe up and threw it at the wall. "What the fuck does a guy have to do to be heard? There were hundreds of women, Maggie. I'm sorry. "Sit back, relax, let me make you feel good," they'd say, then they'd blow me. I was barely more than a kid, at what... eighteen, nineteen... twenty? What red blooded teenager would have turned that down? Is that what you want to hear? As far as I remember I never met your sister. Maggie, since we've been together I've been totally faithful to you. Utterly respectful and devoted. A. Good. Man. I don't know what this picture is or what the fuck she's doing with it."

Striding over to the wall he bent down and swiped his shoe from the floor then came back for the other. Anger radiated through him as he pulled them back on. Two outbursts in one day and I wasn't sure how to handle it, so I cried. It had only been a short time since George had been born and I was tired. Ever since we'd been together, Noah had always been the voice of reason. My rock. I stared like I didn't know him as he extended his arm to the floor and scooped up his jacket, pulling it on as he went.

"Where are you going?"

"Anywhere away from here because if I don't, I'm sure you'll see a side of me you'll never get past."

I edged my way off the bed to follow him, but by the time I reached the landing he was already closing the front door. Seconds later I heard the car pulling out of the courtyard and ran back to get my cell.

Suddenly I was afraid. Had I pushed him too far? The state he left the house in could have led him to the nearest bar... and I knew if that happened it would be a game changer for sure. I called Eamon and got no reply. I left a message hoping he was with Noah and he hadn't gone alone.

My next call was to Steve. He reassured me Noah would have gone to his parent's place. His bolt-hole sanctuary for the times when he felt at his most vulnerable. It was a coping mechanism that he, his sponsor from alcoholics anonymous, and his family had agreed to.

I was beside myself with worry all evening and if I'm honest a little afraid I had made a mistake living with him. I tried to focus on routine and fed George, then I helped Kathleen with Molly and George's bedtime routines. All those tasks were performed with one eye on the phone. Molly asked continuously for Noah which wasn't helpful either, and by the time she settled in bed I was worn smooth. Physically I was still recovering from George's birth and emotionally, I was drained.

Eventually Eamon rang to tell me Noah was indeed at his parents and although I sighed with relief, I felt furious with him for walking away at a time when I had needed him the most. I was infuriated, sulked because he never called before bed, and I was up most of the night with George who had decided he wanted to eat all night. Finally, at around it 5:00 am I managed to catch some asleep.

CHAPTER TWENTY-THREE
Noah

*A*ll I heard in my head on repeat were the words, *Restraining order is revoked*. Everything else washed over me until Lester explained the rest afterward, "You will begin a three-month supervision period which will allow Rudi Haxby time to adjust to the new relationship."

The judge said if this is completed successfully we would reconvene and he'd discuss any future shared custody between Andrea and me. I figured she'd be ferocious in trying to block the decision, but Lester assured me she had to comply.

The second part of what he said had made my heart sink because he said he wouldn't make judgement on Molly until Rudi's custody case was settled. All I remember was turning quickly to eye Lester, alarmed because I wanted Molly as much as I wanted Rudi, but Lester gave me a look that told me not to push my luck.

Afterwards Lester made me see sense. Molly was not already related. Rudi was. Molly already lived with me so her living environment was settled and more able to handle a child being introduced to our home. She'd have one new person to deal with whereas Rudi had five people, including the baby and Kathleen.

Lester said he thought the judge was sensible in his decision, and once I proved I was capable of putting Rudi's needs first—as he was the child whose life was going to be disrupted the most—then with the restraining order revoked I would be given shared parental responsibility for Rudi as the judge had rubber stamped that. I was being watched and I couldn't afford to fuck up.

None of the legal stuff mattered. I felt ecstatic to have been given permission to have my son back in my life. Andrea could no longer control Rudi's future with me by holding a legal paper over my head, and I couldn't wait to tell Maggie that my son would finally be coming home to me... at least for some of his upbringing.

As I got into the car with Eamon, my heart felt like it would burst out of my chest, the relief of years of worry suddenly decompressed and I felt free to breathe unaided for the first time since I could remember. It's impossible to describe that feeling of the unjust sentence that had been imposed on me and how I had carried that around on my back like some huge boulder weighing me down.

There hadn't been a single day where I was free from the shame of assaulting that guy, but it was a reaction not an action to what he'd done to me. I knew from my past there was no point in protesting my innocence after the restraining order was granted and the appeal denied.

"Good job, boss. I'm over the moon happy for you," Eamon said by way of expressing his support, then stuck the stick shift in gear and drove me home.

My mind was chaotic after the pressure of the week and flitted from seeing my new son George being brought into this world and severing the cord between his mother and him; Molly's delight when she held him for the first time; and the fragmented memories of the few times I had gotten to hold Rudi before Andrea cruelly took her revenge on me for not loving her enough.

Eamon hadn't even stopped the car, when I opened the door to get out in my excitement to share the news from the court with Maggie, and I'll admit Molly did take a back seat, but that was only after Lester had reasoned with me. I didn't like how the judge had left Molly's adoption hanging, but I had no choice but to accept it.

Then... when I saw Maggie, I guess the enormity of the whole situation from the previous week hit me like a freight train. I handled it all wrong. If I'd just sat her down and calmly explained what the judge and Lester had said I knew she would have understood. Why couldn't I have had that rational thought when I burst into the house and spewed my incoherent thoughts out the way I had?

Perhaps if Maggie hadn't gone on the defense about Molly, I'd have been able to get my frustration under control enough to explain it in a more palatable way, but instead I allowed my emotions to overwhelm me and it all went to shit.

The curve ball she threw about the picture of the fans pissed me the fuck off. If I had ever met her sister, Shona, I had no recollection of her. We as a band met hundreds of girls every week, and I wouldn't have known them again if I passed them in the street.

Besides, Molly had a picture of her and Shona on her dresser in her room. I've looked at it many times and not once did I ever feel anything about it apart from sadness at her no longer being here for Molly.

I think it was the way Maggie spoke that made me so defensive, challenging me about a picture I'd never even seen or remembered being taken, and I guess the whole tension and pressure of the incidents of that week just made me blow like I hadn't done in years.

Something snapped inside me as my chest tightened, squeezing the air out of my lungs like they'd burst if I didn't do something to relieve the pressure.

My normally controlled temper grew to boiling point, and I did the first thing that came to mind that I felt would relieve it and at the same time, tell Maggie in a nonverbal way not to push me any further. I picked up one of my shoes and threw it at the wall. Dramatic and shameful, but highly effective.

There wasn't a peep from Maggie after I'd done it and when I saw the look on her face, I knew the only thing left for me to do was to get out of there. I stepped into my shoes, grabbed my jacket off the floor and left.

Eamon had heard the row between us—it would have been hard not to—and followed swiftly behind me. I'd grabbed the keys to the

SUV from the bowl in the hallway and as I reached for the handle of the driver's door, Eamon slammed his palm on the window.

"No. You're not driving like this. I'll take you wherever you want to go but you're not driving." He reached over and took the keys from my hand, unlocking the door. I didn't bother walking around to the passenger side, and opened the rear door instead, and slid into the back seat.

I sat with my head in my hands and Eamon prompted me to pull on my seatbelt. I did as he asked, then he started the car and drove us away.

As soon as we passed through the gates and headed into the road, I struggled to keep my emotions in check. My throat burned as I swallowed several times in succession in my effort to keep them back. It didn't work and to be honest by that point I didn't care that I looked weak and I let the tears flow.

Eamon knew the drill and where to keep me safe and even though I felt a failure at running back to my parents at that particular moment, it was necessary to keep me from making the choice that would have killed my relationship with Maggie and my kids completely. They were worth more than any addiction or demon I had to fight and cowardly though it may have looked, it was the best way I knew how at that time, of ensuring I never slipped back.

My mom was already waiting at the bolt-hole by the time I arrived, and I guessed someone in my network had told her the score. For a minute I stopped and wondered who had told her because Eamon hadn't made any calls.

"Steve rang me. Come on, let's get you inside," she coaxed in her warm, affectionate tone.

"I'm sorry... I just..."

"Shh. Glad you're here and you're safe. That's all that matters. As soon as you're settled, I'll go over and see Maggie." My heart ached at how I'd behaved and felt a failure at leaving her to care for our baby son.

"She'll understand, Noah. She'll be proud you've come here instead of some bar to drown your sorrows," she advised, but I wasn't so sure about that. I stared at my mom's face and never spoke. The door opened and Jason, my AA group sponsor stood in the doorway with his backpack over his shoulder.

He shrugged the heavy pack off and threw it on the floor. "Never fear, the cavalry is here," he joked and quickly strode over and hugged me. "Good job, Noah," he praised.

My eyes darted from Eamon, to my mom, then back to him, and I felt ashamed because three people dropped what they were doing to tend to me, and my heart hurt for Maggie.

During that night Jason, my voice of reason, talked everything over with me and afterward my mood was much less dark. His constant reminders that I had so much to look forward to, helped.

Talking about my relationship with Maggie and how much we loved each other helped. All I'd ever wanted was within reach he told me and by the time we went to bed I had decided I was strong enough to go home to Maggie the following morning.

Eamon went to take my mom back to our place, and I'd insisted he stay with them over there. Once Jason had gotten to the crux of the matter and the events that had set me off he called Annalise on my behalf to find out exactly what the reporter who had been snooping around wanted. She explained what Maggie had already told me and had nothing new to add, so I figured we'd have to wait for publication.

The best I could console myself with was that I hadn't lied to Maggie. If I ever had met Shona, I had no recollection of ever doing so.

It was 3:00 am when I finally passed out, only to be roused twenty minutes later from my dreamless sleep by Annalise again.

"Sorry to wake you, Noah, but I didn't know what else to do. I couldn't get hold of Steve. The story that journalist was trying to rake up yesterday is out in the first editions. I've only just had it sent over by Flick in PR."

"And?"

"Vivian Reed claims to be a friend of Shona and states that Shona had your secret baby."

My heart fell to the floor. "What the fuck? Where do they get these people? That's ridiculous. Send me the article in my email," I replied and grabbed Jason's laptop off the coffee table. "Jason, what's your password for your laptop?" I called out in frustration when I saw it was locked.

Jason sleepily padded out of the spare room and took the laptop from me. He tapped in a few letters then turned it around and handed it back.

"What's going on?"

"Some bullshit story from that woman I told you about last night. She's claiming Shona had *my* baby—that Molly's mine," I replied defensively, as I logged into my email and waited for the article Annalise sent me to open. My heart was beating out of my chest and I couldn't even consider for one minute that this girl, Vivian, spoke the truth.

Leaning forward when the pdf picture opened I studied it hard and sure enough George and I were in the background being crude about the girls in the foreground. I stared at the girl who was supposedly Shona and had no memory of her whatsoever. Nothing. My eyes ticked over the details in the photo for clues when it dawned on me it was in our home state of Massachusetts.

I studied the picture of the two girls, both wearing Fr8Load t-shirts and I would never have recognized Shona as Maggie's sister, except for one obvious trait: Shona's eyes were almost exactly like Maggie's and Molly's. I couldn't doubt the similarities between them, but the girl in the picture looked very different from the pictures I had previously seen of Shona.

Calculating the dates in my mind I reckoned the picture was taken around the time I was single and before I had met Andrea. Then I felt sick to my stomach.

No matter how hard I wanted this story to be untrue, from the amount of girls I had one night stands with back then there was the tiniest possibility that I could have... I couldn't bear to think of the end of that sentence because the implications for Maggie and me were enormous. If the story had any credence I was in deep shit. We all were.

My heart pounded wildly as I checked the number for the tabloid running the article and called the newspaper office. I wanted to speak to the journalist reporting the story myself.

"Get Eamon on the phone, Jason. I've got to go home," I said, shrugging my naked ass into my jeans and pulling the day old dirty t-shirt over my head. I was a mess.

"Tell me there isn't any truth in that," Jason said after reading the article for himself while I hung on the line waiting to be connected to the scumbag reporter's desk. I scowled as I gave him a dark look and shook my head in disbelief because honestly—I had no idea what to think.

"Maggie's gonna have your nuts if it turns out to be true," he informed me as he scrolled for Eamon's number, then winced like it was a thought he had, that had made it into words

By the time Eamon had arrived, I had pains in my chest and I could hardly breathe. My heart had definitely been doing a cardio workout since I'd read the article. I took my seat in the passenger side of the car and enquired how Maggie was. Eamon just stared at me for a minute and started the engine. That said everything I'd expected. She was mad.

My cell rang as Eamon pulled away from my parent's place and I headed for home, this time with Jason in tow. He wouldn't leave me, not with so much shit unresolved. My mind was in turmoil and I had no idea how I'd be able to come back from this with Maggie if there was a sliver of truth to this story.

Victor Bright, the reporter, was no friend to me. He'd been the one who had covered the assault trial back in the day.

When I had spoken to him, he'd taken delight in informing me of the damning evidence he had: namely email correspondence from Shona to Vivian and vice versa including pictures from the gig, emails about my sexual performance, and a catalogue of emails containing pictures which document the progression of her pregnancy. I sat in silence, stunned. *If this is true, I'm fucked.*

I demanded Eamon drive faster because I had to get to Maggie before someone else got there first and hit her up with the full story as it was reported. The last thing I wanted for her was to hear it from someone else.

Calling my legal team from the car, I asked if they had obtained the information Victor had been given to authenticate the claim. They had, and I asked them to send it over to me.

Even if it were true, Maggie had to know I'd never have kept this from her, and I had to make her believe that I never knew anything about it... somehow.

～

My mom was in the kitchen making tea for Maggie when we arrived back. It was only 6:40 am, but Molly was already up and dressed and eating breakfast. "Noah," she gushed as she slid down from her chair then ran full pelt into my arms.

My heart cracked right open when her arms went around me because if she were truly my child, then my heart ached for Maggie, and for Shona in equal measure that she'd had a child belonging to me. It was the weirdest, most uncomfortable feeling ever.

I nodded to Mom who looked relieved I was home, and I headed up to see Maggie. The light was on in the nursery and I went in to find Maggie feeding George.

"Thank God, you're okay," she said, and I felt a fresh wave of guilt. Of everything that had happened to her in the previous week, she had brushed it aside with concerns for me.

"I'm so sorry about last night, Maggie. I handled it all wrong."

"Me too, Noah," she replied and shifted her gaze from me to George feeding on her breast.

I was desperate and dreading to tell her what had happened, but I didn't want to disrupt her feed with George and decided I wouldn't even attempt to broach the subject until their task was done.

An overwhelming need for her to accept my innocence about Shona... even if the baby was mine washed over me and I wondered where the Hell I could find the words to explain. First, I had to explain what I had done the previous night to help her understand why I had reacted like I had.

George fell away from Maggie's breast and looked drunk and exhausted from his feed. I scooped him up in my arms, put him over my shoulder and patted his back to wind him. Maggie smiled at the sight of us together and I wished to God I wasn't about to spoil the moment with what I had to say.

Placing George in his crib I took Maggie by the hand and asked her to come to our room. I was worried about her reaction and another argument was a definite possibility.

CHAPTER TWENTY-FOUR

Noah

Maggie sat on the edge of the bed and instead of sitting beside her, I pulled a chair across and sat directly facing her.

"You know I love you with all my heart, right?"

"It's okay, Noah. There's no need to apologize. I guess both our feelings were running high yesterday," Maggie said, thinking I was going to talk about me leaving.

"Oh, honey, there is every need and I believe me I'm sorry, but that isn't what this is about."

She frowned, puzzled at what else it could be.

"You know you told me about the reporter who had been fishing about Shona?" I asked with my heart pounding in my chest.

"Yeah."

"I have something to say about that this morning but before I do, I need to ask you something. Do you trust me?"

Maggie's eyes raked over my face as if trying to read what I had to tell her.

"Yeah, Noah."

"Good," I said and exhaled loudly.

"Then you will believe me when I say I have no idea whatsoever about what I learned this morning," I stated. "I know this is going to come as a huge shock, but you need to hear me out. The girl that went to the papers, Vivian something or other, she has told Victor Bright that Shona had a secret baby... and it's mine."

Maggie's face paled immediately; she breathed rapidly like there wasn't enough air, then she passed out.

"Mom, Eamon," I called from the landing and ran back into the room. Scooping Maggie up in my arms I hugged her to my chest. *What have I done? Everything I touch turns to shit. She doesn't deserve this.*

～

When Maggie came around, she vomited, and I swore to myself if she forgave me for this I'd do anything she wanted just to be with her. Steve turned up at the house having been filled in by Annalise and he was livid that we were put in this position, especially with everything else we had on our plate.

Mom was amazing. She sat with myself and Maggie and her common sense went a long way with helping Maggie to understand that it wasn't my fault. That I never knew about Molly and it was Shona's decision to keep the information to herself.

At lunchtime, my legal team called to say they had attached all Shona's emails to a zip file and had forwarded them for us to read. Maggie and I went into the den to read them from my laptop.

Emails from Victor Bright
6th Feb
Shona to Vivian: ***OMGEEE! Last night was EVERYTHING I ever dreamed of. N is an animal in the sack. I could hardly walk this morning, but it reminds me this one wasn't a dream it was REAL. #fuckedlikeabull. Luvsya S.***
6th Feb
Vivian to Shona: ***I'm dead jealous! Lucky you. George was good, but pretty drunk, and if I'm honest a bit sloppy. Did you go home? (hugs) Viv.***

6th Feb

Shona to Vivian*: Moany Maggie is on my case. I think she's forgotten what it's like to be young. Call you next week. Luvsya S.*

There were daily exchanges following this email between the girls but nothing of significance to the story in those.

4th April

Vivian to Shona*: Can you escape? Got two tickets for NYC gig on the 15th. Will you make it? I need my partner in crime. Maybe we can sneak backstage again. I could always blow a roadie if I need to. (hugs) Viv.*

4th April

Shona to Viv: *Definitely. I've been going out of my mind. I really need to see N again. Luvsya S.*

Then there were a series of emails regarding the concert getting closer and their excitement but nothing else significant other than the impending meeting.

16th April

Vivian to Shona: *Where the hell did you disappear to last night? I managed to get into the Fr8Load dressing room and George remembered me. Squee. He invited me to spend the night with him in Rhode Island. (The sex was insane. I prefer sober George to drunk George.) No sign of Noah anywhere during the time I was there. Did you manage to meet up with him? (hugs) Viv.*

16th April

Shona to Vivian: *We got separated, and I lost my cell. Tried to con my way backstage but came up against that guy who guards N... Eamon. He told me N was already engaged, and I was wasting my time. Hitched a ride back to MA with a guy from Vermont and cried all the way home. Gonna try to get tickets on eBay for the gig in CT next month.*

Again, the girls kept in regular contact with nothing relevant to the story.

17th May

Vivian to Shona: *Didya get the tickets? (hugs) Viv.*

17th May

Shona to Vivian: *Nope gotten beat in the online auction with five seconds to go :(Can't afford to go after the others, they're too expensive. Need new clothes I've gotten fat over the winter. Luvsya S.*

17th May

Vivian to Shona: ***Everything happens for a reason. I'm kinda seeing someone so I'm not sure if I want to ruin that by going all 'groupie to the band' on him. (hugs) Viv.***

There were many more regular emails between the girls until this.

22nd June.

Viv to Shona: ***Been seeing this guy who practices Buddhism. Never been so interested in religion before. Maybe because he's hung like a horse and knows how to use it ;) Decided to go traveling to Nepal and Tibet with him next month. Keep me up to date with Fr8Load. I doubt I'll hear much about them where I'm going. Good luck at college in the fall, Shona. Knock 'em dead. (hugs) Viv.***

Shona doesn't reply and there's a pause in their emails after Vivian leaves the country until these.

22nd November

Vivian to Shona: ***Heyyy girlie! It's been a while, huh? I've been traipsing around these mountain passages and living in love shacks with my man. I love this life and I'm teaching English to the locals for my keep. I'm so happy, Shona, who would have thought this excitement loving groupie would settle with one guy, eh? What about you? I expected to see a long line of emails from you and there isn't one. What the hell are you doing, girl? Fill me in. (hugs) miss ya Viv.***

22nd November

Shona to Vivian: ***How weird that I was thinking about you last night and you pop up in my emails today. Glad you're having so much fun, unlike me. It's been a difficult time here, but I'm getting there. I have something to tell you and I think you are the ONLY one I can trust with my news. Here goes. On the 2nd of this month I had a baby girl, Molly. She's as cute as a button but a demon during the night when she deprives me of sleep. I've barely slept a wink since the day she was born. I thank God she mainly*** *looks like me but I can see little subtle things that tell me she's her dad's child as well. The truth is I never bid for the tickets for the gig in May because I already knew I was carrying her inside. I kept her a secret until I couldn't hide her anymore and I had to confess. My sister, Maggie is furious with me. I get how she feels, I'm pretty pissed at myself for not being more careful, but I can't deny how in love I am with my baby. I may never get to see Noah Haxby again, and I'm okay with that now, because I'll always have something to remind me of the night I spent with him. Take this to the grave, Viv, you are the only person who knows about this. Luvsya S.*

23rd November

Vivian to Shona: ***Sorry I just got your email. Internet here is extremely patchy. No shit! Shona. I'm speechless. You haven't told anyone? Holy fuck, you just blew my mind. You must have known this before I left, and you never said a word. Why not? You shouldn't have to do this all on your own. Maybe you should contact his manager, you never know, Noah may step up... financially at least. I've been catching up on Fr8Load online since your email and saw he's with someone now... Andrea or something. For the record she looks like a bitch. You are far prettier. I bet she's a gold digger. Don't worry, Shona, for as long as you're alive my lips are sealed. I love the photographs you sent, she is ultra-cute and you look adorable in the pictures with your blonde hair. I prefer that to the black and purple style you had when I met you. You're right, I can see Noah in her. What a gorgeous baby. Your sister Maggie will have a hard job staying mad at you when she looks at that little girl. Her eyes are to die for. You are in so much trouble trying to tell that one off when she's older. It must be hard for you seeing Noah on TV when you have kept this secret inside all this time. If you ever need to get things off your chest, you can always message me. (hugs) Viv.***

The girls had kept in touch a few times a year since then, mainly with Shona sending photographs around each birthday, then Vivian received an email from Shona which was dated 21st of December a month before she died.

21st December

Shona to Vivian: *Hi hon, it's been a while since we messaged, but I just had to tell someone my news or I'll burst. I applied to an agency to gain experience with an image consultant and you'll never guess what they threw up. Wardrobe Assistant for Fr8Load's Image team. At first, I thought, no chance, but remember I'm really keen on marketing and advertising and I had done loads of fashion shows in high school. Anyway, I applied thinking I had nothing to lose. I almost fell over when three days later I got a call asking if I would be willing to travel to Australia to support the image team for them. ME! CAN YOU FUCKING BELIEVE THAT? I interviewed and although I lacked experience I had a handle on the band's image and they HIRED me!*

So, I thought... this is fate, right? I mean I get to tell Noah face to face he has a daughter and you know what? I think it will make his world because that bitch Andrea (Yep you called that one right) has made his life a misery by keeping his son from him. (I know I have but this is different. He doesn't know about Molly, so it doesn't affect him the way his son does.) Anywhoo... I'm out of here 3rd Jan to fly to Sydney, AUSTRALIA. I'm scared to tell him because I know he'll think I'm a crank, but I can't wait to see his face when he actually knows about her. I've made him an album from naught to five as she had her fifth birthday last month. Pray for me or send good vibes or whatever Buddhist's do because I hope he'll be happy when I tell him. Why now? I can hear you ask. (See how well I know you?) Well, I'm over that period of insanity, and I don't expect much from Noah, but Molly has asked me many times who her daddy is. I don't want to lie to her so I'm going to give him the chance to know Molly and be her dad. If he doesn't want that then I'm still going to tell her who he is because she shouldn't go through life with that huge a void. That wouldn't be right. Okay, I'll message when I'm there and tell you how it goes. Luvsya S.

26th December

Vivian to Shona: *Damned internet. I've just seen this. Whoo*

hoo. This is insane. I can't wait to hear how it goes. Dream job or what? I can't imagine how you must be feeling. I wish I was there to support you through this. Remember I'm here if you need me. Life here is very sedate, loads of meditation and hugging. Still enjoying the local people, they're so enthusiastic and treat me like a queen. Charlie has gone a bit deep and dull. If it wasn't for the sex, I'd probably leave. (Yep, he really is that good.) (hugs) Viv.

Shona sent one last email to Vivian before she died.

19th January

Shona to Vivian: ***Been here two weeks on the crew and I've never even gotten into the same building as Noah. I'm a glorified laundry maid here and the image stylists are so far up their own asses they could probably give themselves tonsillectomies. If I'm honest, it's getting me down now. There's only one guy here who understands me although all the crew are friendly. Problem is I think he's a junkie because of the mood swings he has. I feel like packing up and going home to Massachusetts. If I don't have any success this week, I think I'll give up and head back. I miss Molly and my sister, and I think I'm just chasing dreams here.***
Luvsya S.

Vivian sent several emails to Shona but when she didn't get a reply, she figured she'd gone home. After that she got caught up in her own life and never knew Shona had died. She only came back to the USA a few days ago to visit her parents. That's when she saw the piece about Maggie and learned about Shona's death in the article. It would appear now Shona had passed, Vivian felt it her duty to share Shona's secret and take her confession to the press as a way of lining her pockets.

Maggie stared, glassy eyed at the screen, tears streaming down her face and I caught her by the chin. Turning her face toward me I was sure she saw the pleading look I gave her. It was all that I had because I was devastated at what I'd learned, and I didn't have the words to begin to talk about it.

CHAPTER TWENTY-FIVE

Maggie

$\mathcal{M}$y heart hammered in my chest when Noah took me into the den and opened the email from his legal team. It started with their explanation of how they've sifted the emails and pulled out the relevant ones to Vivian's account of events. Studying the text, my eyes scanned their part of the email and watched as Noah clicked into the attached pdf copy file of the emails.

When I saw the communications between Shona and this woman, Vivian, a jolt of electricity shocked me so hard for a second I thought my heart may stop altogether. The ache in my chest and my stomach brought me close to tears as a lump in my throat grew, making my airway tighten.

As Noah scrolled down each email one by one I matched the dates and occasions to the events around what happened at home. Every time I calculated the dates as to what Shona said in her emails with recollections of the subsequent events in my head, my heart sunk lower. It became even more painful with what she disclosed to Vivian.

When I saw the email about her giving birth to Molly and the mention of Noah, I almost got out of my seat in panic because I couldn't breathe. Noah was quick to tighten his grip and from the way he covered his eyes with one hand I knew he was as devastated as I was.

The entire contents they had sent us to read took about fifteen minutes of our time and when we were done, both Noah and I looked helplessly at each other. We knew the effect of the words contained in the emails Shona had sent would have a lifelong impact on us.

Tears had flowed from the moment I read the first email because I could hear my sister's voice in her words. Sorrowful thoughts, feelings of loss, and the pain that she kept this from me mingled with anger at God for sending such a horrible and cruel twist to me in my life's journey.

Noah looked desolate... completely lost in his own head. I knew how I felt about Shona's deceit, but I could never imagine the pain going on inside him. It was minutes before his tears came and when they did, he covered his face with one hand again as the other held mine like if I pulled it away he'd never get it back.

The silence between us grew longer, and it felt like an invisible wall slowly building that would drive an emotional wedge between us. During that time, I stared at him, seeing the effects of a storm in him, but in contrast I felt completely numb. It was my body's natural protective reaction to the absurd and punishing information. My instincts were to reject the truths held in Shona's words as lies because I knew if they were absorbed and accepted they would wreck me.

Like all shocks my body had ever experienced, eventually the numbness wore off, and this one was replaced by an excruciating heartache. I sat staring helplessly at Noah as in my head, my world appeared to crumble around me. I'm not sure how long we sat like that —it felt like forever—then Noah swallowed roughly and spoke.

"Maggie... you have to believe me. I knew nothing about this. The emails tell you that." My eyes ticked over his face as I thought about the picture in the news with Noah in the background. Was Molly really his child? "I'm ashamed to say if I slept with Shona I can't remember it. Nothing I can say will make this sound any better will it?"

Noah had never said a truer word.

"How do you think this makes me feel to know this?"

"I can't imagine, but let me say this, Maggie. My heart aches. It aches for Shona who bore this alone. It aches for the fact she had this life changing event and bore my child and I was completely ignorant to that fact. It aches for the crushing pain I know this has caused you. But it explains why I feel so deeply for Molly. I know our situation is completely fucked up, but you need know this, Maggie. Had Shona contacted me I'd have treated her with respect."

"Like you did when you fucked her that night?" Noah winced at my sharp angry tone. "I can't live with you, Noah. Not after this. The shame this has brought me is totally humiliating. My life is ruined, and Molly is now a bastard child of Noah Haxby and classed as the product of a fucked up rock star." I shouted hysterically as I stood up and tried to flee the scene.

Noah's mom came into view and I turned to look at her. "I hope you brought your other five sons up better because this one has behaved like an animal, with the way he's treated women." It was a low blow toward Noah, but I didn't care. I was distraught. My reasoning and reputation had been destroyed because I'd fallen for him.

"You're upset. For that reason I'll ignore your insult, Maggie."

My reaction wasn't rational, but it was the only one I had. *God knows how Shona must have felt after finding out she was pregnant following his one and done session with her. How angry she'd have been with me.*

Suddenly I couldn't breathe again and wondered how I could even live with myself. How I could protect Molly from the constant jibes she would most likely be subjected to in the future? And that was before I even considered George. *What a fucking mess.* I glanced back at Noah who looked grief-stricken and in that moment, I hated him again.

I pulled my hand away, and he reached out and grabbed it again. "No, Maggie." Swiping my hand roughly I tugged free and made for the door. "Don't do this, baby. Don't punish me for something I didn't even know about," he urged as he followed closely behind until I reached our bedroom. I slammed the door, locked it, and sat on the edge of the bed, leaving him on the other side. My heart thudded heavily, and another wave of nausea washed over me.

Noah shook the handle, "Come on, Maggie, this is no time to shut me out. Can't you see I'm as devastated as you are about this? Jesus, I've had a daughter for six years. Six fucking years and she's been kept from me. How do you think that news is sitting with me? It's been hell not being able to see Rudi, and now I know another child has been kept from me. I'm heartbroken."

"I want a DNA test," I screamed at him through the door.

"What? You don't believe her? What the fuck? Open this door, Maggie, or I'll bust the fucking thing down." I heard Doreen on the landing speaking quietly in a stern voice to Noah then her soft calming voice spoke to me through the wood.

"Maggie, sweetheart. Let's think of the children here, okay? I know you're torn apart by this but there are two small children here. Please open the door and let me come in. I've sent Noah down to speak with Molly. Poor child woke frightened by all the noise."

I thought of Noah and Molly together and snickered in irony... he had more right to her than I had. He was her natural father. I opened the door to Doreen and instantly wanted to slam it shut again when I saw the sympathetic look on her face. I didn't want sympathy; I wanted this never to have happened. I cursed Vivian Reed for her greed. If I had no knowledge of Molly's origins, I could have lived in a happy ignorance.

A moment of clarity came to me and I stood, pushing past Doreen as I went into my closet. I pulled out a suitcase and began cramming shirts, tops, jeans, and sweaters into it— Molly and I had to get out of there.

"Maggie, sweetheart, can you just stop for a minute—"

"Stop for a minute? If I'd done that I wouldn't be in the mess I'm in right now. No. If *he'd* stopped for a minute none of us would be here. This isn't a mess; it's a cluster fuck of the worst kind. You think I can carry on as normal, knowing this? You need your head examined. I need to get out of here."

Doreen slammed her palm against the bedroom door as I was about to open it.

"No. Now you listen here, Maggie. Noah may have been a wild one at the beginning of his rock star days but I'm damned sure he never held Shona down to make that little girl down there. Sure, it's a fucked-up situation you've both landed in, but in all of this mess there are two innocent children who need their parents. *Both* parents. God knows how I would feel if I were walking in your shoes, but I'm a mother and I'm not thinking of Noah when I say it, this is about my grandchildren. You both need to deal with this together until it isn't an issue anymore. Not run away from it."

When she swore, it had gotten my attention. In all the time I'd known her I'd never heard her raise her voice. Her calming manner had always made me feel she was in complete control. I stood staring at her inches from my face and watched the fierce protectiveness in her eyes when she spoke about Noah.

"All right, and how in God's name do you think I can do that with the media breathing down our necks waiting for your son to make another fuck-up or another kid to come out of the woodwork? For all I know there are ten more 'Mollys' out there waiting to be discovered."

Doreen dropped her hand from the door when she saw me close to tears again. "Come here," she coaxed and pulled me into her chest. I hated that she was sympathizing with me. "Noah isn't a saint. He never has been, but damn it that boy downstairs is the first to admit that. Has he ever done *anything* to make you feel he's got something to hide?"

I couldn't argue with that, but then again weren't liars great at acting? "How would you feel if you found out Ken had a child with your sister?"

"In these circumstances? All these years later, and Ken had barely known the girl? I'd have slapped his face and called him every insulting name under the sun. Then I'd have cried, and I'd probably have ridden a wave of emotion just as you're doing now. But at the end of it all, when all the crying was done and every last nerve in my body had suffered from the assault of the news, I'd still love him."

"Why?"

"He's the father of my children. He'd still be the man I fell in love with. And mostly because it was at a time when he needed me the most. Look, Maggie, I'm sure you find this all extremely unpalatable. Do you think Noah finds it less so?"

"No, I don't, but Shona—"

"Is dead. And you are here. Forget the press. Forget everything except for how you feel in your heart when you look at Noah. Ask yourself this, can you live without him? Could you share Molly and George with him and perhaps one day see another woman holding their hands?" I don't think I could have dealt with that. I'm not trying to upset you, Maggie. All I'm doing is playing devil's advocate about the consequences of not being with him. He's a young man, Maggie. An incredibly handsome one. It's one of the reasons we're having this conversation today. Girls have always found Noah irresistible. First it was the other moms when they saw him in his stroller, then tiny girls in kindergarten, and you get the picture because this is where we are now."

I broke away from her hold and moved over to sit on the edge of the bed. "She was my little sister."

"And Noah is your partner. Father of your son. Molly's father."

When I heard her say the last part my heart felt like it had shattered inside my chest. I focused on the floor and sat motionless until she opened the bedroom door. Glancing up at her stern expression she shrugged. "You know I'm right, Maggie. Noah loves you like I've never seen him love anyone in his entire life. He's trying to be everything you need. He wants to be a good man. He *is* a good man. All the shit he's endured in the past few years will be nothing in comparison to the effect you'll have on him if you walk away. Now... do I go downstairs and ask him to come and speak to you or do I tell him you're packing your bags?" Her question told me she was finished with what she had to say.

"I'm not cut out for this... to be scrutinized and torn apart like a hound caught at a fox hunt for the pleasure of the press. I should have realized how difficult the impact of being the partner of someone with Noah's background was."

"That's as maybe, but you're here, Maggie. You and Noah must face this delicate situation with a united front. If you love him, you'll stand by him. Screw what the media say. They don't live your lives for you. They don't control what happens. You and Noah and your babies are what matters. Do you think my son has had an easy ride? What those journalists did to him in the past and continue to do is atrocious. So... what is it going to be?"

Despite feeling almost mortally wounded by the situation I took in a deep shaky breath and said, "I'll speak to Noah."

Without another word Doreen left the room, and I sat staring around me. Everything I saw was bought by Noah. I wondered if I had lost my identity being with him. That's how it felt when the press used me as collateral damage to target Noah for his past. I never even knew him then... but the connection to Shona from way back when was still with us in the present time—in their daughter Molly. The room was silent and still but inside my head I screamed loudly.

A soft tentative tap on the door drew my attention as he slowly pushed it open and Noah stood in the doorway, both hands held high, holding the frame. "Baby, I'm so sorry," he said. I could hear the pain in his apology by the sadness in his voice. Glancing up I saw his red-rimmed eyes, and they crushed me. He had been crying since I shut him out. My heart squeezed so tight in my chest with the weight of the situation and I inhaled deeply as I fought for my next breath.

"How do I live with this, Noah? What do we tell Molly? George? Rudi even? You can't fix this... no one can."

CHAPTER TWENTY-SIX
Noah

*A*fter Maggie took off out of the room, I went after her, but I wasn't fast enough. She looked so distressed as she ran up the stairs and took sanctuary in our bedroom. Speaking from the other side of our locked bedroom door I tried to reason with her that I never knew any of what we read in the emails. I was still reeling from the news myself and had to push all of my own feelings aside because her happiness was more important than anything I was going through.

I tried hard to think about the night in question—the one in the picture—every few minutes during that time and came back with nothing. Then I thought in more general terms about what I was like back then and was ashamed of how I'd behaved. I was a player, and of the girls I could remember Shona's face never appeared in any of the images in my mind's eye.

Sleeping around was my way of winding down, a way of releasing all the adrenaline I'd built up by performing. I was impressionable young teen who'd behaved the way I did because of the excess and opportunities around me.

When Maggie spoke to my mom, I knew if anyone could talk Maggie around it was her. The second my mom came back and nodded toward upstairs, I felt the pent-up tension in my neck release and regroup. As I fled up the stairs, I knew it was the most important moment of my life because my future rode on however I handled Maggie's distress.

I was relieved that she'd at least hear me out, but I was afraid that anything I said would add to her hurt as well. I'll admit I had a very low moment on the way up the stairs and I felt as if my life was always destined to be on trial. It appeared to me that no matter how hard I tried to be myself, second chances never appeared to go my way.

Slowly, I opened our bedroom door and saw Maggie sitting on the edge of the bed, directly facing me. My heart sunk to the pit of my stomach, churning with anxiety at the desolate sad figure she cut. Every muscle and fiber of my body screamed instantly for me to wrap my arms tightly around her and crush her tightly to my chest.

My natural instincts with Maggie were to protect her, and I wanted desperately to tell her everything was going to be okay, but as soon as she looked at me and I saw the pain in her eyes I wasn't sure if it ever would be again.

"Do you realize how beyond embarrassing this is for someone like me?"

Despite how much I sympathized, I needed her to understand it affected the both of us. "Someone like you? And you think this news makes me less ashamed? That I'm immune to what's happened and feel less than you do? This has happened to us, Maggie. *Us. You and Me.* Do you think I'm somehow unaffected by the fact I have a daughter? That I missed the first years of her life as well as Rudi's? Do you think I'm happy that your sister never came to me in the years before she died? If she had I may possibly have done something to make life easier for all of you.

"Can't you understand how much this hurts me? It's beyond..." She threw her hands up, lost for words.

"Yes! I do understand. I'm desperately sorry I've hurt you, however unintentional it was, but there's nothing I can do to change what Shona said or to make you feel okay about what we've learned. However, you know what? I'm going to say something that will prob- ably make you hate me more, but it needs to be said all the same. I'm thankful that I don't remember Shona. There—I've said it."

Maggie looked horror-stricken.

"You know why? Because I love *you* with all my heart and we'd never have happened if she'd caught up with me... or if she told me about Molly. Who knows? Molly may have come to live with me after she passed if she had, and where would that have left you?" I asked in desperation.

Maggie's eyes widened, and she straightened her upper body in reaction as the reality of my words hit home. Her face was pinched with worry then it suddenly relaxed when I had nothing else to say. Dropping my hands from the doorframe I wandered over toward her.

"May I sit?" I asked tentatively. She nodded, and I deliberately moved close to her, my leg touching hers in my need for contact. Reaching out I slid my hand under hers and I closed my fingers around it.

In a gentle quiet voice, I said, "Sometimes people make fucked-up decisions and take actions none of us understand... for reasons only they themselves know. You said Shona was infatuated by me? If that was the case, then there are several things that are bugging me about her revelation. Why did she never try to contact me before she came to work for me? If she was so infatuated why didn't she use Molly to get to me?"

"Maybe she did and was discarded as another crank, or more likely because I'd have disowned her for going public with this."

"There you go," I replied agreeing with her. It was highly possible Maggie would have gone crazy if Shona had said her baby was mine.

"Are you're saying I'm to blame? I'm the reason she never told you about Molly?"

"Yes, but not to blame you. It's possible Shona never contacted me until Molly was older out of respect for you. Then... as Molly's natural inquisitiveness took over, Shona felt guilty for not giving Molly a father figure. It appears as if when the opportunity presented itself in the form of being part of the crew, she may have seen that as a chance to reach out to me about Molly."

"What a cluster fuck. Do you know how mortified I feel, Noah? How the fuck are we supposed to get past this? How do I go out there and hold my head high, while I've not only screwed my dead sister's Baby Daddy, but had another child with you myself?"

I turned toward her and clasped her chin between my thumb and forefinger and coaxed her head toward me. Eyeing the worried look on Maggie's face, I took a deep breath and sighed before I tried to reach her again.

"You hold your head up high because you've done nothing wrong. *We've* done nothing wrong. Fuck the press, Maggie. What is more important—the kids and me, or your reputation to people who don't matter? This what it comes down to. I've had more shit and lies written about me than truths, and it's made me cynical. I used to care... and now? I couldn't give a flying fuck what they think because I know the truth in this... I had no fucking idea."

"This is my sister we're talking about. She mattered... Molly matters."

"Maggie, for years my management made me appear like some kind of freak because I was in a band and stupidly I tried to live up to that —look where it got me." I squeezed her hand tighter to emphasize my point.

"What the press did as a result was inexcusable and it changed me as a person. They took my son; they almost took my future—my life. As for the public, they'll forget about this in time and we'll still be together. Of all the times to show the media we are together this is it, baby. If we're completely solid as a couple, we'll be immune to what-ever they want to throw at us. Only then will they leave us the fuck alone."

Despite her anger, I saw her react to my touch. Her eyes softened, and I knew instantly she wanted to believe what I'd told her.

"Neither one of us knew about Molly when we got together. Shona could have told you at any time... she chose not to. I wish I could change our situation, but I can't, Maggie. We've just got to look forward to the one positive in it all—Molly. I've been in that kid's life for a while now, and I've loved her like she was my own... with every bone in my body. Don't you see how amazing this? To find out she's already mine means everything to me."

"Ours," she stated defensively.

"See... *now* you're getting what's important. I know this feels weird. Hell, no one could make this up, it's mind blowing for me and in my line of work I've seen and heard all kinds of shit. Trust me, baby. We're going to be fine. Best way forward is for us to front it out. When the media see they're having no effect they'll move on and leave us in peace."

When I saw her lips quirk weakly in the beginnings of a small smile, I tipped her chin up and looked directly into her eyes. She gave me a soul searching, piercing look that gripped my heart.

"Maggie Dashwood, you are the love of my life. *My queen.* I refuse to let *anyone* destroy what we have. Please, baby... together we can get past this. We have to because I couldn't bear to live without you." Tentatively I bowed my head and placed my forehead against hers.

Her beautiful eyes were cloudy with worry as she pleaded with the look she gave me. Her fingers moved lightly over the shadow of growth on my chin as she drew comfort from touching me. Her hair was tousled wildly from anxiously raking her hands through it as a visible sign that demonstrated how deeply the news about Molly affected her on top of everything else.

The horrible reality of pain and hurt in her eyes made me feel tearful, and a lump grew in my throat because I felt sad and angry at what the news reporters and Shona had done to us. Ultimately, what I had done to us.

"I can only do this if I can say what's on my mind," she said, firmly.

I shrugged and nodded slowly as I waited quietly as she gathered her thoughts.

"Look, I accept you didn't think you'd met my sister. I knew Shona better than anyone and I'm as dumbfounded as you are about how twisted her mind was where you were concerned. I hate it but understand how a lifestyle with no boundaries may have made you act the way you did with all those girls. I forgive Shona for the way she was and for keeping you in the dark about being Molly's father. Hurt doesn't even cut it for how I feel that she never told me. As for this Vivian Reed woman, who claims to be Shona's close friend, I forgive her for being greedy and breaking Shona's confidence as well."

I frowned and squeezed my hand tightly again then looked seriously back at her. Our foreheads were pressed against each other and the touch of skin on skin between us gave me hope.

"When I agreed to be with you, I told you at the time I was scared. That was because I knew of your reputation and I'd already had a taste of what the media could do. Now I've felt their wrath. I always had a feeling something would poke the sleeping serpent and our bubble would burst... and here we are." Guilt riddled my body, and I dropped my gaze to the floor.

"What I want to say now is I know you're nothing like Noah Haxby, the rock star. The reputation that was built around you has done you more harm than good. I will always question whatever they write because the man I know you to be is so far removed from what they've written about you. I find it hard to believe you have the capability to be that person. I know you better than any of them."

"Does this mean you forgive me?"

"Forgive you? There's nothing to forgive. I believe you when you say your lifestyle was pretty hedonistic, and that you took what you could get at that young age. I'm not so old I don't remember the teenage boys in high school, Noah. As for the rest, I'd much rather believe your version than the one that's been spun in the press. I'm not going to say I'll be a doormat about this or that this is going to be easy because it won't, but your mom just tore me a new one on your behalf. She gave me some home truths to think about and like it or not she was right about a few things. Before Shona's emails we were so good together and I know I can't do anything about this, so I have to try to continue with the life we've been building."

Relief flowed through my body and the tension ebbed from my muscles. The imaginary fist I felt squeezing my lungs suddenly released. I dropped her hand and cradled the sides of her head in my hands. "I'll do whatever it takes to make this right." I replied and silently thanked God for another chance.

My eyes focused on her lips before I looked up further and into her eyes. Maggie brushed some stray hair from my eyes and slid her arms around my neck. Tears welled in her eyes then one slowly trickled down her face. I caught it with the back of my forefinger and ran the same finger across her beautiful mouth.

"Shh," I said soothing her. "We'll get past this, baby, life goes on," I said.

Maggie bit her bottom lip, worrying it back and forth and all I wanted to do was make her happy.

"I see the way you look at me, baby. I can feel the love you have in your heart. You're the first person who really got me. The only woman who believes in me apart from my mom," I said with a small chuckle. "You're an amazing person, Maggie. You knew I didn't have custody of my own son, yet you brought Molly here to live in my home. Have you any idea what that meant to me?"

Placing her fingers over my lips she silenced me then pulled them away and kissed me softly on my mouth. She pulled back and stared intently then a small smile curved her lips.

My hand slid from hers to pinch her waist gently as I pulled her closer to me. Suddenly that wasn't enough, and I twisted her from her seated position and lay her gently on her back. Crawling over her I hovered and paused when it occurred to me how gorgeous she looked lying on our bed. Even with tear-stained cheeks she was still the most beautiful woman I'd ever seen.

We shared a silent moment—a period of calm I knew would shift us forward. I wanted to say to her that I hated Shona, but I couldn't— she was the mother of my child.

"You know what?" I asked. Her eyes questioned me, and her mouth opened to speak, "No. Don't say anything," I said cutting her off. An internal struggle came over me because I wanted to kiss her, and I didn't know if it would be acceptable when she was so worked up. Seconds later I couldn't resist and closed the space between us feathering her lips with mine. She rewarded me with a small sigh and it was then I figured we'd be okay.

Surprisingly, Maggie took a leap of faith and drew her tongue along my closed lips, and with that the tender kiss instantly turned predatory. Every thought and feeling that had burned inside me for the previous hour poured into the passionate, hungry, frustrated, and in parts angry, kiss.

I kissed her with everything I had, and she kissed me back, more than matching my level of desire. Her soft warm palms grazed the length of my arms then her fingers tangled in my hair. She sent my pulse racing and my heart burned in my chest at the way she clung desperately to me. By the time I finally dragged myself away our lips were swollen and bruised from our desperate need to find the intensity of our connection. It said despite everything she had learned, she was still mine.

CHAPTER TWENTY-SEVEN

Noah

*O*nce the news died down and the press pack ran off to focus on a cheating NFL quarterback and some Amazonian Supermodel in Rio, I tried to focus on pulling the threads of my life together and incorporating my son into our lives.

Molly's parentage took a bit of smoothing over with the welfare staff and I shamelessly turned on my charm to get them on my side. It helped that the key worker's assistant was a Fr8Load fan.

I tried to balance the story to them in respect of Maggie's loyalty toward her deceased sister because I knew Maggie wouldn't tolerate anyone who spoke in a derogatory manner about Shona.

As Maggie rightly pointed out, Shona had been a teenage mother and as far as anyone outside the family knew, she had made the tough decision to keep her baby and was raising her when she died.

With all the shit going on, our poor baby George was kind of lost in the timing of the disclosure by Shona, the judge's decision about Rudi, and the supervision order. Steve, my manager, added to my load by voicing his frustration because my focus was elsewhere.

Big George—as my bandmate came to be called after the baby's birth—said he thought he may do a solo project until I got my shit together. He felt he was getting stale waiting around. I gave him the nod and told him there'd be no hard feelings if he decided he'd had enough and secretly hoped he would call time on the band.

During the low points in my life I had thought being in the band had brought me more problems than anything positive. Most rock stars enjoyed the tours, using them as their excuse to escape responsibility and let their hair down.

Since my problems with Andrea I had used the tours more to stay sane and have purpose. Tours were a way of making me commit to being involved in life rather than lying in bed staring at the four walls in my room, wondering how I could change my situation with Rudi.

Unfortunately, I knew deep down I couldn't do that and since I'd begun building a life with Maggie, the thought of leaving my family to spend time on the road made me want to turn my back on it all.

When I first talked about touring and taking them along, I figured we could've made it work, but after a short time with a baby in the house I had other ideas about that.

The supervision compliance for Rudi was frustrating. I was hardly a threat to my son, no matter what the judge had said all those years ago.

However, I accepted that even Rudi himself may have had preconceived ideas about me that had been indoctrinated by his mom and because of that fear I prayed I wouldn't have yet another struggle on my hands to gain his acceptance.

Andrea wasn't at all happy about the change to her circumstances and became very obstructive until the threat of being cut out of the visitations altogether brought her into line. She agreed to being present for the sessions and had opted to bring Rudi for the visits watched from a distance by my welfare supervisor.

To say my nerves were shot to hell the first morning I left Maggie and drove off from home to meet my son would be an understatement. No matter how many times I'd walked out on stage without so much as thinking about it, this was a completely different challenge.

Entering the parking lot, I situated my car near the entrance then sat for a moment, taking a few deep breaths. I needed the visit to go well, and I prayed that Andrea wouldn't get a rise out of me.

As I got out the car, with these concerns still on my mind, I noticed the familiar, short dark hair I used to inhale and saw Andrea sitting at a seat near the window. I'd have recognized her by her posture and that ballerina neck anywhere. I fought the feeling of hostility that washed over me, but my body automatically stiffened.

Adrenaline coursed through my veins and the sudden surge tightened my chest and my stomach in a protective reaction. Pressure built in my head forming a constrictive band squeezing my brain inside. *Cool—calm—smile—relax* I chanted over and over as I willed my shoulders to slacken the tension I felt in them.

Mental images of my hands around Andrea's scrawny neck as I squeezed the life out of her was my way of internalizing all the pain she had caused me by taking my son away from me—and me away from him.

Smile. Be charming. Your son is watching you, and by watching his dad he will learn how to treat women. Keep it together and remember Andrea's still the mother of your kid.

None of what happened mattered anymore; the evil wrong she did to me. It had worked to a point and now it didn't. I tried not to look as if I were gloating, but I was... on the inside.

When our eyes met as I walked toward her, I beamed a white smile, teeth and all aimed directly at her because it was the 'fuck you' I had often visualized in my head but never thought would come.

Everything will be okay.

Rudi had been unintentionally hidden from my view, her body completely blocking him from being seen through the window of the inflatables fun house Andrea had chosen for our first contact visit. Personally, I hadn't thought it was a good idea to give her control, then I reasoned to myself she was Rudi's mom, and he deserved to feel secure.

When I reached the entrance, I pushed the cool glass pane on the door and stepped inside the leisure facility. My heart stuttered and skipped a beat, then raced wilder than I was prepared for.

Simultaneously while my pulse raced, my eyes rapidly surveyed the scene scanning all the faces until they halted at my son. He was even more handsome than any of the pictures I'd ever seen of him.

A huge lump formed in my throat—so big I had to look away because I was choked. The last thing I would have wanted was to lose control in front of my son.

Rudi's attention was taken up with a coloring pad and crayons, so I lingered a little longer to savor the moment because I was immortalizing his image in my mind as my first glimpse in person of my son since he was a baby.

Next thing I knew he looked up and straight at me and my world suddenly appeared to stall. During the pause neither of us moved. I stared into his eyes that reflected mine and instantly felt like I had found a precious missing jigsaw piece that completed the picture of my life.

"Is that him, Mom? Is that my dad?" his anxious little voice asked.

Andrea looked older, tired, and if I had to say it, less bitchy. "Yes, Rudi. That's your father."

Rudi smiled shyly, slid down from his chair and walked tentatively toward me. "My mom says you're my dad. Pleased to meet you," he said extending his little hand for me to shake.

I stared down at it for a second and was almost afraid to reach out because I knew as soon as I touched him it made the dream real, and once that had happened I'd kill Andrea before I'd let her keep us apart again.

"Hey, bud. Yes! I'm your dad and I have been so looking forward to spending time with you."

Rudi flashed me a wider smile and my heart melted when I saw one of his front teeth was missing. I couldn't prevent the grin that spread over my face. "Well, champ, looks like you're growing up fast, got a little tooth gone already," I offered for something to say.

"I lost it when I fell off my bike and bashed my mouth two weeks ago."

I felt I'd been struck with a knife when he said he'd hurt himself like that and I'd been oblivious to the event. I felt hurt and angry, but I knew I had to curb my impulse to tear into his mom about it. Frowning, I held him by his forearms. "Were you hurt anywhere else?"

Rudi hesitated then shook his head, and I shot Andrea an angry glare and bit my tongue about my feelings for fear of ruining the visit. The last thing I would do was show any behavior that made the welfare worker feel like I was a threat to Rudi.

My initial attempt at communicating with my five-year-old when all I'd had were two generic 'Your son's doing fine' letters a year and second hand information from my parents, wasn't easy, and I quickly realized the enormity of winning the confidence of a small boy who perhaps knew nothing about me.

"Hey," I said gently, because the last thing I had wanted was any animosity between us. I had to let the past slide to move us forward for our son's sake.

"You got what you wanted, now what?" she asked.

I glanced at Rudi to see if he was listening and when I looked back to Andrea I didn't miss the uncertainty in the way she regarded me.

"Now, we put the past behind us, Andrea. What's happening now isn't about us, it's about what we do next as both of Rudi's parents. I don't want to take your place or to interfere in the relationship you have with our son, I just want to get to know him and let him get to know me."

Narrowing her eyes Andrea scrutinized me like she had difficulty accepting what I'd told her and placed a hand on Rudi's head.

"You have no idea how hard the past five years have been," she informed me in a voice that was more familiar to how she was during the difficult times we'd shared.

"You're right, Andrea, I don't... but I'd have given my life for my son. Staying away was never my choice. I don't want to argue," I said nodding my head toward, Rudi as I shoved my hands in my pockets. "I just want to start fresh and despite what's happened, Andrea, you can trust me never to speak ill of you to Rudi. You are his mother and that grants you my forgiveness to make Rudi's life easier with us both."

A look of shame passed through Andrea's eyes as she lowered them to the ground and I figured she had a lot to think about from then on.

During our first visitation, Rudi appeared reserved but polite, not like Molly with her constant dancing, incessant chatter, and challenging mastermind standard questions. The difference troubled me. It was like he'd never had fun... or wasn't allowed to. Molly was spontaneous whereas every move Rudi took, every comment he made, and every question he asked appeared deliberate.

After the exchange with Andrea I took Rudi off to play on a few of the inflatables and it wasn't long before his behavior became more relaxed and he relished scoring goals at soccer against me into an inflatable goal post.

I wondered if he was worried because despite the fun he appeared to be having he never laughed aloud. I probably wouldn't have noticed had I not been around Molly so much. I compared the two children many times during that afternoon and although I knew I shouldn't, I couldn't fail to because they were both my kids but I didn't know either of them very well yet.

During the three months that followed, the visits got easier, and I almost felt sorry for Andrea as she watched Rudi slip from a one parent child to having us both. As time passed, I felt him gravitate toward me. I reminded myself that Andrea had been his disciplinarian for his whole life so it would have been easy for him to think I was the fun parent due to the unnatural environment I'd been forced into meeting him in. Strangely enough, toward the end of the three months I found myself reassuring her she'd done a good job of raising him thus far.

By the time we were due back in court the judge had decided Molly's case could be finalized by me taking a simple DNA test. It never even occurred to me to do that after Maggie's initial outburst because the picture and emails had said it all and I was surprised the email evidence wasn't enough as the dates all tallied up.

I was thankful for the way it turned out because I wouldn't have wanted to celebrate Molly being mine when Rudi's future with me hadn't been rubber stamped. Maybe the judge was wiser than I originally thought when he'd set the condition about Molly previously.

The day before I was due in court I submitted the DNA sample as requested and went to the studio before I went home to spend the evening with Maggie.

When I arrived home, I was surprised to see Maggie all dolled up in the hottest, clingiest dress, waiting on the front steps. She placed a hand on my chest, gave me a sexy smile and ushered me back into the car. Eamon glanced to Maggie and a knowing smirk passed between him before he drove us away.

Knowing exactly what I needed to take my mind of the events of the following day she had arranged a sneaky candlelit dinner at my parent's place while Kathleen and my mom took care of the kids at ours. It had been the first time we'd had quality one-on-one time since George had been born because life really had been that busy.

The succulent aroma of lemongrass and Chinese spices sent hunger pangs to my stomach as soon as we opened the door of the property. Everything was set: low light, silver and flatware laid on a white linen tablecloth in the intimate setting and security of my bolt-hole.

Maggie knew me very well, for she'd taken me to my safe place to reduce my level of stress in anticipation of my vulnerable emotional state, on the eve of what was probably the most important day of my life. If things went my way, it would be a major step forward in restoring some of my damaged reputation.

Being with someone as grounded as Maggie was as effective as any therapy or pills I could have taken. There had been only one occasion where I had thought drink was the answer since I'd met her. Even then I'd felt the strength to seek seclusion rather than fall back into that trap.

Dinner was delicious, but the company was even better. Maggie was witty, and I found myself completely focused on her. It was like she had cast a spell on me where I could think of nothing else except to kiss her beautiful mouth as she told stories of her days in high school until my sides were sore from laughing so much.

Eventually it wasn't enough to watch, and I caught her chin between my thumb and forefinger as I leaned toward her and pressed my lips to hers. "Mm, best course of the night," I mumbled then kissed her for real. My tongue played along the seam of her lips and as they parted, it invaded the warm space inside as her tongue curved around mine.

Without breaking the kiss, I slipped my huge hands under her tight little ass, lifted her clean out the chair, and staggered blindly in the direction of the leather sofa in the den. I inhaled her scent deeply as she curled her arms around me and buried her face in my neck. An exquisite sensation ran down my spine when Maggie's nails scratched my neck then curled up into my hair. She fisted a handful tightly as she wriggled her ass against my hands.

Oh, is that how it is?" I asked playfully as I stared into her eyes. She shrugged but didn't say anything... she didn't have to.

Her body heaved as her uneven breaths belied how quickly she became aroused. My cock was rock solid. She always had that effect on me. No real effort necessary. The chemistry between us was fire and ice, electricity and water. Each burning or shocking us with shivers and chills to pull at our cores.

Reaching the sofa, I spun myself around, dropped clumsily to the soft leather, and slid back on it. Maggie's center landed directly over my erect dick and it felt good. It was pleasurable and painful at the same time. Like a bruise that aches at the slightest touch but you know the feeling can only get better.

When she rubbed herself teasingly against me I strained for greater purchase. I knew from the moment I touched her that night I'd struggle to make it slow and easy as my desperation to get inside her was too hard to control.

Within less than a minute I'd flipped her onto her back, my rough hands gliding up her smooth and silky thighs to reach nirvana. Grabbing the waistband at each side, I frantically tugged her panties down her legs. The material creaked under the strain until I suddenly felt the strain leave them at the same time as a loud tearing sound cut into the silence between us.

Maggie broke the kiss. "Did you just rip my panties off me?" she asked, amused.

"Hush, woman, lie back and let me spread you wide. I want to look at you," I said in a low, wicked, half whisper.

"You did not just say that!" Maggie said, chuckling.

"Wanna bet?" I joked as I hurriedly bunched her dress up around her waist and buried my face between her legs. Maggie was giggling until my tongue connected with her clit, and I heard her breath catch in her throat. "Mmm, delicious," I mumbled playfully as I continued to languish long deliberate strokes and short teasing licks with my tongue.

Pushing my head back, Maggie sat up and reached for my belt buckle then frantically opened it quickly followed by my jeans. Her cool hand slid into the searing heat in my pants and she wrapped her fingers delicately but firmly around my cock.

She began to rise off the sofa and shoved me forcefully like she was taking charge and I knew she wanted to love me, but I couldn't allow that... not that night. With all that had gone on and the anticipation I had contained inside I needed to take control.

Grabbing her by her wrist, I shook my head and her eyes bore into mine. A silent conversation happened between us and she understood I needed to do it my way that day.

Shrugging my jeans down my legs I pulled them and my socks off in unison then knelt before her on the sofa. Next, I gripped her by the legs bending them up toward her shoulders. My cock brushed her thigh igniting all the pent-up raw carnal feelings I'd been harboring inside.

Our eyes locked, and she smiled, the gesture melted my heart, but fueled the desire to take her to unbearable heights. I'd never looked into the eyes of someone so calm and full of desire at the same time, so I bowed my forehead to rest on hers and angled my cock just right. The way her beautiful vibrant eyes widened before her gaze grew in intensity almost ended me. My cock stretched her pussy walls as I pushed my way into her body... the feeling never got old.

No one had ever looked at me like that... not that I noticed them looking before Maggie, and no one could ever have replicated the powerful connection we had because we owned one another heart, body, and soul.

I took Maggie twice in the hour that followed. The first wasn't sensual and giving, but rather demanding. She was as clued in as I was and gave as good as she got, her ass rose to meet each thrust. Reaching over, I pulled out a cushion, lifted her hips, and slid it underneath increasing the depth as I sank balls deep to her core. That sexual encounter took our connection to a new level.

If I was rough the first time around, the second time I took her was almost spiritual in contrast. It was slow, sensual, and sexy. I treasured her, taking her with care. I lavished her with attention and worshipped her body. Every moan, whimper, and intimate sound Maggie made tightened her hold on me like a warm blanket of love enveloping my heart, and making it an intense session for both of us.

Covered in sweat, Maggie's face and neck glistened, her face flushed from the effort of our lovemaking. She curled up on the sofa and rested her head on my lap and she shoved her dress down her legs after we'd tidied ourselves up. The scent of our steamy session hung in the air.

"I can't believe tomorrow could be the final decision about the kids. When I look back at the week of George's birth, I honestly didn't think we'd survive. I've learned to accept you as Molly's dad and I'm glad you never said anything to her before. I can't wait for tomorrow to tell her. She's going to burst with excitement," Maggie murmured and circled a finger around the hairs on my bare thigh.

"Hell, baby, it's me you'll have to watch. If the judge gives me the final nod, I may strip off my clothes and do cartwheels across the floor of the courtroom naked."

I burst out laughing at Maggie's don't-even-think-about-that look and shook my head. "Maybe the press expected that of me, but I'd never do anything to jeopardize my kids from coming home."

Maggie inhaled deeply and gave a long sigh, "One more day, Noah. Then everything's going to be okay."

CHAPTER TWENTY-EIGHT

Maggie

The night I planned for Noah was designed to take his mind off the pending court hearing and it went even better than I'd expected. I was happy to see how relaxed he appeared considering what was at stake. I trusted him, but I wasn't complacent of the pressure I knew he must have felt. I worried it may have affected his depression and because of that and his history with alcohol I removed all possibility of Noah losing control. I didn't think he would; however, it did no harm to be mindful of his past.

By arranging a meal at his safe place, it minimized the risks of him being overwhelmed. I think Noah knew why we'd gone there and if he had an issue with that he never said, and if he did, he got past that quickly because we had a fabulous time.

It wasn't until we were back home in bed that Noah showed any sign of uncertainty. I could tell by how restless he was that the decision of the judge played heavily on his mind. When I tried to encourage him to open up about that, he became introspective, shrugged his shoulders, and didn't reply. He knew nothing I said would improve his chances because his future with Rudi depended on a legal decision.

Even his welfare worker had tried to reassure him he had nothing to worry about; the visits with his son had gone well, and she assured him the next step of unsupervised visits and sleepovers would feel much more natural.

However, I knew Noah would continue to err on the side of caution until the judge told him differently. He had been disappointed so many times in the past. His protective mechanism wouldn't allow him to take anything for granted.

Supervision became a dirty word in our home and I was glad that part had come to an end. I agreed with Noah it wasn't a natural setting for him to get to know his child in front of his estranged ex-girlfriend and with a social welfare worker hovering in the background. The good thing was he and Rudi had grown closer.

Each time Noah visited with Rudi he came home buzzing and gave me a minute by minute account of what had been said, how he felt the visit had gone and then he included comments such as which of his brothers Rudi looked like the most.

It was evident in the way he spoke about his son that his feelings had grown deeper. The brightness in his eyes coupled with how animated he was about Rudi, warmed my heart and I saw true happiness in his smile. It gave me a glimpse of the man he was before all the sorrow had affected him and that made my heart ache for all he'd gone through.

As I got to know Rudi through Noah, I became excited for his visits to our home and prayed the kids all got along when the time came. I wasn't surprised when he expressed some concerns about Rudi's personality because he was very accustomed to Molly and the way she interacted. However, from what he told me I wasn't worried, and I explained that sometimes boys were less forward than girls, especially at that age.

Being a schoolteacher, I had dealt with more than a few quirky behaviors from very young children and then reminded him that Molly had been given a lot more input with her communication due to my training. If I compared her to other kids her age, she appeared streets ahead.

I had envisioned more strain between Noah and I after we found out about Shona and the secret she'd kept hidden. My immediate reaction to her news devastated me and I reacted both irrational yet completely appropriate at the same time given the circumstances.

When Noah asked me to forgive him, I became rational and felt there was nothing for me to forgive. How could I blame him when he had been ignorant to Shona's decision to keep Molly's existence to herself? I apportioned more blame to her for not telling me the facts and Noah could hardly take responsibility for something he knew nothing about.

Since the night we'd ironed it out, I had ignored the press and pushed my anger at Shona to the back of my mind. I was surprised at how quickly our relationship appeared stronger than ever, despite the pressure Noah was under from his management, his band, the family courts, and trying to form a proper relationship with Rudi.

He coped amazingly considering all of that, and at home Noah remained the even-tempered, patient man I had known him to be since I had first met him. Sometimes I would lie and stare at him in bed wondering how this ordinary man I lived with had ever lived his life to excess. Then I'd look at how handsome he was, how amazing he was as a musician, and how sexy and charming he could be... then it wasn't difficult to imagine at all... and sometimes that part frightened me, and my insecurities would creep in.

There were times I'd listen to him on the phone with his bandmates, with the language and banter they had, and it would leave me chuckling heartily or in awe when he'd discuss his ideas, or a song he had written. It was there I knew how exceptional he was compared to other men. And then there were some occasions when he'd say something to me on the fly and it left me... breathless.

On the odd occasion I felt like I didn't know him at all because I had never seen the excesses of the rock star lifestyle he'd led because his band hadn't done much since I'd met him. There was one thing I did know for sure; Noah had grown happier in the time that I'd known him. It made me think when Noah said how much he loved being with me and added his break from the band was the first time in years he'd had the opportunity to think for himself.

Apart from when George and the guys dropped by, Noah Haxby, the front man from Fr8Load, never made a personal appearance in our home. Instead I had the gentle but strong family man who was fantastic with Molly and George. Molly adored him, and I reconciled myself with what I'd learned from Shona's emails because when choosing to accept Noah as Molly's father, I was certain I could never have found anyone better.

~

When Noah went to court the following morning, I tagged along and held his hand. Lester called Noah from his car to ours and informed him the DNA test result was back. Noah stiffened then stated we already knew the answer to that. Apparently, Lester couldn't confirm it as he hadn't seen it himself and only knew it was included in the emailed checklist of reports that had gone to the court.

Glancing down at my slender fingers in Noah's strong warm hand I felt a swell of love for him in my chest and squeezed his hand. When I looked up, his serious eyes met mine and I could see his concern hidden there.

Apart from the call from Lester, we rode to the courthouse in silence. Noah stared out the window deep in thought and I left him to manage those without interference from me and before long Eamon drew up at the front of the building. Noah stiffened again and sat bolt upright in his seat. Assembled on the steps were a pack of photographers and reporters.

"Fuck." Noah muttered, "They're like fucking vultures. Don't they have anything better to do?"

Eamon eyed Noah with a serious expression on his face. "Boss, if there was ever a day to keep your cool, this is it, right?"

Noah tensed further then sighed heavily. Dropping his shoulders he slowly nodded. His eyes ticked over the faces in the crowd and his hand gripped mine tighter. I glanced out to see what he'd seen that had drawn that reaction.

Andrea, his ex, was talking to a group of reporters on the steps of the courthouse. "Jesus, I can always count on her to create a fucking spectacle of us. She never thinks of our boy when she does this shit. Get the fuck out and listen to what she's saying," Noah barked at Eamon in frustration. At his request Eamon quickly got out of the car, locked the doors with us inside, and moved swiftly into position at the back of the reporters to hear what she was saying.

Eamon's presence drew attention to us and the press swarmed around the car like bees on honey. I was frightened as I listened to them banging on the windows, their voices slightly muted as they fired questions to Noah inside the car. Camera bulbs flashed incessantly in their effort to get the 'money shot' even though it was light outside.

Noah ignored them completely, his neck straining past one of the reporters while his eyes were fixed on Andrea. I wondered what he was thinking watching her. I took his lead and tried to ignore the press. Also, I tried to study Andrea. I had only seen a few pictures of her online and those hadn't done her justice. She was absolutely stunning—catwalk stunning—and I felt self-conscious of how I'd be compared. We were practically opposites to look at and the only thing I had in common with her was we had both carried a child fathered by Noah.

Minutes later Eamon came jogging back, shoved his wide arms apart and spread a path through the press. Ushering them back to a safe distance he called out, "Back off," before he gave them a menacing growl. I jumped at the fierceness in his voice.

Once they had retreated a few feet, Eamon gave the window two knocks then opened the door. Noah yanked me out of the car, then took the stairs at a faster pace than I was used to as he dragged me along, wrapping a protective arm around me when we reached the top. He made no comment as we made our way into the court.

Eamon murmured into Noah's ear, and I figured he was probably explaining what Andrea had said as we walked the sterile oak-paneled passageway down to the courtroom. The high ceilings and empty space enhanced the echo of our hurried footsteps as Noah marched determinedly toward Lester who was stood outside the heavy oak doors at the far end of the corridor.

Andrea's mouth dropped as we passed because Noah completely ignored her presence and as soon as we reached Lester he ushered us straight into the courtroom. He directed Noah to sit at a table at the front and Eamon and I sat directly behind Noah and his legal briefs. I sat in silence as I watched a short exchange between Lester and another member of the team.

Minutes later Andrea entered with her legal representation and sat on the other side. Lester turned to speak to Noah as the judge arrived, so their attention became diverted to him.

Noah turned to look at me and I instantly smiled and mouthed, "I love you." He gave me a small rueful smile in return before facing the judge. As I watched him sitting there at the mercy of the court, my heart almost tore in two as I sat quietly and waited to hear what the reports had to say.

We sat through several minutes of legal exchanges between the judge and the council before the judge breathed impatiently and stared pointedly over his half-spectacles at Andrea. My curious eyes followed his, and I watched her straighten up in her chair as she sat looking innocently back at him.

In that moment I had insight to the kind of person she was. She was using her sexuality to entice the judge, and I wondered if he could see through her smart clothes and perfect makeup to see what I did—a manipulative bitch who had put Noah through hell for years and deprived her son of his father.

When he cut to the chase, the lawmaker said he had three decisions to make. The first was in Rudi's case, the second the question of biological paternity in the case of Molly, and the third regarding Molly's adoption. I figured the third would be moot after the second was decided as we knew already Noah was her father from Shona's emails.

The summary he read covered the observations, comments and recommendations made by the welfare officer in Rudi's case, and was listed in bullet points. When he finished, I'd heard a lot of praise for Noah in the supervision reports.

I almost missed what the judge said because I had been thinking on those when it sunk in that he had granted parental responsibility in equal parts to both Andrea and Noah. His final comments were that the welfare team felt they had all the evidence they needed, and no further assessments were deemed necessary.

Noah's shoulders sagged with relief before his hands flew to his head. Placing his elbows on the table his hands moved from his hair to his face and he broke down in relief. It was heartbreaking to see him reduced to tears, and I glanced at Andrea with disgust. The effect of the wise man's comment on her was clear, after a shocked gasp of disbelief she looked like she'd been slapped—hard.

Lester gave Noah a side hug, said something I couldn't hear, and patted his back a couple of times. Noah slowly pulled himself together and took his hands away from his face. Turning to look at me he swiftly flew out of his chair, leaned across the small wooden balustrade, and gave me a tight hug.

"Thank God," he whispered.

Calling Noah to order, the lawmaker turned to look at Andrea, who still looked stunned, and leaned forward to give her an angry glare. He then preceded to dress her down for the way she had manipulated a situation to her advantage and probably swayed justice for Noah in the past.

Pointing out that Noah had paid a more than generous allowance for Rudi and paid for the home she lived in, he then said he'd considered this when he awarded custody to Noah. He went on to say Noah had shown how responsible he was in taking care of Rudi—even after the restraining order had been granted.

Then he unexpectedly stuck his neck out and said he had reviewed the paperwork around the assault and had he been the judge in the case Noah would never have been found guilty in the first place. He said in his opinion the evidence presented was biased. It probably helped that the original judge was dead because he'd taken an unusual course of action to voice that for the record.

It was obvious he had the measure of Andrea and stated that the custody agreement would be drawn up by the welfare worker in consultation with both Noah and Andrea and any such order must take into consideration Noah's schedule of work.

Andrea was about to protest when he silenced her by holding up his hand. "I will expect these arrangements to be served for consideration no later than fourteen days from today's date in the best interests of the child. The sooner this is ironed out, the better for Rudi's emotional welfare."

Leaning back in his chair he dismissed Andrea from the court because the second part of the hearing was about Molly and she was not an interested party to that.

Andrea stood, gave Noah the stink eye, and left with a facial expression that would have turned milk sour. The judge waited until the doors closed then turned back to address Noah. He waved a piece of paper in the air as he looked down at his notes to prompt him.

I have here the results of the DNA test provided by you Noah Lockwood Haxby at the medical facility to the court yesterday. From the paperwork I understand a sample from Molly Dashwood was also submitted by Molly's adoptive mother, Margaret Dashwood. I believe the question of paternity has been raised after you, Noah, were named as the biological father of Molly.

He asked the Clerk to the Court to approach the bench, and he passed the single piece of white paper to him.

Without waiting the clerk unfolded it and cleared his throat.

"These are the results from a DNA sample provided by Molly Dashwood, child, and second sample of DNA submitted by Noah Lockwood Haxby to determine biological paternity. The results are as follows," he added and cleared his throat again.

Result—Combined Paternity Index Result (CPI) zero percent. Probability of Paternity (POP) zero percent. The alleged father is *excluded* as the father of the tested child. This conclusion is based on the non-matching alleles.

It went on to say the alleged father lacked the genetic markers that must be contributed to the child by the biological father.

Noah leaned over from the waist and spread himself flat on the table. Clearly floored by the results revelation. Turning his head to the side I saw more tears flow, but not in relief. The shock of the outcome hit me square in the chest and I gasped. For a few moments I couldn't think. A few seconds passed and Noah sat upright with his palms flat on the table. He looked behind him to me and then back to the judge.

"We have evidence... the emails—"

"I asked them to check the samples twice. There has been no mistake, Noah. I can see how that has distressed you and that leads me to inform you, Noah Lockwood Haxby, that this application is dismissed on the grounds of the physical evidence to refute your application to be recognized as Molly Dashwood's biological father.

When I saw Noah hang his head and close his eyes, my heart shattered into a million pieces at the cruel lie which had given us such a difficult dilemma to bear. Shona's emails almost cost us our relationship. I didn't understand any of it and I had no words of comfort for Noah.

"Now, Noah, I can see how the impact of this information has affected you and how disappointed you are; however, I am in a position to address the issue of Molly Dashwood's adoption. I would understand if you wanted to go away and digest what you've been told here today?"

Noah glanced at me through his red-rimmed eyes and the hurt I could see he felt in his heart radiated into mine. Turning back to the judge he said, "I'd like to hear that now if it's all the same to you," Noah bravely advised him.

"Noah Lockwood Haxby, in response to the adoption application you submitted with the agreement of Margaret Dashwood, adoptive mother of the child, in relation to the child Molly Dashwood, I am now in a position to recommend this and grant you joint parental responsibility for the child. This official adoption will be entered onto the Registry of births, deaths, and marriages in the name of Noah Lockwood Haxby, adoptive father of Molly Dashwood. All that's left to decide is whether Molly continues to be known as Dashwood or Haxby."

Molly's adoption by Noah was bittersweet because he had begun to think of her as his biological daughter and I hoped the negative DNA test wouldn't impact on his relationship with her going forward. Neither of us had time to absorb everything as it happened. Noah turned to me and mumbled through his tears, "Haxby? You'll take my name when we marry, yes?"

It wasn't how I'd have liked to decide but I nodded through my blurry eyes as my tears began to fall. What should have been a long awaited positive decision suddenly felt like a consolation prize because I had resigned myself to Noah being Molly's father and I realized how comforting that had been to finally know who the other half of Molly was. With the DNA result being negative the question of who her biological father was had been opened once again.

CHAPTER TWENTY-NINE
Maggie

Noah stood and turned as I rose to meet him. He scooped me to his chest as soon as the judge stood from his chair and headed toward the door. Separated by the balustrade we did our best to hug each other, "I don't know what to say," Noah admitted.

"Me neither... other than Shona lied. Why would she do that? Why would she go to the length of chasing you to Australia unless she truly believed you were Molly's father?"

"I fear that's the one question in all of this that will never be answered now," he replied.

We stood in silent reflection for a moment then I decided to put it out there, "Molly's adoption must feel second best to being her biological dad. I can't imagine—"

"No, Maggie. You heard the judge. I'm her dad. Biological or not. I'm the man she sits across from at the breakfast table, the man who teaches her Math. The man who raises her onto his shoulders when she's too tired to walk. I'm who she knows loves and protects her. How do you think she sees me? Do you think it matters to her at this minute how I got to be her dad? I'm still the same man who cheers for her when she's doing well and the one who comforts her when she's sick. The fact we can go home and tell her she can call me dad will mean the world to her. It doesn't matter how we got there."

A lump formed in my throat and I swallowed it back because he'd said everything I needed to hear and even though he'd been dealt a major blow with the news we learned, none of it seemed to matter. If I ever doubted whether he'd show preference to Rudi and George over Molly he'd obliterated that thought from my mind with his words.

Long after the judge had left the courtroom, we stayed in the sanctuary of the quiet place absorbing everything that had been said and it was an hour after the hearing before we left the court.

In contrast to our arrival there, Noah didn't shy away from the press when he saw them lurking but met them head on. To show those reporters our united front, Noah put his arm protectively around my waist and held me close.

"I've only got a few words to say and I'm not taking questions, but there are things that need to be rectified for your information, then it's our wish that you leave us alone."

Some of the press gang had been standing at the bottom of the steps and came clambering up to join the huddle already assembled around us. Eamon pushed one back when his microphone got shoved too near to Noah's face.

"For years I have been subjected to many mistruths and fabrications at the hands of the media. I'll admit at the beginning of my music career there were acts which I don't deny and indeed were sensational enough to attract extra attention for Fr8Load as an up-and-coming band. As time went on, the interest around me in particular, became so distorted it contributed to the separation of me from my son. Through biased reporting at the time, my trial for assault should have been handled with a better degree of factual information than that which was recorded, because I was in fact defending myself during a sexual assault. Since then, from the time I met Maggie there have been several inaccuracies which had led me to take legal action to defend myself and Maggie's position. For a few months, Maggie and I were placed in a very difficult position due to reports which emerged from various sources who had been paid to disclose information. Despite the media's interest in those events no evidence of conclusive proof has been provided to substantiate the validity of the information reported. This has caused me and my family unnecessary distress and heartache. A highly respected judge recently saw fit to revoke the restraining order granted following my guilty verdict of assault. Following this I was granted visitation to meet and build a relationship with my son. Today, the same judge has granted me joint parental responsibility for my son in the belief his esteemed colleague in my previous case was not privy to all the facts when he made the initial decision."

Collective gasps came from the reporters as they feverishly wrote on their writing pads.

Noah cleared his throat then continued, "I'd also like to inform you as a direct result of a story published which raised the question of paternity toward Maggie's sister Shona's daughter I submitted DNA. Today, I can confirm for you I am not the biological father of the child as per those emails." The press gasped again then fell silent. Noah had their full attention.

"I only have one more announcement to make today and this will come as a surprise to many. As of today, I am stepping out of public life. This morning I emailed my manager after discussing with the other band members my intention to leave Fr8Load. Since I was seventeen years old my character and reputation has been manipulated by many who sought to make a living from the little talent that I have. It is a God given talent, but many have lived better lives than I have simply by being associated with me, writing about me, or from selling products connected to me. This stops now. Thanks to the careful handling of my career by many of those others, I have no desire to perform in public again. I will be retiring from Fr8Load to focus on a more sedate career behind the scenes."

Sliding his arm from my waist, Noah grabbed my hand and nodded to Eamon to inform him he was done. Turning away from Noah, Eamon parted the crowd of reporters who were initially stunned;

however, once the news had sunk in, they began to chase us toward the car.

Eamon opened the SUV door and Noah shoved me in then jumped in himself and Eamon swiftly shut the door behind us.

"Have you lost your mind, Noah?" I asked as I stared incredulously at him with raised eyebrows.

"The opposite. I promised myself if the court decision went my way today, I was never going to put us in a position that could destroy us as a family again."

"Don't you think you're being hasty? That your emotions are running too high to make a rational judgment about your future this way?" I asked.

"No. This decision isn't about what happened in court, Maggie. It's what happened after that guy grabbed me by my balls. It's about how those fuckers hounded you when your sister wasn't even in the ground, it's about my son being kept from me because they listened to a jilted pissed off woman who got pregnant as a way of forcing my hand. But most of all it's because of the fear I felt about losing you when the story broke about Shona's emails."

"What did Steve say? Why didn't you tell me what you were thinking?"

"Steve... I can't repeat what he said because it was so fucking insulting it makes me want to choke him. You... I didn't tell you because I knew you'd talk me around to a wait-and-see situation. I'm taking full responsibility for my life for the first time as an adult, Maggie. We get to make the decisions from now on, not those who are self-serving and want to make a buck out of what you wear, how we dress, what fucking furniture is in our homes, or which car we drive. You have no idea how far reaching this shit is, Maggie."

"You're right, I have no idea, but that doesn't mean you take decisions about our lives without even consulting with me."

"What are you saying? You're no longer interested now that I'm quitting the band? You want to be married to a rock star is that it?"

I slapped him hard across the face and his hand flew to his cheek.

"Don't be so fucking obtuse. How dare you talk to me like that. I'd support you no matter what you do, Noah." I shouted, enraged he would throw such an insult at me. "I'm going to excuse what you just said to me because I know your emotions are running high, but I will remind you I hated Noah Haxby the rock star, remember? And like you said, I have no idea who he is because I have never known you personally during that phase of your life. Since I've been with you I've only met the band on what? Four or five occasions in passing, and I've never heard you sing live apart from with Molly. So, don't you dare rant at me like I'm one of your groupie bitches you've been with in the past."

Eamon stopped the car and turned to address me. "Can you both stop shouting, I'm trying to concentrate here. And Maggie, if it's any consolation he kept this so close to his chest I heard it for the first time when you did." I heard how hurt Eamon was when he spoke.

I stopped and saw the worry etched on Eamon's face and realized the implications for him. "God. I'm sorry, Eamon, I thought you knew."

Noah huffed loudly, slid back in the car seat, and scrubbed his hand down his face like he'd realized how badly he'd fucked up.

"Hmm. And you wonder why we're pissed at you? We're the two closest people who have your back the most in this world and you kept us in the dark about your intentions? Do we even know you at all?"

"It was precisely because you both know me so well that I never said anything. I'm still going to be famous after I leave the band. We'll still need protection every day. That shit doesn't just disappear because I say so. If you're happy to work with someone who's not a high-profile artist, Eamon, then I would be honored if you'd stay with me. I'm sorry if you think I took you for granted. It never occurred to me you'd be anywhere else."

Eamon didn't reply and turned to face the front, restarting the engine. Gripping the steering wheel, his fists tightened like he was holding back his thoughts as he began to drive again.

"Look, I didn't decide this on the fly. Long before I met you, I was tired of all the shit that went with the band, Maggie. I've been making noises for a while and it came as no real surprise to George. Between you and me, he's relieved I had the balls to draw a line. He wants to do his own thing."

"So, he's going solo?"

"He wants to. He fits the rock star mold better than I do. Most rockers are highly charged alpha males who get off on cheating or dominating their women, taking me on and doing what they want, and they never apologize for the idiotic decisions they make. I'm not made that way. I've pretended to fit in for so long I almost forgot who I really am. You changed that. When I met you... something shifted and made me who I wanted to be... the real me, rather than who others wanted me to be."

My eyes softened, and I felt a sudden empathy for his situation. "What will you do?"

"Write, collaborate, set up a recording studio... maybe even run an independent label or hold masterclasses... hell, there's a lot of work for a guy like me."

A silence stretched between us and although I still wasn't totally convinced he had made his life-changing decision for the right reasons, I kept my mouth shut.

The rest of the journey felt slow because the atmosphere between the three of us was heavy after the exchange of words and I felt disgusted with myself for lashing out the way I had, and I acknowledged the possibility that my own emotional state was less than even as well at that time.

Eamon was quiet but polite when he opened the car door after we arrived home. Noah slid out of the back seat and turned to help me step down. "I never got to say it earlier, Noah, I'm glad about your boy. I know more than anyone how badly it affected you when they said you couldn't see him."

Dropping my hand Noah stepped forward and hugged Eamon, who stiffened then patted his back awkwardly like he wasn't used to his affection.

"I'm sorry if what I said today hurt you, Eamon. I've had it to the brim with those fuckers. I know I've probably hurt a lot of people by the decision I made today, but for my sanity and my family it had to be done. You more than anyone knows what they almost did. You were there and saw me at my worst. I guess unless you have been in the position of knowing you don't care whether you live or die you may not understand how I feel. Thing is... I do know... and I never want to go back to that. Leaving the band is my way of ensuring I've done all I can to keep my life moving forward the way I want it to. When it was just me, I didn't care what happened to me. Now it's a case of caring what doesn't."

Stepping back, Eamon broke the hug and looked slightly embarrassed by Noah's show of affection. He scratched the back of his head and averted his gaze to the ground. "Thanks, it was just a curve ball I never saw coming, although if it's all the same to you, I'll stay."

"You have a job for life, buddy. No one has had my back the way you have. George... well you know how I love that guy, but he's a different breed. He and Jason have watched me closely, but you've been the one who has pulled me off the floor, shoved me in the shower and dragged me to be wherever I had to be. That's beyond your scope of responsibility and I'm thankful. There were many times when no one knew the extent of what I'd stooped to because you protected me by covering for me."

"Like you said, Noah. You were a good person that had a shit thing happen to them. I would never have let you sink."

"And for that reason, I'm eternally grateful. I'm glad you're sticking with me."

Noah stepped in and gave him another hug and this time Eamon's response was less stilted and much more genuine. "Thanks for keeping me around," he muttered before breaking free again. Eamon turned and jogged up the stairs to avoid an awkward moment and opened the front door for us. As we entered the hallway, Molly came running with an excited look on her face. "Noah, Mom, you're back," she shouted with a beaming smile on her face.

CHAPTER THIRTY

Noah

When the moment came for me to tell Molly the news about the adoption I had wanted it to be as memorable as I could for her. It had been a long time coming to a kid as young as she was, and to be honest it had felt like a lifetime for me as well.

When she ran toward me bursting with excitement for no other reason than we'd arrived home it had melted my heart to see her so happy. For a second I wasn't sure I could say the words to her without choking up, but I knew I wouldn't keep her waiting a moment longer.

Taking a deep breath, I knelt down to embrace her and held her face in my hands. "Hello, cutie," I whispered and kissed the end of her nose. I could hear the raw emotion in those two words. Molly looked back bashfully at me. "Yep, we're home, and you know what? I have a little surprise for you, young lady."

Shaking her head slowly she stared wide-eyed, her excitement growing with my question. "What?" she asked.

"Not what, *who?*" I replied.

Molly looked confused, narrowed her eyes, and scrunched her nose. "I don't know what you mean why are you trying to muddle me?"

"The surprise is *who* not what," I repeated.

"You mean *someone* is the surprise not the *something?*" she asked with her hands on her hips.

Her sassy attitude made me smile. She was chalk to Rudi's cheese. Where she was bossy and organized, he was messy and passive. The would compliment each other perfectly, and I figured once Rudi found his feet with her they'd be great friends.

"You know how you keep asking me when I am going to get to adopt you?"

"Yeeeeeeeeah?" she said accentuating the word, tilting her head, and narrowing her eyes again.

"Well... I guess it's time you did what I asked you to... now that I'm your daddy," I answered with a cheesy grin.

Clasping her hands together she held them to her chest like she did when she was overwhelmed, and her eyes turned glassy. Turning to look at Maggie, she bubbled up and wailed. Through her tears she sobbed, "Is this true, Mommy?"

Maggie had teared up as well and nodded frantically 'yes', too choked to speak. I leaned forward and scooped my sobbing little girl into my arms. The name she called me didn't matter to me, but the sense of belonging I had from seeing her reaction almost did me in.

Crying through hiccups she took a deep breath and asked, "Daddy? Can I call you my daddy forever now?" Her pleading eyes searched my face waiting for confirmation, and I thought my heart would burst out of my chest with the love I felt for her. "I'd be honored if you called me Daddy," I replied, my voice husky with emotion.

"Daddy," she said again and cried harder as she wrapped her arms around my neck and wailed into the crook of it. I tried to soothe her by rubbing her back and she mumbled, "I asked Santa for a daddy when Mommy helped me write a note, but he gave me a bike instead. Maybe his elves were still making you then," she reasoned.

Maggie's watery eyes softened, and she stepped forward and joined me next to her, "I guess they were because you know Santa, Molly, he wouldn't give a child a dad unless he knew he was perfect."

I grinned at Maggie as Molly lifted her head and smiled sweetly then she looked adoringly into my eyes. "Yep, Mommy that's right, and you're a lot smarter than you look." Both Maggie and I chuckled at

Molly's reply and Molly cupped my chin in her hands and kissed my nose.

"Don't worry, I know you've never been a daddy before, just like I am new to being a Daddy's girl. I think we'll be fine because if we get stuck we can always Google it."

~

Quitting the band wasn't quite how I imagined it, and I was naïve to think they'd simply let me walk away. Instead there were contractual obligations to consider, and we were halfway through an album. I was leaving because I didn't want to be a part of the attention Fr8Load attracted, not to leave my friends in the lurch.

Therefore, I finished the album and a couple of other small but important events, then the band decided to fold. George supported my decision and although the others were more than a little pissed, I knew had it been the other way around they'd have done what was right for them too.

Once I had left performing behind, my life became more than I ever imagined it could be. Being a father to three kids came to me like it was the most natural thing in the world. My home life with Maggie and the kids was sheltered and sedate in comparison to my time with Fr8Load and I relished in it.

Initially, Maggie was worried I'd get bored after the lifestyle I'd previously led, but with each day that passed, with us spending it together with the kids, she became convinced I'd made the right choice.

From the age of seventeen I'd been on the road with the band for most of my career and I had almost forgotten what it felt like to wake every day knowing exactly where I was. Between that and the shit Andrea put me through, it shouldn't have come as a surprise when my mental health suffered.

Being able to reflect on those times and how much happier I felt since I stayed home with my family helped me to heal. There hadn't been one single time since I left the band that I had craved alcohol.

During the months following my departure from the band, my

confidence grew about living in peace and away from the public eye. That's not to say there wasn't the occasional mob of fans whenever I went anywhere. However, the fans and the followers of Fr8Load weren't the issue for me; it was the press.

It was nice to have the time to stop and chat about music with fans... something I rarely had when I was one of the band being shipped from one place to the next gig on the schedule. I felt relieved to have left all that behind, but I knew if I did nothing before long I'd procrastinate. Fortunately, my brother, Phil, didn't allow the grass to grow under my feet.

A few times in the past, Phil and I had spoken at length about building and designing a recording studio, and once he was sure I was never looking back, he pushed again about us going into business together. He was relentless in his pursuit to make it happen and I knew eventually I'd have to do something else with my life so once he'd twisted I agreed.

A couple of weeks later life got busier as my brother began ordering mixing boards and acoustic glass panels and there were surveyors roaming around the west wing of the house. Next I knew, I'd filled in official papers that Phil had filed then Haxby NP Recording Studios was born.

Several weeks of upheaval to our household resulted in a working studio and I had to admit Phil certainly knew his shit. The sound was pure, the equipment was sick, and as soon as George clapped eyes on the place he begged us to produce his first solo album.

Obviously, I was honored he thought we up to producing someone of his caliber but I was a little apprehensive because at that point the most we'd done was mess around and produced a few tracks of mine. It was Phil's confidence in his own ability that sold me on it and led us to produce George's first solo album with George's own money.

Not that money was an issue for us. It was just that George had plenty, and we figured if he could pay it would leave more in the pot if we ever found a young start-up via the internet that we wanted to back.

Besides the recording work to keep me busy, I continued to pen some of my own songs. I found the words flowed once the pressure was off. Some I kept for my own collection but others I wrote with artists in my mind. I surprised myself with some of the subject matter; however, I supposed that was what happened when my mind was clear of anything else to think about.

~

"We're number one, we're number one," Molly and Rudi screamed when they came bursting into the studio, closely followed by a smiling Maggie with George hanging on her hip. They had been to watch Rudi play in a little league tournament.

Staring bright-eyed they were overflowing with excitement.

Reaching forward, I grabbed Rudi around the waist and pulled him in for a hug. Molly, never one to be left out, immediately swooped forward, and made it a group one.

"That's fantastic, son. Go, Rudi. You're a champion," I shouted loudly, my voice full of enthusiasm and praise.

"No, Daddy, not Rudi—the song," Molly's high-pitched voice yelled.

I bunched my brow, puzzled at what they were talking about.

"*Free to Breathe*, the song we wrote," she replied impatiently. Molly changed a word and then felt that gave her royalty rights. Maggie named the song after a term we had both used when we'd weathered some heavy shit and came out the other side and it was perfectly fitting. Glancing up at Maggie I kind of knew what they meant, but waited for the full story from Maggie.

"Almost a quarter of a *million* downloads since midnight," she said accentuating the number like she found it incredible... so did I. Everyone held their breath while I digested the news. Once Maggie's words sunk in, I stared nervously at my kids smiling faces and prayed to God I hadn't started another rollercoaster ride with the press.

I'd forgotten the release date of Junior Sweetman's country tune. Since I had left the band the one thing that hadn't changed was losing track of events. I had been working between the studio and home and hardly ever knew what day it was, never mind the date.

"Seriously?" I asked unblinking.

"Yes! We heard about it in the car. Straight in at number one in the charts. The man on the radio said you were a genie. You're such a clever cookie, well done," Molly said, mimicking the same words Maggie said to her when she was good. I stared at the proud look she gave me, and Maggie drew breath.

"A genius, Molly," Maggie said correcting her and chuckled.

My heart clenched with affection at my kids reveling in my success. George wriggled in Maggie's arms, stretched his arms out toward me, and began to whine in a way no parent can ignore. Setting him down on the floor she turned him toward me and he ran over, hugged my knee, and grinned before I lifted him onto my lap.

"Don't you have anything else to say?" Maggie asked incredulously when my focus turned to George.

"It's a good song," I mused, still concerned that it would bring attention to us as a family again.

Maggie scoffed, "I'd say a quarter of a million downloads makes it more than a good song, honey. We need to celebrate. What do you say? Should I call the family together for a barbeque?"

Before I could reply, Molly and Rudi were bouncing on their toes. "Barbeque!" they squealed in unison. "Can Lori Ann come, pleeease?" Molly whined with her hands clasped in prayer. If ever a child could spot an opportunity to use for her own benefit, she was the one. "Can James and Bruno?" Rudi asked, following her lead.

Maggie smiled at the kids then glanced back to me, "Guess that's settled then. I'll ask Kathleen to manage the kids and I'll call your mom," she said not waiting for me to reply. "Don't worry there's plenty of food in the pantry and fridges," she added, like I'd even thought about that.

I knew it was pointless trying to get anything else done that day and if I was honest I'd say I was more than a little apprehensive that the song had gone to the heights that it had. It was the fifty-first song I'd written but a first in country music for me.

Fr8Load were used to topping the charts with songs I had penned but "Free to Breathe" was one I had not intended to write—had never thought myself capable of writing. However, the words had flowed with no effort at all and once I'd begun, the raw emotion of the story just came to me.

It was very different from anything else I'd ever written, like a story unfolding in my head. I relived every scene as I wrote it. It was the story of my sad lonely life as a singer in a band and the only music that appeared to fit and give it the right vibe was a mournful catchy tune that was so full of misery it tugged at your heartstrings.

Normally when I wrote a song, the lyrics spoke for themselves, but with "Free to Breathe" it was different because instead of clever rhymes the words were the story of my personal, sometimes agonizing, journey.

I'd never written anything like it—where a song played like a movie inside my head. It was a painful exercise because it made me relive some of my darker experiences in life.

Writing it really affected me as I tapped into my emotions and I became somewhat withdrawn and difficult to live with.

Several times Maggie almost tore me a new one for my mood swings. Then there were times when she wondered if I missed the band. I put her straight on that account, it was the one decision I was one hundred percent certain I had gotten right.

During that time, she became suspicious and thought perhaps I had been getting emails or other communication that had sunk my mood. I'm not sure she believed me at first when I had nothing to say, until I realized the words of the song had dragged me down.

Recounting the unjust treatment I'd experienced had still been able to affect me. It was only after I set it to the emotional catchy country tune that I realized the full effect of the song because I struggled to finish it when my emotions suddenly engulfed me.

For a while I saw it as a therapeutic outpouring and almost shelved it, but then I sang it to Maggie because I felt it explained why I'd been so down; she was also overwhelmed and pleaded with me to share it with the world. Her reaction was the most animated I'd ever encountered for my music and it changed my mind about sharing it with others.

Junior Sweetman was a massive country music star and the only person I could trust to sing it the way it was intended, and to Maggie's mind he was the only country artist that could sing the song that way and do it justice were I to release it. His reputation was solid as a family man and a much-respected artist and I appreciated that fact.

It was a bold move for someone like me—a hard rocker—to write a country tune; even if it wasn't intended, and an even bolder one to approach the management of, in my view, the greatest country artist of the century to sing it.

Being at the top of the food chain as the front man in a band did not mean the same thing as being in the food chain at all when it came to songwriting. Sure, I had a reputation as a good singer/songwriter but that was in the rock music genre. Country music was a whole other ball game. Added to that was the pressure I felt from the media's reaction if I'd called it wrong.

For weeks I mulled over Phil's request to send a demo tape. It was the one thing I loved about my brother, he was pushy, but he never took it upon himself to do anything without consultation. In the past, with anyone else my opinion hadn't mattered, bucks did. However, neither Maggie nor Phil put pressure on me because they both accepted I had to be master of my own destiny.

It was an unexpected visit from George that changed my mind about "Free to Breathe". I'd been writing for George for his second album when he made a social call and naturally the topic came up about the country song I'd written. Phil began to spout off at the mouth about how awesome it was and after some persuasion I had reluctantly agreed to play it for him.

We'd done some insane shit together, yet I had felt shy about sharing the song—especially as the subject matter was very personal to me—and I wondered if George would think I'd flipped or been whipped, or both. It truly was that deep. I didn't even stay in the room while he listened to the track.

"Where is he?" George called out. His voice had an urgency to it as he bounded down the hallway to the kitchen. "Fuck me!"

"George... the kids," scolded Maggie as she followed him into the kitchen.

"Oh, sorry," he cringed, "You gotta get that out there, dude, it's fucking brilliant. Nothing like anything you've done before and even better," he gushed, his hands up to accentuate what he said.

I watched his expression to look for the truth and the gleam in his eyes told me he thought it was a winner. George was a 'no bullshit' kinda guy, and I knew he'd never let me take a punt unless he believed in me.

"You're with them? My fan club of two on this?"

"It would be a travesty if no one heard it, buddy. It's a once in a life-time song."

My eyes flicked between his and Maggie's and a smile crept onto her face, "I may not know anything about music, Noah, but trust me I'd want that on my playlist if I was feeling a sense of melancholy about life."

I stood in silent contemplation and my nerves almost ate me alive because if it went wrong the press would hound me down and the last thing on this Earth I wanted was to be subjected to their attention again.

Life had been sedately beautiful since I'd left the band. But I had to decide whether they controlled me, or it was the other way around.

"All right, but be prepared for a knockback. The only person who can sing this song is Junior Sweetman."

George ran past me down the hall to where Phil was sitting in my little home studio. "He's going for it; quick get the demo tape over to Sweetman's management before he changes his mind."

I smiled knowingly at Maggie, because like she said, even though she knew nothing about music, she believed in me... and that was worth any teardown the press may deliver.

Phil sent the track off by email and we waited. George said he wouldn't leave until he heard their reply... I told him that could be weeks and he shrugged it off. "No fucking way. You send a tape they'll listen as soon as they see your name. They're gonna piss their pants with excitement when they've heard it," he replied with a level of confidence I never felt.

Maggie made lunch and was clearing away when Phil's cell rang. Taking his weight on one butt cheek he reached into his front pocket and pulled it out.

"It's them," he said, smirked secretly to himself, then took a deep breath and calmly answered.

"Haxby NP Recording Studios, Phil Haxby speaking," he said sounding much more official than we really were.

Everyone watched him as he listened intently to the call then he gave us the thumbs up and a huge toothy grin. George punched the air looking ecstatic, then mouthed, "Told you."

"Ah, I'm happy you like it. We love the song and know it'll be a massive hit, but I think It's only fair to warn you we offered to two other parties we thought may be interested as well. The response has been overwhelming, so I guess it's down to the figures for the best deal and royalty rights."

A further period of silence ensued as Phil listened carefully then he did a silent jig, "All right. Thank you for your interest. Noah is in the studio now. I'll speak with him and get back to you as soon as I have an answer for you."

After concluding the call, he threw his head back and chuckled. "Junior Sweetman wants to donate his right nut for the song... and is willing to negotiate your package."

"Doing a song contract is one thing, Phil, but I think Maggie would have something to say if you started to offer Noah's package as part of the deal," George added when his head went straight to the gutter at the first opportunity.

Maggie shook her head, "Ha! Next you'll be dragging out toilet humor jokes," she said in a patronizing way.

Phil and I talked numbers then he followed through with his game plan, pushing hard for the best deal for the upfront fee and my royalties from the sales. Junior asked to meet with me, and Phil quickly and politely shut him down by offering a conference call because since leaving the band it had been my wish to lead a purely private life.

That part was true, talking to someone on the phone or over the internet was fine by me but I drew the line at meeting another celebrity in public. I'd made it my mission not to court that kind of attention.

Phil then put Junior on speaker-phone so we could hear everything he said and the man damn near had an orgasm when Phil said the song was his to record. And since it sounds like the tune has found great success, I guess it put my rock career to bed and eased my path to that of songwriter and producer for other artists.

CHAPTER THIRTY-ONE
Maggie

*a*fter the court hearing I had a hundred conflicting feelings swimming in my head. Shock, denial, and disbelief were the ones that consistently repeated at the news we heard from the court. The day the emails arrived replayed over and over, in particular my reaction to the possibility of Noah's relationship to Molly.

When the judge disclosed the results, I may have looked quiet and calm—I had no choice except to portray that exterior for Noah's sake —but inside my head I had hundreds of unanswered questions: images of Shona at various stages of her pregnancy, at Molly's birth, and over the years since. For years I had pressed her about who the father was and every time Shona had responded with, *"What does it matter? He'd probably deny her anyway, and I don't want her growing up feeling rejected."*

It was the one thing I remained angry with her about after she died. I should have been angry about the emails, but they were never intended for me to see, so who knew, she could lied to make her life sound more interesting to someone she obviously thought she'd never see again.

Her damning disclosure had almost wrecked Noah and I as a couple, but after the result from the test I had put her ambiguous emails to one side for the sake of Noah and the children. From that point onward not having a definitive answer to the question about her and Noah was something I'd learned to live with. It wasn't like she was coming back... or that he'd remembered being with her if he had.

I wasn't blind, I knew they had met from the picture her friend had shared with the world, but that was the only piece of evidence that was undeniable. If her friend was with her and Shona believed it was Noah's then I had to entertain the possibility that they may have slept together.

I had to balance that information with the woman Shona was and if she had lied about Noah being Molly's father then it was possible the whole emails about sleeping with him were a fabrication of her mind. Not to speak ill of my dead sister, but Shona had always been a fantasist, and she was fanatical about Noah. Whatever the truth was, sometimes not knowing was better.

Leaving Fr8Load was the best thing Noah could have done for his emotional health. From the moment he made the decision, I saw tension I never knew he had within him ebb away. In the early days of him quitting, I had huge concerns he'd taken a knee jerk reaction because of how the media had treated him.

It made me want to know how deeply rooted the issues went, so I went back and read about the man I was with and I poured over every article I could get my hands on. I concluded with absolute certainty the reporting around him had been written with a biased slant aimed at causing the maximum shock value to the reader.

Many argue that public figures have no right to privacy, that they court the attention of the press, and in the early part of his career that was certainly true of Noah. However, the media should have been responsible and reported information to the public about when he was on the clock instead of stalking him in his private life.

From everything I had read— the good and the bad, I believed the public had been sold a damaging version of Noah that most certainly wasn't true of the man that I had come to love.

Having been on the receiving end of their malice a couple of times due to the stories they ran about us, I was surprised Noah was as balanced as he was. He put that down to the calming effect I had on him, but personally I thought he was very young when all the bad things happened and by the time he'd met me, he'd grown up. As soon as the media turned on me it made me understand how they twisted information and bent the truth just far enough to stop short of a lawsuit.

Like Noah, I had no respect for them after that. My dad used to say, *"Don't believe everything you read in the papers."* I had thought him a cynic when he told me that; however, since knowing Noah, I wished more people could have benefited from that advice.

Another saying I'd heard repeatedly was, "Never judge a book by its cover." I had always thought myself as a fairly liberal, non-judgmental person, until I learned how a biased opinion based on the hearsay of others could impact so negatively someone's life. I had judged Noah the same way as most before I knew who he really was.

Everyone knows that beast called rumor wasn't an easy thing to tame. Even an eminent judge was swayed when Andrea was granted a restraining order to block Noah from seeing his son. It taught me how full of humility Noah was when he still managed to be cordial with her for the sake of his son. I'd never met someone as fair as Noah, he never harbored a tiny grudge toward his ex-girlfriend once Rudi was in his life... at least not outwardly from how he behaved. I was humbled by his approach.

Andrea wasn't an easy person to communicate with as I found out when I answered the phone the first time Rudi was staying over at our place. If I said I hadn't been a little concerned about Rudi joining us as part of the family for every other week it would have been untrue. Not because I didn't want him with us... of course I did. I only wanted everyone to be happy.

My worries were borne from a lack of information from Andrea. Neither Noah nor I really knew his routines, and he appeared to be a very quiet little boy in comparison to Molly. The last thing I wanted was for him to feel overwhelmed and I didn't want Molly to become attached and then pine on the weeks he was with his mom. Above all,

I was concerned about all the changes Molly had already dealt with on top of the separation and loss of Shona.

Despite Andrea's attempts to control all aspects of Rudi's every waking moment during his first few visits, with constant calls to him with urgent questions that couldn't wait; I'm pleased to say that Rudi integrated without a hitch. He and Molly clicked within minutes, and they were both very caring toward their brother George.

Rudi's reservations at the beginning were quickly replaced with a newfound confidence when Molly offered praise and high-fives for every little achievement from remembering to wash his hands before dinner to much bigger achievements like when he scored a home run at softball.

The two older kids became inseparable, and I was pleased that Rudi made no fuss about returning for the weeks with his mom. Molly didn't like it much, but she accepted it as a normal part of our routine. Even Andrea began to accept that Noah was good for Rudi, but I knew we'd never be friends because of the look of longing still there in her eyes. I never regarded her as a threat because Noah barely gave her eye contact. His ex would never be anything more than Rudi's mother to Noah and as far as he was concerned the only reason they breathed the same air was because they shared a son.

Watching Rudi blossom under Noah's fatherly guidance and Molly's bossy ways had been one of the most rewarding parts of my journey in our family life and every day that passed I watched Noah's love grow for of all our kids. He was a funny, compassionate, understanding, and fair father and he had the measure of each of our children's strengths and weaknesses. He was a natural when it came to understanding what each of them needed.

Having found a balance in his life was everything to Noah and because of this he always ensured we had our special time as a couple as well. He never ceased to amaze me with his little romantic surprises when I least expected them. Funny and attentive were two of the sexiest traits I'd ever found in a man and Noah had the whole skill-set to make me feel like the luckiest woman alive. He kept me on my toes with his wicked, playful ways as well as curling them whenever we had the time.

One of the most important surprises was when Noah arranged a train ride for the kids. It was the sole topic of conversation for weeks after Rudi had asked several times if they could do it as a treat. After speaking to Phil and another brother David to make some covert arrangements, the birthday treat was set for Rudi for the following week.

Andrea tried to manipulate the situation by asking for Rudi for half of the day and Noah understood more than anyone how it felt not to see him on his birthday, so he compromised and told her Rudi would be home to spend the night with her from around 6:00 pm. As Noah said, a child should get to spend time with his father and his mother on his birthday... pity Noah's insight had never occurred to Andrea to let Noah see his son.

The trip to the train station involved leaving home in the dead of night and I wasn't happy that the kids routines were being disrupted because of Noah's paranoia over the press. Goodness knows how I managed to keep my thoughts to myself when Rudi's birthday treat involved pulling my sleeping children from their beds.

We set off for New York City at 3:00 am, with three tired, grumpy kids but their tetchy moods dispersed when we arrived at the train station and were met by a magnificent vintage Pullman train with all the guards in authentic uniforms from the Victorian period.

Rudi and Molly immediately hugged each other in a show of mutual excitement and Noah chuckled, looked at me, and wrinkled his nose in a tell of how their togetherness affected him. Walking toward the train, Kathleen took Molly and Rudi's hands and Noah picked George up into his arms. The guard helped Kathleen lift the kids onto the train. Once on board, two young girls in period costume stood to escort the children down the long, carpeted corridor.

Surrounded by the luxurious wooden paneled interior and rich tapestry drapes, class oozed from every inch of the train carriage. Noah smiled warmly, looking delighted he'd got us all there in one piece and passed George to Kathleen. As they walked away from us, Noah pulled me back by my forearm and turned me to face him. When he took a step forward, I had to take a step in the other direction and my back hit the wall.

"Hold on, baby. I want to ask you something," he said. He looked nervous, and I searched his face as I tried to figure out what was so important he'd allow the kids to walk on ahead without us?

"Yeah?" I said as my eyes searched for the kids who were almost out of sight.

"Don't you think it's time we got married? You're the only one without my name in the family now."

"Can we talk about this later, Noah? The kids have gone on ahead."

"It's okay, they're being well taken care of," he said and smiled as slid his hand around my waist and kissed me slowly.

"So?"

"Is this your way of wearing me down, Noah?"

"Only if it's working," he replied and snickered as he peppered kisses around my neck.

"Keep going, I'm thinking," I teased as a broad smile spread on my lips with the thrill of his ministrations.

"Are you close?" he asked, sliding his hands to my butt as he pulled me closer.

"Mm-hm," I replied as shivers ran down my spine and my core clenched with want.

"Is that a yes?" he probed.

"I'd be a fool to pass up a man who asked questions like this," I whispered and grinned wider.

"So... that's a yes?" He asked, pulling back as he regarded me with wide eyes.

"I've said yes, before... absolutely—"

Before I could say anything else he stepped back, grabbed my hand, and began running down the corridor of the train pulling me behind him as he shouted, "We're on."

He turned to look over his shoulder and chuckled again at the look of what must have been pure confusion on my face because I had no clue what the hell was happening.

Two carriages later we stood in the stateroom of the train surrounded by his brothers, their girls, and his parents. My eyes flitted around the room in a stunned confusion and then I saw his parent's pastor who I'd met once at a family barbeque.

"You meant now?" I asked in an incredulous tone.

"Did you need someone else here?" he asked knowing there wasn't anyone other than Mrs. Richie who was important to me. I glanced around again and noticed her sitting in the corner of the room nodding with a smile of delight on her face.

Glancing to the kids I saw Molly had changed into her Disney Belle dress from home and Rudi was dressed as Woody from Toy Story, then I looked down at myself dressed in the woolen pant suit I'd pulled on for a day crawling around on a train.

"There's a bridal store shopper next door with an assortment of dresses in your size. Mom helped me with that, and there's a beautician for hair and nails and—"

I got it—Noah wanted this to be completely private. It was partly my fault because I'd once joked when he pressed for us to get married during a date that he should just surprise me to make it happen—so he had.

Looking at Molly, Rudi, and George, I knew we had all that mattered; being married wasn't about fancy dresses and immaculate hair, it was about the joining together of two people who wanted to share the rest of their lives together.

"No... I think I'm dressed perfectly for this... let's do it," I replied and smiled affectionately at my family.

Noah's eyes widened, and he looked suddenly hesitant, "Yeah?"

"Yeah, I'm ready. I don't need to put on a dress to make today the best one of my life. All I need is right here. The people who are important to us."

It was sudden but entirely appropriate that Noah had managed to keep the most important day of our lives away from the press. Afterward he told me even the staff of the train and the bridal shop people had no idea who they were attending that day. Everyone had to leave their mobile phones in special boxes before boarding the train to ensure nothing was leaked about our event.

I surprised everyone when I cried as Noah read me his vows and I was so choked the only sentence I croaked out was, "Everything you said, and I love you more every day," then I sobbed into his arms. I had wanted to marry Noah from the moment he asked me, it was only that on every occasion he'd suggested it I felt the timing was off.

To me, the stability for the children and Noah's recovery came first, but when the opportunity presented itself it didn't matter to me where we were or the fact I wasn't in some fancy assed dress. It was knowing the lengths that Noah had gone to, to ensure our day was about us, and how determined he was to make me his that were the most important factors of the day.

Besides, wedding dresses were two-a-penny, but how many brides would be able to say they got married in a black woolen momsy-looking suit attended by Belle from Beauty and the Beast, and Woody from Toy Story?

When I thought back to my darkest day when I saw Noah on the plane, I felt ashamed at how I regarded him then, because my feelings were borne out of ignorance, hatred, grief, pain, and his maligned reputation. Recalling how I felt without knowing all the facts made me as guilty as the media who demonized him. It was amazing how far we had come together.

I believed wholeheartedly Noah did what he had to do to give himself space to breathe, space to recover from the hurt that almost destroyed him, and he took the only decision he could that would enable him to live his life free from those who were ever ready to use hearsay and fabrication to tear him down.

There's a truth to what they say, "*The bigger they are the harder they fall*," because Noah's management used the power of the press to build him up as one of the biggest, most prominent hellraising rock stars on the scene at that time, and the very same people that made him almost destroyed him.

I guess what they never figured on was Noah's sense of self, that inner voice that told him enough was enough, and led to him ultimately shocking them by quitting as an impact of all their stalking and lies. From rock star to rock bottom, Noah's journey took his drive, his desire to perform live music, and most importantly to his fans—his talent—away from the public eye.

Fortunately, through the support of the people who loved him, Noah found happiness in a quieter life and a way of taking control of his own future. Due to his true talent he was able to resurrect his passion for music in a way that he could create and share it with the world without being constantly targeted as a sensational front-page splash.

His experience taught me to look twice when we, as the public, were given a glimpse into the celebrity world of a rock star because I knew firsthand we're often fed the most sensational titbits syphoned out of a much bigger picture and twisted to fit a particular trend the journalist wants us to accept as truths.

They usually covered the excesses of extravagant wealthy lifestyles, the salacious parts of a sexual relationship, or other sensational stories that shifted tabloids and magazines off shelves and newsstands, created material for TV shows, and trended further on social media.

What we miss is the rest of that story or how the subject of the story has been manipulated or mistreated—they never show the unhealthy lifestyles those bands endured, such as the sleepless nights, long distance flights, pack up meals, vitamin injections or sometimes worse, just to keep them on their feet to perform their roles. I'd considered how that would have felt if I went to sleep in one country and woke up in another every few days... and was still expected to look and feel my best.

After witnessing the muted shift in attitude of the journalists from the moment when Noah told them he wasn't Molly's biological father, it demonstrated their unwillingness to accept responsibility for the story they had wrongly reported because instead of a page one retraction to follow up the next day there was only a tiny boxed withdrawal apology to Noah on the lower left-hand corner on page thirteen. It would have been missed had I not looked for it.

No one challenged the lies of a dead girl or her friend who had brought the whole sorry story to the world. And I would always hold some anger in my heart toward Shona for refusing to tell me who Molly's father was.

For years Noah was newsworthy, and his management left them to run with it. Noah said if he could go back to before he was in the band he'd have turned out differently. Then again, perhaps he was as great as he was after what had happened to him.

No one knows what the future holds. We don't have a crystal ball, but I do know one thing for sure, Noah will never trust a journalist so long as he lives after the agonizing personal pain some of them put him through. Not one of them recognized Noah's vulnerability as a young impressionable man during those years.

It took the death of my sister and the malicious lies that followed before Noah's tolerance limits were reached and he took a stand against them in the most dramatic of ways. Since then he had challenged every article and won each one like some small battle in the war he'd waged against them.

Music is still important to him and he's fortunate to have found his new niche, but he told me that even if his new career died a death tomorrow, it's me and his children that matter the most to him. The only grey cloud that hangs there for him is how Molly's happiness could be tainted when the question arises as to who her biological father is, and she reads the reports of what happened around her mom.

My reply when he said this was, "You're her dad, Noah. The only one she's ever known. Anyone can become a biological father in minutes, but to Molly, her dad will always be the loving man she knows would give his heart to make hers happy.

By that time Noah will be the man who has guided and protected her, the one who took the time to teach her, praise her, and one who has built a lifetime of memories in her mind. You'll be able to tell Molly the truth; that you were ready to accept her as your child whether or not she shared your blood and how the DNA test affected you when it came back."

Noah has insisted that working with Molly as she grows, will help minimize any negative impact for her in the future. In my view this the mark of a man who will go to any lengths to protect and preserve her happiness. In a way I'm happy there is no competition to challenge Noah's position because biologically connected or not, it's already plain to see, Noah will always be the father she adores.

The End

OTHER TITLES BY K.L. SHANDWICK

THE EVERYTHING TRILOGY

Enough Isn't Everything

Everything She Needs

Everything I Want

Love With Every Beat

just Jack

Everything Is Yours

LAST SCORE SERIES

Gibson's Legacy

Trusting Gibson

Gibson's Melody

READY FOR FLYNN SERIES

Ready For Flynn, Part 1

Ready For Flynn, Part 2

Ready For Flynn, Part 3

OTHER NOVELS

Missing Beats

Notes on Love

ABOUT THE AUTHOR

K. L. Shandwick lives on the outskirts of York, UK. She started writing after a challenge by a friend when she commented on a book she read. The result of this was 'The Everything Trilogy'. Her background has been mainly in the health and social care sector in the U.K. Her books tend to focus on the relationships of the main characters. Writing is a form of escapism for her and she is just as excited to find out where her characters take her as she is when she reads another author's work.

Printed in Poland
by Amazon Fulfillment
Poland Sp. z o.o., Wrocław